...ous trilogy yet!

Danger & Desire
Shipwreck, Scandals and Society Weddings

Leaving the sultry shores of India behind them,
the passengers of the *Bengal Queen*
face a new life ahead in England—
until a shipwreck throws their plans into disarray…

Can Alistair and Perdita's illicit onboard flirtation
survive the glittering social whirl of London?

Washed up on an island populated by ruffians, virginal
Averil must rely on rebel captain Luc for protection.…

And honorable Callum finds himself
falling for his *brother's* fiancée!

Look for

RAVISHED BY THE RAKE—February 2012
SEDUCED BY THE SCOUNDREL—March 2012
MARRIED TO A STRANGER—April 2012

from Harlequin Historical

Author Note

I loved writing about the immediacy and the drama of the wreck of the *Bengal Queen* in the first two books in my Danger & Desire trilogy, but I found it equally challenging to explore the effect of that several months later on two more people whose lives are changed forever after the ship hits the rocks. Sophia Langley is miles away, safe in a Hertfordshire village, but after years of believing she knows her destiny, now she is forced to come to terms with her very uncertain future. Duty and desire both seem to pull her in the same direction—is it the right one to take? Meanwhile Callum Chatterton has to make a decision that satisfies his sense of duty but threatens to completely overset his careful plans and equally carefully guarded heart.

One of the joys of writing a series is that I can continue to follow characters from earlier books, and it was fun to encounter Dita and Alistair from *Ravished by the Rake* and Averil and Luc from *Seduced by the Scoundrel* again, and to glimpse their new married lives. They were as eager for a happy ending for Callum and Sophia as I was—I hope you enjoy reading about their journey to find love as much as I enjoyed writing it.

LOUISE ALLEN

MARRIED TO A STRANGER

TORONTO NEW YORK LONDON
AMSTERDAM PARIS SYDNEY HAMBURG
STOCKHOLM ATHENS TOKYO MILAN MADRID
PRAGUE WARSAW BUDAPEST AUCKLAND

Recycling programs
for this product may
not exist in your area.

ISBN-13: 978-0-373-29684-2

MARRIED TO A STRANGER

Copyright © 2011 by Melanie Hilton

First North American Publication 2012

Available from Harlequin® Historical and
LOUISE ALLEN:

The Earl's Intended Wife #793
The Society Catch #809
Moonlight and Mistletoe #830
A Most Unconventional Courtship #849
Virgin Slave, Barbarian King #877
No Place for a Lady #892
*The Dangerous Mr. Ryder #903
*The Outrageous Lady Felsham #907
*The Shocking Lord Standon #911
*The Disgraceful Mr. Ravenhurst #951
*The Notorious Mr. Hurst #955
*The Piratical Miss Ravenhurst #959
The Viscount's Betrothal #982
**The Lord and the Wayward Lady #996
**The Officer and the Proper Lady #1020
†Practical Widow to Passionate Mistress #1052
†Vicar's Daughter to Viscount's Lady #1056
†Innocent Courtesan to Adventurer's Bride #1060
††Ravished by the Rake #1076
††Seduced by the Scoundrel #1080
††Married to a Stranger #1084

Other works include:

Harlequin® Historical *Undone!* ebooks

*Disrobed and Dishonored
†Auctioned Virgin to Seduced Bride

Harlequin Books

Hot Desert Nights
"Desert Rake"

*Those Scandalous Ravenhursts
**Silk & Scandal
†The Transformation of the Shelley Sisters
††Danger & Desire

Titles by this author are also available in ebook format.

To all my friends in the Cambridge Chapter
of the Romantic Novelists' Association—
thanks for the support and the fun.

LOUISE ALLEN

has been immersing herself in history, real and fictional,
for as long as she can remember, and finds landscapes and
places evoke powerful images of the past. Louise lives
in Bedfordshire, and works as a property manager, but
spends as much time as possible with her husband at the
cottage they are renovating on the north Norfolk coast, or
traveling abroad. Venice, Burgundy and the Greek islands
are favorite atmospheric destinations. Please visit Louise's
website—www.louiseallenregency.co.uk—for the latest
news!

Prologue

Hertfordshire—1799

'I love Daniel and I will wait for him and marry him!' Sophia Langley glared at Cal. Her small bosom—Where had that come from all of a sudden? he wondered—rose and fell within the bodice of her unfashionable gown; her nose, as usual, was smudged with charcoal.

'It is ridiculous. You are far too young, both of you.' He resisted the urge to pick her up like the small, under-fed kitten she resembled and give her a good shake to try and get some sense into her. Why on earth his twin would fix on the daughter of one of their gentry neighbours to fall for defeated him. The chit wasn't even out yet.

'You do not understand me, you have taken virtually no notice of me when we visit, and now you know what is best for me? I am seventeen and Daniel is the same age as you.' Indignant blue eyes, her best feature, narrowed at him.

The retort that she was only seventeen and three days old and that he was ten minutes older than his twin was childish; he bit it back unsaid. At just eighteen he was a man and he did not bicker with girls. 'What do you mean, I take no notice of you? We played together as children, didn't we?'

She snorted. He supposed she was refraining from observing that she had trailed around after them and had been tolerated as a fielder at cricket and as a suitable maiden to rescue while they were defeating dragons or Saracens or half the French army, but that hardly made them soul mates.

'We are both going to be away for a long time. You will meet someone else, fall in love properly when you grow up.'

It was, he realised as soon as he had said it, tactless in the extreme. Sophia drew her skinny frame up to its full height somewhere near his chin.

'You pompous, unfeeling wretch! How you can be the twin of someone as wonderful as Daniel, I have no idea, Callum Chatterton, but I love Daniel and I swear I will marry him and I hope you fall in love with someone who breaks your heart.' She stalked away, the dignity of her exit marred by catching her toe in the edge of the rug. He laughed. She slammed the door.

Cal shook his head and went back to packing for India.

Chapter One

Glebe End House, Hertfordshire—5th September, 1809

'It is from Callum Chatterton.' Sophia Langley looked up from the single sheet of paper flattened under her hand between plate and cup. Her mother, a slice of toast suspended halfway to her mouth, looked as puzzled as she felt. 'He says he will call this afternoon.'

'Then he is back.' Mrs Langley frowned. 'I do not think he has been back to the Hall since March.'

'It appears not.' Why the man who would have been her brother-in-law was calling now, six months after the funeral of her betrothed, she could not imagine. 'Lord Flamborough has said very little about him, now I come to think of it.'

Will Chatterton, the Earl of Flamborough, elder brother of the twins, was a near neighbour. He had always been a good friend—too good for Sophia's conscience once he had brought the news of Daniel's death. Her betrothed had perished in the wreck of the ship bringing the twins back to England after their ten years in India in the service of the East India Company. Will did not owe them anything now she would not be marrying Daniel.

Sophia looked down at her ringless hand and the tight cuff of her morning gown of deep mauve lawn. She had worn black for three months and had just moved into half-mourning. She still felt the most terrible hypocrite every time any of their friends or neighbours, reminded by her attire, sighed sympathetically over her loss.

With the reading of the will after the funeral it became clear that Daniel had neglected to amend it to recognise his betrothal. Neither Callum, who had been so outspoken about the engagement at the time, nor the earl, whom she suspected of not approving either, seemed to realise just how this left the Langleys.

Daniel had made no provision for her at all. Callum, who had seemed almost frozen with grief over the loss of his twin, had tried to explain that this was simply the result of Daniel's carelessness about business, his unwillingness to confront unpleasant matters such as his own mortality, rather than any lack of love or care for her.

But her heart told her differently. Daniel had fallen out of love with her, just as she had realised, too late, that she had with him—not that she could say such a thing to either bereaved brother. And if they had not loved each other, then, in all conscience, she had no claim on Daniel. If she had been honest with herself and ended the engagement sooner, she might well have found a husband and her family would have been secure.

She would probably have a family of her own by now, she thought with a pang of longing.

Perhaps Callum or the earl would have made over some funds to her if she had asked, but pride, and the awareness of her own youthful folly in ever agreeing to the betrothal, stopped her mentioning it.

Will had called regularly to offer assistance—the loan of a gardener from the Hall, his carriage when they needed to go into St Albans, a surplus of vegetables from the gardens. But in the face of her constant, polite refusals his visits had grown fewer. She worked hard to disguise their poverty and so far, just, she was succeeding. But the stack of bills in her bureau was growing and the polite requests for payment were becoming more abrupt. Sophia knew they were reaching a point where she was going to have to make some very hard decisions about her own future.

'Perhaps he has decided to do the right thing and make over some of his inheritance from Daniel to you,' Mrs Langley said. She sounded brighter than she had in weeks at the prospect.

'There is no reason why he should, or could,' Sophia explained patiently. 'The estate he inherited from Daniel was entailed, he cannot part with any of that even if he wanted to and he has his own career and future to consider. No doubt he will be marrying soon, especially if he is not returning to India.'

'Ah, well.' Her mother sighed. 'Never mind. Dear Mark will complete his studies soon and be ordained and then he will have a parish and everything will be all right.'

Sophia did not point out that Mark was hardly likely to find a parish with a stipend large enough to support

himself, her and Mama *and* deal with their debts without an influential patron backing him. Her brother had
neither the drive, nor the engaging personality, to seek
out a good position for himself; a curate's place in some
industrial town or rural backwater was more likely. It
was up to her to deal with this.

She gave herself a mental shake and focused on the
letter again. The note in the strong black handwriting
was brief and without explanation. Callum Chatterton
would do himself the honour of calling on her—not
on Mama, she noticed belatedly—that afternoon and
trusted that she would be able to receive him.

Sophia scooped up the rest of the post before her
mother could realise just how much of it appeared to be
bills. How could there be so many when all she seemed
to do these days was make do and mend and search for
economies? 'I will deal with these this morning,' she
said brightly. 'How interesting it will be to see Callum
Chatterton again.'

Her desk was in the corner of her bedchamber and
she closed the door with a sense of finding sanctu-
ary. Sooner or later she was going to have to make her
mother understand just how serious matters were, but
not yet. One more month and then she must write to
a London agency and seek employment. The shock of
having to dismiss their solitary footman had been bad
enough for Mrs Langley who felt the loss of status very
sharply. Explaining that her daughter was going to have
to start earning her own living would doubtless result
in hysterics.

The room was simple and light, hung with white
and primrose muslins. *A girl's room,* Sophia thought,
as she closed the door. *And I am no longer a girl. I am*

six and twenty. I am on the shelf, stuck in the back of beyond with no eligible bachelors for miles around.

If only she had had the sense to face up to the fact that she had fallen out of love. She should have written to Daniel, explained, and they could have broken off the engagement amicably with no scandal; everyone had been surprised that her late father had allowed it in the first place, with her so young.

She had been too passive in accepting the betrothal as final. But in other ways she had changed so much in nine years. She had grown up and matured. Grown independent and forward, Mama would say. But what was a girl to do when she was neither a spinster on the shelf nor a wife? She had knowledge now, and her own thoughts and ideas, her own interests and beliefs.

For nine years she had waited, not happy about the length of time, but resigned and patient, learning to keep house and improve her mind. She wondered now with a sudden attack of conscience if it *had* been patience. Perhaps she had been selfish, enjoying this luxury of time to learn to be herself. When her friends had sympathised with her wait she had been uncomplaining. Her art was her escape and she had focused all her free time and energy into improving her skills.

On the desk lay her sketchbook open at the self-portrait she had attempted the other day. It had made her look at her reflection critically and the outcome was not likely to make her vain, that was certain.

In the years after Daniel had left she had grown upwards, if not much outwards. Now she was rather too tall for the mode, rather too slender, without much to fill out a gown in front. Her nose was a trifle long and her mouth a fraction wide, but her eyes were satisfactory, she thought. They were bluer than they had been, or perhaps that was just because her lashes had darkened with her hair which was virtually black now, no longer the deep brown it had been.

She flicked over the page to a study of the head and shoulders of a man. When she had received the letter that had told her of Daniel's imminent return she had studied the miniature she had painted of him before he and Callum left. It was poor work, she knew. So she had taken up her pencils and a drawing pad and began to sketch the twenty-seven-year-old man the boy might have become. And that had been when she had finally accepted—or perhaps *allowed* herself to accept—that she did not love him. She had waited for Daniel because he would make her his wife, give her a place in society. His family and resources and position in the East India Company would finally silence all their creditors.

It had been a shock to see the echo of that picture in Callum's drawn countenance on the few occasions she had seen him before he'd left Flamborough Hall in March. He had grown into his looks; his body was no longer that of a gangling boy, but a hard, fit man. The intelligent hazel eyes, darkened with pain, held years of experience, his mouth was firmer, his expression more guarded. Only the thick dark brown hair was the same, still apt to fall across his brow, just as Daniel's had.

That confrontation with Callum the day before he and Daniel had left for London and their new lives with the East India Company came back to nag at her conscience. It was strange how often she had thought of that and those clear hazel eyes summing her up and then dismissing her. *I love Daniel and I swear I will marry him,* she had vowed. And she had broken that vow. The acceptance of the true nature of her feelings had shaken her as though she was a butterfly breaking out of its chrysalis into a bright, dangerous, exciting new world. 'I do not love you any more,' she had whispered to the portrait. 'What if I do not want to marry you when I meet you and know you again?'

The dangerous idea had been niggling at the back of her mind that perhaps she could earn her living by drawing—not teaching girls, but actually selling her own work. It was not love for a man that made her heart beat faster now, but the act of creation as a picture took form on the page, when the visions in her mind came to life at the point of her pencil. She had toyed with the idea of approaching some book publishers—the famous John Murray or Mr Ackermann who produced so many prints, perhaps.

But there was no choice, not realistically. The idea of making her own living in that way was a daydream. Ladies did not become commercial artists; it would be one step up from the stage and the scandalous reputation that carried with it.

Nor could a lady jilt a gentleman; it would be a shocking and ungrateful thing to do now she had let things run on for years. No one expected marriages to be love matches, so that was no excuse. Nor did a dutiful daughter throw away an alliance that would secure her family's fortune—and certainly not if she would be left an old maid of twenty-six in the process. Whatever sort of man Daniel had grown into, saint or sinner, she must marry him and do her duty. But then tragedy had released her in the only way that society would accept, making her emotional turmoil even worse.

Sophia tossed the bills on top of the sketchbook and

paced across the room. But there was no escape, for that brought her to the trunk that was full of linens, each sheet and pillow sham and towel embroidered in the corner with *C* and the cat's mask that was Daniel's family crest: a pun on the French *chat* for Chatterton. There were underclothes and handkerchiefs, nightgowns and sachets, pen wipers and gloves. The trunk represented nine years of collecting and embroidering and carefully ticking off each item on the list in *The Ladies' Compendium and Housewife's Remembrancer.*

That had been almost a fantasy. She had played at being betrothed while she got on with the rest of her life, as independent as any woman with limited means and a reputation to maintain might be. But now this was real and the folly of a young girl's infatuation was coming home to roost. It was all her fault. She should have broken off the engagement years before, found another match. If she had she would not be an old maid now, her husband would be supporting her mother and she would not be afraid to open the day's post or look at the accounts book.

Sophia squared her shoulders and went to sit at the desk. Ignoring the mess they were in could only make it worse. To throw herself on Lord Flamborough's mercy and ask for a loan would be to sacrifice every iota of self-respect and pride. To try to make a living by her art would scandalise all who knew her.

'Mr Chatterton. Good afternoon.' Sophia dropped her sketchbook and pencil into the flower trug beside the rustic seat and walked across the front lawn towards him. She had been pretending to gather flowers for the past half-hour rather than have the front door opened to him by the maid of all work, the only servant other than Cook who was left to them.

'Miss Langley.' Callum swung down from his horse and threw the reins over a spike in the picket fence before opening the gate into the small front garden. He removed his hat and his face was serious as he took her proffered hand. 'I hope I find you well?'

'Very well, thank you.' She smiled brightly as though the brilliance of it might distract him from her limp and much-washed gown. 'You look… I mean since I last saw you…'

He had lost some of the colour that India and a sea voyage had given him, but the lines of strain and grief had gone from his face, leaving him, she was almost startled to find, a remarkably good-looking man. She should have expected it—she had seen him six months ago, after all—but now, with his full attention on her, the effect was disconcerting. Her pulse fluttered, her tongue was twisting itself into knots and Sophia knew she was blushing. Obviously she did not mix with gentlemen enough.

Callum must think her a complete ninny, but if he did, he did not let it show on his face. 'It was a difficult time,' he acknowledged. 'I think it is behind me now. I find I can look back with gratitude for the memories and even forward to the future.'

She found her hand was still in his and that she had no desire to remove it. 'I am glad the pain is healing. I can imagine that, dreadful as it must be to lose a brother, the loss of a twin is even harder to bear.'

'Yes. That is perceptive of you. Not everyone realises.' He shifted her hand to the crook of his arm. 'Is the summer house still standing?'

'The summer house? Why, yes.' Startled by the change of subject, she turned and let him lead her around the side of the small villa. 'How strange that you recall it. Daniel and I used to hide in there and talk and talk and imagine that my parents had no idea where we had got to. It is just the same as it used to be, just rather more rickety.' There had been tiny yellow roses around the wide doors again this summer, roses she had thought to pick for her bridal flowers.

The doors were unlocked and she opened them, went inside and turned as he followed her slowly into the small, rather dusty space. 'It is not quite the romantic bower we thought it then; you must excuse the spiders and earwigs.'

'I am still surprised how small insects are in England,' Callum said, and his mouth curved into the first smile she had seen from him since his return. 'Might we sit here and talk?'

'Yes, of course. Shall I ask the maid to bring out some refreshments? Perhaps I ought to call Mama.'

'Thank you, no refreshments.' Callum set two chairs near the doorway, dusted off the seats with his handkerchief, put down his hat gloves and whip and waited for her to sit. 'Do you feel you need a chaperone?'

'Not at all. Why ever should I? I have known you for years. You were almost my brother.'

Callum raised one eyebrow. 'I can assure you, Sophia, my feelings for you were never brotherly.'

Flustered, Sophia took the left-hand seat. Now he had put the idea of danger into her head he seemed altogether too male and too close in the tiny structure. 'Is the earl well?'

'Yes, thank you. I gather it is a while since he has seen you.'

She had been avoiding Will and his kindness, afraid that she would humiliate herself and ask him for help, knowing that once he realised in what straits the Langleys found themselves he would feel honour-bound to bail them out.

'He has been very kind,' she murmured. 'You have been in London since—'

'Since the funeral. Yes. I was offered a senior post with the Company, one that is based at East India House in Leadenhall Street. The hard work helped at first. Since then I have found it fascinating.'

'I am delighted for you,' Sophia said politely, wondering what this had to do with her, but glad that he was recovering from the tragedy. 'How gratifying that your talents have been recognised.' This was not the gangling youth she remembered hitting a cricket ball all round the lawns of the Hall, nor the intense young man setting out to seek his fortune in India.

'Thank you. I have taken a house in Half Moon Street—a fashionable area by St James's Park.'

'Indeed?'

'And now I have concluded that there is one thing missing from my new life.' He was looking out over the tangled shrubbery, but she sensed his mind was not on horticulture or even on the unkempt surroundings.

'Hmm?' she prompted as encouragingly as she knew how.

'A wife.' Callum Chatterton swivelled round and faced her, his air of abstraction quite gone.

'A wife?' Sophia found herself caught by his eyes, eyes that seemed now to see nothing but her.

'A wife. I wondered if you would do me the honour, Sophia?'

Chapter Two

'Me?' Sophia's surprise was almost comical. For a moment she gaped at him and Cal wondered whether he had made a mistake and she was not the intelligent and poised young woman he had thought six months ago. Then she shut her mouth—her wide and generous mouth—thought for a moment and asked, 'Why should you wish to marry me, Mr Chatterton?'

Ah, yes, the intelligence was there, and the courage. Her chin had come up; she was taken aback, almost alarmed by his unexpected proposal, but she was not going to allow him to fluster her. He recalled the first time he had seen her after he had returned home. He had been half-drowned, battered, bruised, hoarse with shouting through the long, desperate night for the brother whom the sea had taken, and he had been in no state to be gentle with her.

Sophia had fainted when he'd told her the news, but when she had recovered her senses she had been calm, undemanding and firm with her mother who was indulging in hysterics. From the depths of his own misery Cal had found himself unable to care very much about Sophia and her feelings, only to be grateful for her restraint and the way she retreated behind the mask of the civilised things that one says and does to somehow hold the wild expressions of grief at bay.

He told her a little of what had happened and he had been unprepared for the generosity of her response when she could well be blaming him for failing to save her betrothed.

'I was on the deck, Daniel was in one of the boats, helping the women down,' he had explained. 'A great wave took it. I could not find him.'

'You went in? You tried to save him?' she had asked in horror. In her wide eyes he saw again images of tumultuous seas, of darkness and rocks, and heard rending timber and screams.

'Of course.' Cal recalled staring at her blankly. 'Of course I did.'

'Please.' She had reached out and touched his cheek, her fingers burning hot against the chill of his skin. 'You must get warm or you will take a fever.' Weeks later, as the deep cold inside him had begun to thaw, he had recalled that touch, her instinct to comfort and nurture instead of demanding comfort herself.

Other memories had come back as he learned to live with his loss and to remember Dan. He had nagged his brother to remake his will when he was putting his own affairs in order and Dan had been evasive. He would get round to it, he promised. Nothing was going to happen to him, after all. He had shrugged off all the illnesses that India could throw at a man, had missed being bitten, stung, eaten or mauled by the assorted lethal wildlife—what was Cal worrying about? Besides, if anything did happen, his twin would look after Sophia, he knew that.

'Yes, of course,' Cal had agreed. 'I would care for her as though she were my own, I swear it. But even so—' But Dan had not done anything about his will and then, when it had come to it, Cal had done nothing to help Sophia. He had been sunk in grief and shock and with a black hole where the consciousness of his twin had been for his entire life. As he recovered that promise came back, niggling at his conscience.

He pulled himself back to the present and the young woman in her drab gown who watched him from behind wary blue eyes. She had grown and filled out from the scrap of a girl he remembered almost ten years ago, but she was still too slender, too pale.

'I found myself looking forward for the first time in months and I thought it time I married. I am almost twenty-eight, I have estates now to consider as well as a career that involves entertaining. A wife seemed... logical.' Dull, perhaps, after the high-fliers who had been warming his bed and helping fill the long night hours when he would prefer not to sleep, and certainly not to dream.

'I can see that,' Sophia said, a trifle tartly. 'But why me? You are the brother of an earl, you are in London where you may meet any number of eligible young ladies who, if you will pardon my frankness, will have several more childbearing years ahead of them than I have. I assume an heir is one of your considerations when you talk about estates?'

He liked the sharpness, her honesty, and answered in kind. 'I had not thought of a long engagement. We could, as it were, make up some lost time.' She caught his meaning, blushed, but her mouth twitched. Sophia possessed a sense of humour, then.

'I repeat,' she persisted with a frown of reproof, 'why should you want to marry *me*? The Season might be over, but I cannot believe you could not find a wife in London if you are minded to marry soon.'

'I think you would be very suitable. And I feel it my duty,' he stated. 'Daniel would expect it. I promised to look after you and I have neglected that in my own grief.' This was the woman Dan had once loved, however carelessly.

'What?' Sophia interjected. 'No! It was a tragedy and an accident and no one owes me anything. And I do not expect anything either—least of all to marry you, Callum Chatterton. You never showed the slightest interest in me when we were younger.'

Sophia got to her feet, her cheeks flaming, a martial glint in her eye. Cal stood too, but made no move to touch her. She was mortified, he could see, and hurt pride was making her angry. Animation improved her looks, he thought, even as he tried to repair the damage of his bald statement.

'I am proposing a…shall we call it a marriage of convenience?'

'It is very noble of you,' she said. And he felt a momentary flicker of admiration for the way she controlled herself. She had dignity as well as courage, he thought and then saw her expression waver into uncertainty. 'Let me understand. Do you mean that you would not want to…I mean, that you would not expect to share my bed?'

'Why, certainly I would want to share your bed and

make love to you in it, Sophia.' The blue eyes widened. Was she completely unaroused, completely innocent? How very interesting. And stimulating. He had so far been seeking the company of the skilled and the sophisticated, but an innocent wife would be just as distracting provided the essential sensuality was there.

She recovered her composure with visible effort. 'Forgive me if I cannot find it in myself to accept such a flattering offer.'

'I think you have more common sense than to accept some romantic flummery from me,' he said drily. 'I could protest feelings that we both know I do not have, any more than I expect them from you. But let us be frank. I assume you have not taken some vow of chastity.' The haughty look became a frown. 'So who will you marry now? Some country squire? The curate? Instead you could be the sister-in-law of an earl and have the comfortable life I will give you.'

'Let us leave aside what I might gain from such a match,' Sophia said, her back turned to him as she stared out over the untidy garden. 'What possible benefit could it be to you to marry a woman of my age without influence or wealth, other than to salve your conscience? Any wife will warm your bed as well as I.'

He should stop teasing her. 'I would gain a wife with elegance of manner, intelligence, courage and poise,' Cal said. Her cheek, all he could see of her face, became peony pink. He was laying it on rather thick—she hardly looked elegant in that gown. 'I would have the satisfaction of knowing I have done as my twin would have wished.' He hesitated, then decided that he owed her frankness, if nothing else.

'I do not look for a love match. If I am to be honest,

I do not think myself capable of that kind of total emotional commitment any longer. I feel, since the wreck, that part of me has been ripped away. You knew us both once, you showed some understanding of how a twin must feel—I wonder if you can comprehend that now I do not think I will ever be able to love anyone wholeheartedly again. Not my brother, and not a woman.'

Sophia moved away, her movements jerky, and came to rest with one hand grasping the frame of the door. She did not speak.

'With you, with your maturity and our shared loss, I can hope for some acceptance of that. I am not sure I can ask it of some young girl looking for first love.' Still she did not reply. How much was he wounding her by speaking of Dan and her lost dreams?

He thought of her faint when she had heard the news. For nine years she had clung to the promises she had made. She had been faithful and loyal, just as she had sworn that day in 1799 when he had tried so clumsily to put a stop to the betrothal that had seemed premature and ill founded. He had not sensed then any deep emotional involvement from his twin and the passing years had proved him right.

Dan should have come back and married Sophia years ago, even if he hadn't wanted to risk her health out in India. She'd have had status, the estate, probably children by now, if he had only come home when he had had the opportunity. There was no excuse, not really. There had only been Dan's desire to have his freedom and his total lack of responsibility towards anyone but Callum. And Cal could have made him come back and do his duty, and he knew he had not because it was good to have his brother beside him and not to have to share him with a wife and children.

He would marry Sophia if she would have him, because that was the right thing to do and it was convenient for him, but he did not want to have to agonise over her feelings. It had been hard enough dealing with his own grief and the aching void where Dan should have been.

But soon he must find a wife and settle down. Besides anything else there were two estates to consider, the one that was in trust for him until he married or reached thirty and the one that had been Dan's on the same terms and which was now his, too. He felt depressed and weary at the thought of setting out to find a wife, courting a woman, pretending to love a woman. So much simpler to marry Sophia and solve all their problems.

It would help if he could feel any positive emotions, but they seemed to have deserted him, leaving only a black, aching hole even now, six months later. And so had empathy. He felt his brother Will's pain at a distance; Sophia's, hardly at all. And yet in all other ways he was back to normal. He worked hard, his brain was as sharp as ever, he had ambition, he planned for the future, he welcomed the company of friends and colleagues. He was eating properly, looking after himself and creating a home, not lurking in bachelor lodgings.

Sophia moved again, as though she checked herself from flight, and the sunlight caught the shine of her hair, outlined her figure vaguely through her thin skirts. She turned and looked at him and he saw a speculation and awareness that had not been there before. Cal felt a sudden heaviness in his groin, a stirring in his blood.

'Well, Sophia?' He moved closer to her until the hem of her skirts brushed the toes of his boots. 'Shall we fix a date?'

'Mr Chatterton—Callum—I cannot marry you.' Sophia realised there was nothing else she could think of to say. She could not argue with his sense of duty, with his desire to fulfil a promise to his twin. But how could she accept him when it was her own folly that had allowed the betrothal to endure? Daniel could not have broken it off, not as a gentleman.

'I realise that your feelings for Daniel might make this somewhat awkward,' Callum continued, as dispassionately as though he was discussing the price of tea. 'However, I will endeavour to make you a good husband. I am certain now that I will be remaining in England, which will relieve your mind on the score of either the unhealthy climate or the likelihood of long separations.'

In love with Daniel? She blinked at Callum, distracted from his ruthlessly practical catalogue. *Of course, how could he know how inconstant I had been? I swore to him, so long ago, that I would always love Daniel. What else is he to assume?* Appalled, Sophia realised that she could hardly disabuse him of the notion now; it would be dreadful to announce that she did not love her betrothed when Callum's loss was still so raw.

He was saying something else. She pulled her attention back with an effort. '…a sensible and amiable wife and you require a husband. We could marry quietly by licence.'

'You appear to have thought it all through very thoroughly,' Sophia said, her mouth dry. 'How efficient. I must confess I do not feel much inclined to be sensible, let alone amiable, just now. As for what the intelligent thing to do might be, I have no idea.'

Screaming seemed tempting. *You require a husband,* indeed! Certainly she did; she lay awake in the panicky small hours thinking just that thing and wondering how they would manage when their creditors woke up to the fact that there was no well-connected male in her future to pay the bills. It would be a long while before the pittance she could earn as a governess or a put-upon companion would pay off the debts. But to marry a man who was proposing out of a chilly sense of duty…

'I cannot marry you simply because you have a kindly impulse.'

'I do not commit to matters of importance, of honour, on an impulse.' His mouth curved into something that was almost a smile.

'Certainly not a kindly one,' she tossed back at him.

'I am not much given to impulse,' Callum confessed, and she became aware of his eyes on her body, assessing her.

He was so certain that she would do what he said. Sophia bit the inside of her lip to stop herself flaring up. It was ungrateful, but she was the only one who would decide what she was going to do. 'My feelings for your brother do not concern you?'

'No.' He did not appear willing to expand on that. Perhaps, because he felt nothing for her, he did not care if she still loved another man. It argued that he did not see marriage as involving any exchange of deep feeling, of passion beyond the physical.

She averted her eyes from his broad shoulders and long legs and the distracting prospect of physical passion. He was an attractive man. That was not a good reason for making a marriage, especially as he would hardly be entertaining the same feelings of physical attraction for her. A wife was a warm body in a bed who would perform her marital duties and produce children. Apparently she passed muster, even if she did not drive him wild with desire.

This was as bad as the prospect of marrying Daniel had become, only colder. Sophia reminded herself that Callum was, by business and training, a trader. He was approaching marriage, she supposed, in the same way as any other contract, rationally and with good sense.

'Financially there are problems, are there not?' he asked.

She had to be honest about that, never mind how her pride revolted. 'Yes. There are debts, more than we can cope with any more. I had intended to apply for a post as a governess or perhaps a companion.'

'I expected that,' Callum said. 'I had not realised it was quite that bad, however. Be assured that I will take care of all of it.'

She would get by far the better part of this bargain, for she would bring Callum nothing but herself and she could not pretend that she was much of a bargain. This was the answer to her prayers. Why, then, was every fibre of her being revolting against it? It was an excellent match and any well-bred and delicately brought-up young woman would expect nothing more than what Callum was offering her. Most would snatch at it, deeply grateful to have a second chance.

But she was not anyone else, she was herself and she ached for a meeting of minds and for companionship and for love. Her heart told her to refuse, politely and firmly and put an end to this humiliation, but her head held her back from an irrevocable decision.

'I must think about it,' she found herself saying.

'What is there to think about?' Callum seemed genuinely baffled by her prevarication. 'Is it your mother? You must have planned for her future when Dan returned. Surely there is a relative who would make a congenial companion for her.'

'Well, yes, Cousin Lettice would be delighted to move here, it was always the intention.'

He nodded. 'Excellent.'

'How can you not mind that I was betrothed to your brother?' She stretched out her hands as if she could somehow reach him through the glass wall of practicality he was erecting between them. 'Would I not remind you of Daniel?'

Callum stared at her hands without taking them. 'I have told you how I feel. I have come through the grief and I do hope I would not be so foolish as to be jealous of your feelings for him,' he said eventually. 'If you tell me that you cannot marry me because of those feelings…' He left the sentence hanging. Her escape route.

But it would be a lie and the escape would be into deeper debt, misery for herself and Mama, difficulty for Mark. Sophia shook her head. 'No, it is not that. I know he is… I have accepted that he is gone. It is just that this is so sudden, so unexpected. I need time.'

'Time is not on your side. It is not as though you are a widow who has children already,' Callum said with such flat practicality that it did not hit her until several seconds later that he was warning her that she was letting her only chance of motherhood slip by. 'It will help you decide if you saw where you will be living. There is the town house, of course, but there are also two estates to choose from for when we are out of London. We could drive over and see them together and decide which to live in and which house to rent out.'

'Choose?' Everything was going too fast. 'But Long Welling was always yours, was it not?'

'It was managed by my father and then by Will. I have been in India, remember, and in London for six months. I have no great attachment to it and both houses are vacant at the moment.'

The house where she would live with this man. An insidious little voice was murmuring that Callum's arms would be strong around her body and that he would always stand by her. She could experience physical passion at last. He would give her children. Security. But was it right?

'You need time to think it over,' he said and she realised he had hat, gloves and whip in his hands. She had been so deep in her thoughts that she had not noticed him move. 'I will return tomorrow morning. Goodbye, Sophia.'

'Goodbye,' she said. 'Callum—'

'Of course, how remiss of me.' He bent his head and kissed her, firmly but fleetingly, on the mouth. 'Is that what you wanted?'

'I don't know.' Sophia stared at Callum, somehow managing not to run her tongue over her lips to taste him. 'I have no idea what I want. What I ought to want. You have turned my world upside down.'

'Excellent.' He strode away across the lawn without looking back.

Sophia gave way to the urge to lick her lips. There

was a faint trace of something alien and disturbing over-lain with coffee. *Excellent?* 'Oh, you stubborn, impossible man! Were you listening to me at all?'

Chapter Three

Sophia sat in the front parlour the next morning and tried to work through a muddle of thoughts. There was resentment at the way that Callum simply made assumptions about what was best for her—and the fact that he was doubtless right did not help. There was respect for his sense of duty and loyalty to Daniel and the nagging consciousness that her own duty to her family lay in making a good marriage. *This marriage.*

If only they had a little money and she had room to think. Her mind kept running over and over the lack of money like a dog in a turn-spit wheel. Tradesmen had been understanding about the settlement of bills since her father's death, because of her betrothal to a son of the Hall. But for the past six months they had known that was not going to happen. Nor, unless she married well, would her brother have the influence of a great family behind him to help his career. And if she did not marry Callum, who could she marry?

The prospects locally were hardly promising—some

yeoman farmers much older than herself, the curate, a widower or two, none of whom had shown any particular interest in her. There was no denying that marriage would widen her world very greatly. Mama would be happier if she was well married.

And there was the uncomfortable awareness that she found Callum Chatterton physically attractive. She could not even summon up the will to feel shocked at this, only a conviction that if he actually tried to make love to her she would be stricken with shyness. Duty and a scarce-understood desire said *Marry him*. Every emotional fibre of her being, coupled to pride, said, *No, not when he has no feelings for me and is only offering out of a sense of duty to a man I had not even the constancy to love until death.*

The crunch of gravel under wheels brought her out of her brown study as undecided as when she had drifted into it.

'Mr Chatterton,' the maid said and closed the door behind Callum. In buckskin breeches, boots and riding coat he should have looked every inch the English country gentleman. Instead he seemed faintly exotic, dangerous even. Perhaps it was the remnants of the tan and the way it made his hazel eyes seem green. Or perhaps it was the sense of focus about him. He was a hunter and she was the prey: all for her own good, of course.

'Good morning, Sophia. I have the curricle—shall we drive? It is a pleasant day and we will be more able to say what we mean, perhaps, if we are free from the risk of interruption,' he said. 'I thought you would like to see the two houses.'

Don't be missish, she told herself. She was never

going to decide whether to marry this man if they met only to have stilted conversations in the parlour.

'Very well. I will just go and fetch my hat.'

In the hall she said, 'I am driving out with Mr Chatterton, Lucy. I do not wish to disturb my mother; please tell her where I am if she enquires. I may not be home for luncheon if Mr Chatterton decides to call in at the Hall on the way back.'

'Yes, Miss Langley.' The maid's eyes were wide with speculation. 'I'll take pains not to disturb her.'

Oh dear, now she thinks she is assisting in a love affair. I just wish I did know what this was. Am I wrong to encourage Callum? But I do want to be married, to have children. If the man was someone I could like and respect. If I did not think I was imposing on him to an outrageous extent.

She was weakening, she could feel it. She could certainly respect Callum Chatterton's achievements. He was intelligent, hard working and courageous. But could she like him? What was he like under the emotionless carapace that seemed only warmed by disturbing flickers of sensuality? Perhaps he was as cold and hard and logical as this all the time. He admitted to finding it hard to feel for other people now. *I think I want him. I certainly need him. But perhaps not as a husband.*

Callum was standing by the curricle when she came down and there was no groom up behind. It really would be rather fast to drive ten miles to Wellingford with him, even in an open carriage.

'Is it not acceptable for you to drive with me like this in the country?' he asked. Apparently her doubts were clear on her face. 'It would be in India, if the man is approved by the family. Your mother would approve of me, I believe,' he added with the first hint of a genuine smile Sophia had seen.

'Yes, she would,' she agreed, as he helped her up into the seat. 'Mama would approve of any eligible man who showed an interest in me now, let alone you!' she added and provoked a small huff of amusement from him. She had been evasive last night when her mother had asked her about Callum's visit. Mrs Langley had been left, she was guiltily aware, with the impression that he had called briefly to see how Sophia was getting on.

There was so much she was feeling guilty about. If she could only let go and just do her duty... Callum handed her the reins while he walked round to mount on the other side.

'And, yes, this is a trifle fast, but not so very bad in the country.' She handed the reins back, taking care not to touch his hands as she did so. She wanted her mind unclouded by the disturbing *frisson* of physical awareness that brushed her senses when she looked at him—to touch him would be worse. If only she knew what was right.

'It is certain that you will remain in England?' she asked as Callum looped the reins and turned on to the road to Wellingford.

'I was not certain, when we left India, but now the position in London is confirmed. One of the directors was travelling as supercargo and spoke to me at length about my career and the opportunities with the Company. He survived the wreck and I believe I owe much to his influence in gaining this post.'

'He would not have exerted himself if you did not merit it,' Sophia said. 'I am glad you will stay in

England. I certainly do not wish to bring up children in the Indian climate; I have heard too many stories of the illnesses they succumb to.' For a long time she had told herself that was why she had not pressed Daniel about marriage; now she knew it had been an excuse.

'Ah, we are discussing children now?' Sophia looked sideways and found Callum was smiling. Faintly, it was true. She realised she was staring at his mouth and switched back to looking straight ahead. 'Should I take that as a promising sign?'

'Not necessarily,' she said, wary that this was going too fast again. 'I am merely considering all aspects of your proposal.'

'But if you are convinced I am not returning to India you will marry me and if you think I might go back, you will not have me.'

'Callum Chatterton, you are harassing me! I said no such thing and this is not a matter to be bargained over.'

'Very well, let me be clear then. I need an heir; I would like several children, in fact. But I would not expect you to live in India and certainly not bring up a family there.'

'And I would not wish to spend long periods separated from my husband.'

'Flattering,' he remarked and she jabbed him in the ribs with her elbow, suddenly the small girl again.

'I did not mean that!'

'I can assure you, that eventuality is highly unlikely to occur.' When she did not reply he added, 'I am prepared to promise you that I will not take a posting in the Far East again without your express approval. You see how convinced I am that you will suit me?'

'Why, thank you, sir,' Sophia muttered and caught

sight of that elusive smile again. *But would you suit me? Does that really matter?*

'Here is the turning to Wellingford village.'

'And Daniel's estate,' Sophia said, pulling herself together. This is where she would have lived if she had married Daniel.

'Yes. It is years since I've been there. I have no idea why Grandmama left this one to Dan and the other to me. She used to reside here and Great-Aunt Dorothea had Long Welling. There have been tenants in until recently, so they should both be in good repair, but as for decoration, I have no idea.'

'Paint and fabrics are easily dealt with. The question is, which feels best to you.' But her heart was beating a little faster at the prospect. A home of her own, finally. *I am deciding on marrying a man, not a house,* she reminded herself. There were any number of changes one could make to a house, but not to a grown man, not one as single-minded and stubborn as Callum Chatterton. But she must stop thinking about this as a marriage of love, or even affection. This would be a marriage of convenience with most of the convenience on her side. It would be up to her to accommodate herself to him, not the other way around.

'There.' Callum reined in the pair at the crest of a small hill. The valley opened up before them, green and lush; the fields were interspersed with coppices and a larger beech wood crowned the opposite hill. Smoke rose from the chimneys of the village and on the slope directly across from them sat a neat brick house.

'What do you think?'

'It looks smug,' Sophia said instantly, startled out of her reverie by the force of her reaction. 'So symmetrical and tidy.' Two windows either side of the front door, five on the floor above, five peeking out from the roof behind the parapet. The drive swept round at the front in a perfect circle with a central flower bed. Service buildings flanked the house in carefully balanced order on either side. It was like a doll's house or a child's drawing.

'And that is wrong?' Callum was studying it with his head on one side. 'Everything looks so different after India, I am still not used to it. Except the Hall, of course—that just feels like home.'

'Shall we look at this one inside?'

'Isn't that rather shocking?' Callum kept his face perfectly straight, but she guessed he was teasing her.

'I might as well be hanged for a sheep as a lamb,' she said. 'Driving around in the curricle is rather fast, going into an empty house alone with a man is shocking. But I have come this far; I may as well give you my opinion on the inside as well if you think it would help you make a decision about the house. *Your* house.'

Callum moved the horses into a walk again and they wended their way down the hill, along the village street where they were much stared at, and up the opposite slope to the gates.

Close to, the air of immaculate formality was reduced somewhat by a rather ragged garden, a drive in need of weeding and dull window glass. Callum drove round to the deserted stables, tied up the pair and offered her his arm as they walked back to the front door. 'The last tenants left two months ago,' he said. 'Will did not re-let because he knew I'd want a free choice.'

'This feels like intruding,' Sophia said with a shiver

as they stood in the front hall. 'I half-expect someone to appear and demand to know what we are doing.'

'Yes.' Callum threw open the doors on either side. 'Odd, is it not? When Grandmama lived here it always seemed a friendly enough place. The rooms are well proportioned and the view good.'

Sophia followed him. 'I suppose we should look at the kitchens and servants' quarters.'

Those proved to be perfectly satisfactory. Callum did not, to her relief, suggest they look at the bedrooms. 'It is a very good house,' Sophia said as they returned to the front door.

'And you do not like it.'

'It is not for me to say,' she responded, earning a sideways look from those penetrating hazel eyes. 'Do you?'

'Not much. It is…dull. I cannot imagine us living here.'

'What are houses in India like?' Sophia asked, steering the conversation away from marriage as they went back to the stables.

'The Europeans live in single-storied houses called bungalows, with a wide and shady veranda around the sides. You spend a lot of time out on the veranda. When I was holding court I would sit there and the petitioners would assemble in the courtyard in front. In the evening that is where we would all sit and talk and drink.

'There are wide windows covered with slatted shutters to let in the breeze, and each room has a big fan in the ceiling that is moved by the *punkah-wahllah,* a man who sits outside in the passageway and pulls the string with his toe. The bathroom has a door to the outside so the water carrier can come and fill up the tanks and take away the waste. The kitchens are separate because of the heat and the risk of fire. Servants are very cheap so one becomes lazy easily,' he added.

'How?' Sophia asked. Callum, she thought, would not take to a life of indolence. Now, recovered physically from his ordeal, he gave her the sense of suppressed energy. Or perhaps it was simply impatience with her indecision.

'Oh, you could be carried everywhere if you wanted. You reach out for your glass and someone puts it into your hand. You forget something and a bearer scurries off to get it the moment you frown, apologising as though it was his fault and not yours. Some of the memsahibs—the European wives—had constant battles with their cooks, wanting them to make English dishes. If you get used to Indian food it is much easier.'

'Would you want Indian food in England?' she asked, seized with trepidation at the thought of explaining dishes she did not understand to a temperamental English cook or, worse, a French one. *Stop thinking like that! It is not my problem. Not yet.*

'I could always employ an Indian cook, I suppose,' he said.

'Of course,' she said, politely, and then saw the amusement in his eyes. 'You are teasing me, are you not? Seeing how far I would be prepared to accommodate your whims.'

'Whims? A man's dinner table is almost the most important priority.'

'What is more important?' Sophia asked. 'No, do not answer that! I walked right into it.'

'I cannot imagine what you mean.' Callum sounded

all innocence. But the man had a sense of humour, thank heavens, even if he was using it to bait her with.

Sophia tried to recall the brothers nine years ago. Daniel was usually laughing and joking. He rarely took anything seriously, except when they were together. Callum, as he had grown up, had become quieter, more intense. More private, she supposed. Or perhaps he was simply being tactful and not intruding on his twin's courtship.

At least, he had kept out of it until that last day when he had tried to stop her tying herself to Daniel. Why had he done that? At the time she had been too hurt and indignant to puzzle over it, too distressed at Daniel's departure to worry about what Callum thought. He had been perceptive, it seemed, and had had his twin's best interests at heart. The love had not lasted—at least, not on her part. She could not guess at Daniel's feelings.

She brought her mind back to the present and found Callum was taking a back lane through the woods. 'This is charming. And mysterious,' she added as they came out of sunlight into shade. The great beeches soared on either side; their smooth grey trunks rose like pillars in an outdoor cathedral, and the tracks that led off on either side wound their way deep into the wood.

'I came this back way because I wanted to see if the house is still as I remember it, and this is the way we came when I was a child,' Callum said. 'You are going to love it or hate it, I think. It is not possible to be indifferent.'

The lane became a track, swung round to the right and opened up into a wide clearing. To the left there were views over the valley and a decent metalled carriage drive heading off to the valley road. To the right stood the house. Or, rather, there it grew, for it was hard not to think about it as anything but organic, rooted in the earth. It was built mainly of soft pinkish-red brick with a section of white stone that looked as though it might have been robbed from a ruined castle, and here and there were the signs of an oak frame, twisted with age. The roof was of clay tiles, moss-covered and irregular, and chimneys sprouted in profusion.

'I love it.' Sophia stared, enchanted, not realising that she had put out her hand until she found she had covered Callum's bare fingers. He did not move away, and after a moment he curled his fingers into hers. She wished she was not wearing gloves, could feel the texture of his skin, whether he was cold or warm, sense his pulse. She gave his fingers a little squeeze, needing to share the moment.

'I like it, too. I have only a vague recollection of it; we did not come here very often, for Great-Aunt had fallen out with Grandmama and was a trifle eccentric.' He freed his fingers and jumped down to tie the reins to a branch. 'Shall we see if it is as welcoming inside?'

'You feel it? The welcome?' That was good: they seemed to be in agreement over it. *I am thinking as though I have decided. Too fast...I need more time. He is a stranger after all these years.*

Callum reached to lift her from the seat, his hands hard at her waist, and she caught her breath as his eyes darkened. He let her down, slowly. Her toes brushed against his boots, her hems must have touched his thighs. Her heart thudded and she was uncertain whether it was more with nerves or desire. 'I am down now,' she said after a moment when he still held her.

'On *terra firma*?' His thumbs just brushed the underside of her breasts and a strange aching shiver ran through her.

'I am not certain I have been on that since you walked back into my life,' Sophia confessed and Callum laughed and released her.

He opened the door with a huge old key that had been left under a stone by the path and stood aside for her to enter. The house was not musty exactly; rather it smelled of old wood and fabric, faded lavender and the ghost of wax polish and wood smoke. It creaked a little as they stood there.

Somehow it swept away her jittery nerves. 'I love it,' Sophia repeated as they stood in the hall. 'It feels warm, as though it wants to hug us.' It sounded fanciful as soon as she said it, but Callum did not laugh, only looked at her a trifle quizzically.

'Perhaps it does. It sounds almost alive. Listen. Like a ship riding at anchor,' he murmured. 'Shall we explore?'

They wandered through the old house, drawing back the curtains, peering into cupboards, finding odd flights of stairs that went to one room only, almost falling down the cellar steps.

Sophia caught Callum by the wrist as he peered down the precipitous, dusty steps into the dark beneath. 'Don't you dare go down there! Do you remember that day we played hide and seek together at the Hall and I hid in the wine cellar and you and Daniel pretended you didn't know I was down there and locked the door?'

'And left you to those great big hairy spiders and the mice and the mouldering skeletons that hung in chains, which is what you accused us of when we relented.'

'Did I say mouldering skeletons?' She tugged him firmly back into the kitchen passage and closed the door.

'No, that's what you were screaming about when you threw a bottle of Papa's best crusted port at Dan's head.'

'You caught it.'

'Of course,' he said and for a moment there was something unspoken, more than just the recollection of a childhood prank. Callum had saved the port, saved his brother from a possibly serious injury and her from the consequences. 'If you will not let me explore downstairs,' he said, 'I dare you to come up to the bedchambers.'

'Why?'

'To assess their suitability and condition.'

'You did not want to look at them at Wellingford,' she said.

'We had agreed by then that we did not like the house. There was no point.' He cocked his head to one side and studied her. 'Are you suspicious of my motives?'

'Yes,' she said frankly.

'My dear Sophia, if I was intent on seducing you I could do it as well on the drawing-room sofa, the kitchen table or here and now.'

'You could? Is that not very uncomfortable?' Disturbing images flitted through her imagination. Callum raised one dark brow and took a step forwards. Sophia threw up both hands. 'Oh, no, that was not a challenge! Come along then, let us see what is upstairs.'

Finally, they arrived in a great bedchamber dominated by a four-poster of age-blackened carved wood, so high that there was a wooden stool set to help the sleeper climb into bed.

'Well?' Callum stood in the middle of the room, hands on hips, and studied her face.

'I adore it,' Sophia confessed. 'I want it. But that is quite irrelevant; I cannot marry a man because I have fallen for his house.'

'Liking the house is surely on the positive side of the scales. There are other reasons to marry. You would not permit me to attempt to seduce you downstairs, but this is a proper bedchamber and a very comfortable-looking bed.'

'You are not going to seduce me!'

'Am I not?' Callum tossed his hat and gloves on to a chest and came purposefully towards her.

'You are far too much a gentleman to seduce a virtuous lady,' Sophia said with all the conviction she could muster.

'Certainly not one I have no intention of marrying,' he agreed.

Sophia edged around a stool. 'But I haven't said *yes* yet.' It came out as an undignified squeak.

'True. May I not kiss you? Are you quite certain you wouldn't like to be kissed, Sophia?'

'Well, yes,' she said so promptly that he blinked. 'Now don't look so shocked! I am curious. Here I am at six and twenty and I have hardly been kissed, certainly not for ten years. The prospect of a good-looking man demonstrating how it is done properly is undeniably intriguing.'

'Are you always so honest?'

'I hope so.' Of course, to allow Callum to kiss her when they were not even betrothed was a shocking and unwise thing to do, but she had been wanting to kiss him for the past hour at least, despite that.

Partly it was curiosity, as she had admitted. But mainly it was the good-looking gentleman himself. He annoyed her, he teased her and she sensed a deep inner darkness in him that he was hiding and showed no signs of wanting to share. On the other hand he would, she was certain, make her a good husband and, when she was not feeling like she wanted to shake him, she found him curiously easy to get along with. Perhaps it was simply the shadow of their childhood acquaintance.

Sophia bit her lip and looked at him standing there patiently for her to make up her mind. As patient as a cat at a mouse hole, she thought.

'Shall we get rid of that bonnet?' She began to untie the bow, her fingers all thumbs. 'If you are considering marriage, you must expect your husband to want to kiss you,' Callum remarked. Sophia turned her head away, unable to think of a single sensible thing to say. She was beginning to find her focus was oddly blurred, as if she might be coming down with a fever, and it was difficult to read his face. 'But, if this is making you uncomfortable…'

'No. I would like to be kissed, I think,' Sophia said, placing her hat beside his on the chest. It was only a kiss, after all. Another fast thing to be doing, but hardly something to be frightened of. It was ridiculous, at her age, never to have been kissed properly. 'But that's all.'

'I thought you might say that,' Callum said. She had no time to wonder whether that was a joke or whether he was deadly serious before he pulled her into his arms.

Chapter Four

It was a disturbingly pleasant sensation, being held by Callum Chatterton. Part of her was shocked at being so intimately close to a man, but it was hard to summon the appropriate outrage when she was being held fast against his body and he was tipping up her chin to look down into her face. After all, she had asked for this.

He was very good-looking, even more so close up. Now she could study the fine lines of his lips, the subtle colours in his hazel eyes, the uncompromising masculinity of his bone structure. He was not a pretty youth, he was a man, complete with a bump on his nose which looked like a break, several small scars and faintly tanned skin that gave him a most exotic air.

Callum let her study him, his face as serious as hers must be, then he bent his head and took her mouth. Sophia almost jumped at the intrusion of his tongue between her lips, the pressure that opened them to him. Was this normal? It felt indecently intimate. She quivered and his arm tightened around her, supporting her, almost, not quite, constraining her. He felt very determined.

She could taste him, which was shocking. And she could smell him, which was even more so. He was clean, of course, but under the smell of ironed linen and good soap there was something dangerous and faintly musky, overlain by spice and sandalwood.

He was holding her very firmly, which might have been frightening. Sophia flirted for a moment with a feeling of alarm, the instinct to struggle, then let herself relax into Callum's hold. He was too strong to fight. His mouth was insistent now and she let him do as he wished, and, increasingly, what *she* wished, as her tongue learned to play with his.

It made her body feel most strange. There was an ache, low down, and the urge to mould herself tightly against him *there* as though that would ease it. She realised that his body was hard against her belly and that was…worrying. It made the ache worse and so did pressing against him. Then Callum's hand cupped her breast and he began to play with her nipple through the fabric of her bodice and the ache turned into a stab of sensation that had her whimpering into his mouth.

This is far more than I expected. Far more. But it was a fleeting thought, easily dismissed. This was the man she was going to…*no,* might marry. She must learn to respond to his lovemaking. Then the kiss deepened, became more demanding, and Sophia lost awareness of everything except the sensation that was singing through her, the strength of Callum's hold, the urgency of their bodies. So this was proper kissing… She was drowning. It was overwhelming.

'Sophia?'

'Oh.' Callum had stopped kissing her. How long had she been standing there, her brain reeling, her heart pounding and her senses quite disordered? What must he think of her? She wanted to run and hide, from herself as much as him.

'Have you *ever* been kissed before?'

She blinked and he came into focus. He looked pleased with himself and faintly amused. Amused by her old-maidish ignorance, she supposed.

'Not like that, no.' It seemed she could articulate, at least.

'Dan never—'

'Certainly not. We kissed…but it was different. We kissed a little and held hands. He put his arms around me. He touched my…my breasts once.' She felt her cheeks getting hot. She wanted Callum to kiss her again, to touch her. And he knew it. He must be feeling sorry for her, poor frustrated spinster that she was.

Gradually her pulse calmed and she felt her colour rising under that steady gaze. She had very little experience of men, but she knew he was aroused. That was only to be expected, she supposed. But had he thought she was so…so desperate? Frustrated? Potentially wanton that she needed to be kissed until her legs trembled?

She felt the anger sweep through her and know it was for herself, not really for him. She had been frustrated and she had not realised. She had been desperate for a man's caresses. What might she have done if he had not stopped—or would the apprehension that was trembling just under the confused desire have made her flee?

'Are you all right?'

'No,' Sophia said. 'No, I do not think I am *all right*. What have you done to me?'

'Kissed you,' he said. 'There is some basic attraction between us, I think.' From the way he smiled he seemed to find that amusing. 'Sophia, that was passion, that is all.'

'Very basic,' she snapped. 'I am obviously far more ignorant and innocent than the women you are used to associating with,' she added bitterly. 'I did not want passion! I only wanted a kiss in a decent manner. There was no need to virtually ravish me,' she hissed and slapped him, hard, right across his handsome face. She might not be heavy, but she was fit and tall and she put a great deal of feeling into the blow. It rocked him back on his heels, she was pleased to see.

Callum lifted one hand to his face and touched his cheek with his fingertips. 'A *decent* manner? That was the sort of kiss that lovers exchange. The sort of kiss married couples exchange. If I had wanted to ravish you, believe me, we would be on that bed by now.'

Bereft of words, Sophia turned and walked down the stairs and out into the sunlight. And now she was going to have to sit beside Callum for half an hour, so close that she could feel the heat of his body next to hers and all the while he would be smirking with male superiority over reducing an ignorant spinster to such a pitiful puddle of need.

The horses looked up and whickered softly at the slam of the front door and she stared at them in sudden speculation. Perhaps she was not trapped here after all. She could drive a gig with one horse. How much more difficult was it to drive a pair? These had been well exercised and seemed biddable enough.

She ran across the clearing, untied the reins and climbed up on to the high seat. It took a moment to sort out two pairs of reins, but she had been watching Callum's hands as he drove and she found the knack of it.

'What the hell are you doing?' He had come out at last, but there was the width of the clearing between them now. 'Sophia!'

'Get up.' Sophia clicked her tongue and the pair responded as Callum began to run. She slapped the reins down and they broke into a trot, then a canter. As the carriage swayed up the rutted track she heard a shout behind her, but by now she was too concerned with not overturning the curricle to heed him.

The track sloped uphill, which helped, and she had the pair steady by the time it turned on to the road. They settled into a walk again and she did not try for more speed. As it was, the instinct to hang on to the side of the vehicle with her free hand was hard to fight.

But the pair's docility calmed her. It left her with nothing to do but brood on what had just happened. *How could he? Why did he not ask? But he did, in a way,* a small voice cut into her tumbling, angry thoughts. *He asked to kiss me, it was not his fault that I was so shamefully carried away by it. I gave myself up to his kisses far too easily. I did say I agreed.*

She managed a wry smile. Now she knew something about herself that was a revelation. She had felt physical desire and she had also been frightened by the force of it, the sheer physical power of him. His brother had never made her feel like this, needy and shy and confused and almost out of control of where her passions might take her. Memories of Daniel had not made her want to moan with frustration. The gentlemen she encountered at the modest country gatherings had never tempted her in the slightest, she admitted as she negotiated the village street and a flock of sheep. Her body kept murmuring that it expected more. Sophia tried not to listen to it. *More* meant surrendering everything to Callum Chatterton.

'Confound the woman.' Cal stopped at the top of the hill and surveyed the lane down to the village; it was mercifully free of wrecked carriages. The breath rasped in his lungs from running for a mile, but he took a grim satisfaction that he was not panting. He had dragged himself from the lethargy of grief and had thrown himself into physical activity, those past months in London. Boxing, fencing, riding. Sex. They had all helped heal him, helped bring some balance back as well as strengthening his body.

He surveyed the road. If Sophia had got this far, then she was probably sufficiently in control to get home safely. He had chosen steady horses so he could concentrate on her and they had been well exercised. Now he should stop worrying that she had broken her neck and face the fact that he had badly mishandled that kiss. She truly was an innocent and he had shocked her, not so much by what he had done, but by the reactions he had provoked in her.

He had not set out to shock her, Cal told himself as he strode down the hill and into the inn yard. He had intended to kiss her, with restraint, and convince her that marriage to him was nothing to be afraid of. And then she had quivered in his arms and he had sensed the innocent natural passion and sensuality so he had given a mental shrug and found himself taking, demanding, far more than he should.

Sophia's total surrender in his arms would be flattering if it were not for the fact that she had probably simply been overwhelmed by the novelty of it all. And now the physical desires he had been suppressing when he was near her were all on the surface again. The taste of a woman, the feel of her in his arms, was as powerful as a drug. No, not just a woman. *This* woman. He wanted Sophia Langley very badly indeed.

'Anari murkha,' he muttered in Hindi. 'Worse than a fool.'

'Sir? Sorry, sir.' An ostler emerged from the stables.

'Not you.' Cal unclenched his teeth and tried for a more pleasant tone. 'I require a horse to get to Flamborough Hall; I'll have a groom bring it back later today.'

Having to deal with a suspicious ostler who could not understand why a gentleman should arrive sweaty, horseless and without his card case or more than a crown in his pocket, and then riding a slug of a nag home, did nothing to improve Cal's mood.

He had tried to be honest with her. He could not find it in himself to love, to risk caring so deeply, ever again. Life was too uncertain—how could he cope if he allowed himself to feel for her and then lost her?

Did she understand the difference between physical passion and love? He did not want to hurt her, break her heart all over again. And yet… An errant smile curled the corner of his mouth as he thought of Sophia's reaction to his kisses and caresses. She had felt glorious in his arms, despite her inexperience.

He was still musing on that as he rode up to the front of the Hall and tossed the reins to the groom who ran forwards to take them. 'This belongs to the Black Swan in Long Welling. Have someone take it back at once, will you?'

'Yes, sir. Miss Langley called with the curricle, sir. Wilkins drove her home.'

'She has won her wager, then,' Cal said lightly. 'Most improper. You and Wilkins won't speak of it, I trust.'

He strolled into Will's study, his mind full of interesting memories which his body, relaxed by vigorous exercise, was eagerly endorsing.

'There you are! How did it go?' His elder brother tossed down his pen and looked up, his expression lightening. 'You look better—so much colour in your face. Sophia said *yes*, then?' Will had been enthusiastic when Cal had returned to the Hall and told him of his intention to marry Sophia. Cal suspected that he had been worried about the Langleys, but had been unable to penetrate their polite reserve.

Cal found himself staring at the triple portrait of the three brothers that hung over the fireplace. There was the man Sophia had loved. He forced his attention back to Will. 'At first she said, *maybe*. We went for a drive and decided we did not like Wellingford and we did like Long Welling. Then there was an…incident and now I do not know.'

'Incident?' Will's left brow arched up.

'Incident,' Cal repeated, returning a look devoid of expression. 'She will, however, be marrying me whether she likes it or not.' He looked away from his brother's speculative gaze to Dan's painted smile. Once, just thinking about Daniel had been enough to trigger the instinct that he was there, listening. Now the void inside echoed with emptiness. He stamped down on the feeling.

'I will let her sleep on it,' he added. It was tempting to go straight over to the Langleys' house and have this out, but years of negotiating contracts had taught him to wait and keep the other party guessing. Sophia was angry and embarrassed now; by morning he would wager she would be unsettled.

I need an heir; I would like several children, in fact. He had said that to her and, until the words had left his lips, he had not realised that they would be true at a deeper level than the simple need for a successor. And the way she spoke about children made him think she wanted them, too. He glanced back at the portrait. A wife and children. More hostages to fate.

There was a silence, then Will said, 'She deserves happiness.'

'Of course,' Cal agreed. He would do his best to make her content, just as long as she did not expect love.

Sophia paced up and down the bedchamber floor. *I will say no,* she thought, sinking down on the end of the bed. It was shameful how he had made her feel— wanton and vulnerable and yearning. And ignorant. She was playing right into Callum Chatterton's wicked, clever, hands. *He* had not been shaken to the core by that kiss, that was for sure. Mr Chatterton knew what he was doing. No doubt being bedded by him would be a shattering experience. Not that he was likely to enjoy it much, for she could hardly measure up to the skills of the women who had been his mistresses over the years.

A husband who loved his wife would not be disappointed in her ignorance, would be faithful to her. But this was to be a marriage of convenience and under those circumstances a wife was not supposed to take any notice if her husband took a mistress.

Which was not fair. But then life was not fair and she was not some young girl who could afford to dream of fairytales and princes.

She would refuse to marry him. He affected her too much on too many levels. She desired him, he had demonstrated that clearly enough. There had been moments today when she had simply relaxed and enjoyed being with him. He could make her like him and that would hurt if he would not let her close to him. He reminded her of Daniel and of a long-ago innocent time and of her own guilty conscience.

Sophia threw the window open and leaned her elbows on the sill, shivering a little in the cool night air. It washed over her heated skin and with it came a sobering flood of reality. She could fume and plan and curse Callum Chatterton and her feelings about him all she liked, but her own fate was not the only thing at stake here and her anger over what he had revealed to her of her own nature and desires was almost irrelevant.

Even if she found paid employment she would never earn enough to pay off their debts and keep Mama in genteel comfort. Her mother and brother would have to sell this house, pay off the bills and settle together in whatever humble parish Mark found himself. But if she was married into the Chatterton family, then a whole world of influence would be opened up to her brother, her mother would bask happily in the assurance of status and connection and she could have a family of her own.

The same results might come if she married someone

else, of course, but it was a daydream to imagine she could easily find another eligible suitor at the age of twenty-six, shut away in the depths of the country with no dowry and no connections.

She turned back into the room and found her sketching pad and began to draw. A church interior, the long aisle, a challenge in perspective, a man at the far end, waiting at the altar rail, his face a blur.

'Mrs Callum Chatterton,' Sophia said to herself. 'I suppose I had better get used to it.'

Chapter Five

By three o'clock the next day Sophia was hard put not to range up and down the parlour like a caged animal. Where was Callum? There was no sign of him, not so much as a note. Had he changed his mind and decided that after yesterday when she had slapped him, insulted him, stolen his horses and abandoned him in the middle of the woods that she was impossible, duty or no duty?

When the clock struck the half-hour she could stand it no longer. 'I must go out for a walk, Mama,' she said. She stuffed the half-hemmed pillowcase that she had been mangling into the workbasket and almost ran out of the room. She snatched up a straw villager hat, jammed it on and was out of the front gate before she could think where she was going, or why.

She stepped straight out into the little lane, aiming for the stile into the field opposite and the footpath through the woods. The sound of hoofbeats only registered when the horse was almost upon her. No one cantered down here—Sophia spun round and the rider wrenched the animal to one side, but not before it caught her with its shoulder and knocked her to the ground.

Sophia sat in the mud at the edge of the lane, her hat over one eye, and tried hard not to scream. It was too much. This was her best afternoon dress, worn in the expectation of receiving a proposal of marriage. Her bottom hurt where she had landed on it, her heart was thudding like a steam engine and she wanted to give in and weep.

Instead she found herself being hauled to her feet by a man who was becoming all too familiar. 'What the devil do you think you were doing? Don't you ever look where you are walking? You could have been killed!' He looked as furious as she felt.

'You were going too fast, Mr Chatterton,' Sophia snapped back. 'Or perhaps you cannot control your horse any better than you control your lusts?' She pushed her hat straight and glared at him.

Callum stared back, his eyes narrowed, his mouth grim. He looked dangerous, irritated and impatient. 'Where were you going?'

'Out. For a walk, if it is any of your business.' He was still holding her with a big hand wrapped around each arm, just above the elbows. 'Will you kindly let me go?'

He ignored her demand. 'Out? When you were expecting me?'

'Expecting you, Mr Chatterton? Why should I be? I assumed you would not make another assault on my virtue in my own home.' As she said it she felt something contract inside. Was this really the man who had made her drunk with desire, so incoherent that she could not think? Yes, it was and being this close brought back an unsatisfied ache to add to her discomfort.

'You should have been expecting me to come and finalise the arrangements for our marriage,' he said, his voice even. It was infuriating that she could not get him to raise his voice and show some emotion, even if it was anger.

'Oh. You still intend to marry me?' *Thank goodness.*

'Do you mean to be deliberately provocative, Miss Langley?'

'Yes,' she said, lifting her chin. *I might have to marry him—I do not have to like him.*

'And what are you attempting to provoke, I wonder?' he said, his voice silky smooth. A quiver of something that was not quite fear and not quite desire went through her and she knew he sensed it from the way his eyes narrowed and his mouth curved.

'Some genuine emotion,' she flashed. 'Not cold duty, not manipulative lust, not sarcasm. The truth. Do you truly *want* to marry me or not, Mr Chatterton? I should warn you, I meant it when I said we have considerable debts. And Mama will need support; I do not expect my brother to be able to do that.'

The question hung there in the warm air. Then Callum smiled. 'Yes, I want to marry you, Sophia. I think it is the right thing to do. I think we can deal well together. I cannot pretend that I love you, that I ever will love you. And I do not ask that you will love me—how can I expect you to be so fickle as to forget Daniel that easily? And, in any case, I suspect love to be a much overrated emotion. That does not mean I will not do my utmost to be a good husband to you. And I understand about the debts.'

She tried to block the surge of guilt at his mention of Daniel. It was easier to think how he had made her feel yesterday. How, shamefully, she wanted him to make her feel today. The desire to touch him, to feel those muscles shifting under her hands, to smell his skin again, to taste him against her lips… She was going to marry him, so those sensual promises would be her reward for doing her duty. She only hoped that if the need to provide for her family had not been so great she would have had the strength to refuse him and that she was not doing the right thing for all the wrong reasons.

She twisted away, but something must have shown in her face, for Callum caught her by the shoulder and turned her back to face him as he untied her mangled bonnet strings and removed the crumpled hat. His hand as he brushed her hair back from her face was gentle and she closed her eyes against the intent in his, breathing in the smell of horse and leather and the spicy scent she was coming to know as *Callum*.

'I wish to marry you, Sophia Langley, because I believe it is the best thing for both of us. I also wish to marry you because I promised my brother I would look after you if anything happened to him.

'And I believe that you know you will marry me and, not surprisingly, you are angry and frustrated at having your hand forced by someone else telling you what is right for you. Especially when that other person was somewhat clumsy yesterday.'

'I—' He had summarised it perfectly. So efficient, Callum Chatterton. 'You have left me very little to say, sir.'

'That was my intention. You could say, yes,' he suggested.

'Yes. Yes, I will marry you.' Surrendering to the inevitable was an odd sensation. A sort of dizzy relief mixed with fear.

'Excellent.' Callum bent his head. She held her breath, closed her eyes. He kissed her, lightly, on her cheek.

Sophia gave a strangled gasp of disappointment, relief, surprise, but his hands still held her upper arms. She opened her eyes to find his face already far enough away for her to read the cynical amusement in his eyes. *He knows I want him to kiss me properly. How humiliating.*

'Later, Sophia,' Callum murmured.

'You know how to tease, do you not?' she asked, almost tempted into smiling at his effrontery. There was a noise behind her, some kind of disturbance, but Callum continued to hold her. 'Sometimes it makes the conclusion sweeter,' he murmured.

'Sophia Grace Miranda Langley!'

'Mama.' It sank in that she was standing—or perhaps sagging—in a man's arms in the middle of the public highway, her skirts mired, her hat gone and her hair a tumbled mess.

'Thank heavens! Oh, how wonderful!'

'Mama?'

'Come inside, both of you, before someone comes along.' Mrs Langley flapped her hands as though rounding up chickens.

Callum stooped to hand her the bedraggled villager hat, tossed his horse's reins over the gatepost, replaced his own hat—which, of course, he had safely in his hand—on his head and opened the gate for her. Elegant, controlled, serious. If he so much as let his lips twitch she would… No, he would not make such a tactical mistake. No giving way to smug triumph or foolish passion for him.

'Thank you, Mr Chatterton,' Sophia said with as much frigid politeness as she could manage.

'My pleasure, Miss Langley.'

'I fell in the lane, Mama. I will go and change.' She whisked upstairs, leaving her suitor to break the news to her mother. With any luck Mama would be over the worst of her transports of joy by the time Sophia rejoined them in the parlour.

'Here you are at last.' Her mother beamed at her when she finally came down, some composure restored along with a fresh gown and tidy hair. 'Well! There are many details to arrange, but I am sure we can work everything out over the next month or so.'

'I intend us to marry in two weeks' time,' Callum said, perfectly polite, perfectly implacable.

'But that is no time at all!' Sophia gasped.

'I would have thought you had already waited long enough,' he said with a lift of one eyebrow. He swept on without waiting for her reply. 'I will go to London tomorrow, deal with various pressing Company matters and make sure the house is readied for your arrival. I will speak to the butler and have him find a maid for you. I must do some shopping. Then I shall return to the Hall for the wedding.'

Was there no hesitation, not even for a second? Sophia wondered, watching the hooded eyes, the long fingers lying apparently at rest. *This is your marriage you are talking about,* she wanted to say to him. *Our future. How can you be so calm?*

But Callum swept on. 'The wedding will be by common licence and, under the circumstances, very quiet. Six months has passed, Sophia is in half-mourning, there should be no adverse comment, but I would not wish to attract gossip. I trust two weeks will be sufficient time for your cousin to join you, Mrs Langley? Sophia said that was the plan for a companion.'

'Yes. Dear Lettice can come at any time; she will be delighted, I know. But Sophia's bride clothes—'

'She may shop all she likes in London,' Callum said. He did not shrug, Sophia thought, but he might just as well have done.

'So romantic,' she muttered and saw by the lift of an eyebrow that he had heard her. She raised her voice. 'And if I do not like the house you have in London, or the servants?' Of all the arrogant, cold, *practical* men! 'I thought we were going to live at Long Welling. I *like* Long Welling,' she added rather desperately. Her friends were close, St Albans was a familiar and friendly little town that she knew her way around. How was she going to cope, all alone in London with just a virtual stranger of a husband for company?

'My business requires me to be in London for the present,' Callum said in a tone of finality. 'It will take time for Long Welling to be got into a state to be our country home. If you dislike the London house, we will move to another. If the staff fail to please you, you may dismiss them.'

But we cannot dismiss each other, she thought. Yet would it have been any better with Daniel? He would have been almost as much a stranger as Callum and there would have been the disillusion of acknowledging that their love had evaporated with time and distance. Here, at least, there were no illusions to begin with.

'You will not object if I do that?' she asked, curious at this willingness to accommodate her. Obviously his emotions were not at all engaged with any of this, not even the house he had been living in for six months.

'The home will be your concern.'

Well, that was plain enough. It sounded lonely, though. *Oh, pull yourself together,* Sophia, she scolded. *There will be balls and parties when the Season starts and exhibitions and libraries before then—the whole of London to explore. You will make friends soon enough.* She was shaken by yesterday's experience and today's fall and her resilience was low, worn down by months of worry, that was all it was.

'It all sounds wonderful,' she said with a polite smile. Callum stared back at her, his gaze steady and unreadable under level brows. He made her a slight bow. Acknowledgment of her compliance? A genuine desire to marry her—or just a cynical satisfaction at getting his own way?

Sophia felt a little shiver run through her and the smile stiffened on her lips. Opposite her, the man sitting at his ease in the wing chair lowered his lids over the clear hazel eyes and she realised she could not read his thoughts in the slightest. Then he looked up again, directly at her, and she saw the heat and the desire in his look and knew she could interpret one thought at least: he was thinking about yesterday afternoon. Was desire to be the only heat in this cool marriage? She shivered.

The falling notes of the hymn died away. The choir, who a moment ago had looked like a flock of cherubs, their innocent, well-scrubbed faces turned up towards the stained glass window of the east end of the church, became once more a group of freckled village boys, nudging each other as they sat down in the ancient oak stalls.

No doubt they had mice in their pockets and catapults hidden under their cassocks, Cal thought, amused by the normality of their barely disciplined naughtiness. Beside him Will cleared his throat and on his right hand Sophia closed her hymn book.

In a moment they would leave the high box pew and walk down the aisle to shake hands with the vicar who would be marrying them in three days' time.

And Will and I can both get dead drunk tonight, Cal hoped. He was tired. Beyond tired, he thought, contemplating restless nights, hectic days and miles of travel.

Now all he wanted was sleep and to get this wedding over with. He had done everything that was needful, he thought. At the East India Company offices he had consolidated his position in a post that brought status, a doubling of what his salary had been in India and the opportunity for endless profitable investment in return for his total commitment to the Company's interests.

He had reorganised his house in fashionable Mayfair to receive its new mistress. The rent was high—twice what he would have paid in the City—but they were going to move in the best society, not mingle with the cits. He had given his most superior butler *carte blanche* to appoint a fashionable lady's maid and to make all ready for his return and he had come back here and endured Mrs Langley's endless list-making and insistence on discussing every aspect of the wedding in wearisome detail.

Then there was a rustle of silk beside him as he walked up the path between the leaning gravestones and he looked down at Sophia, silent in lavender at his side. He held the lych gate for her and then offered his arm as they waited for the carriage to draw up. It was necessary to stand there and shake hands with some of the congregation who had gathered round, to agree that after such a terrible accident, such a tragedy, that it was a blessing that he was comforted by the support of Miss Langley, who had so bravely put aside her own grief to marry him.

No one appeared to think it strange that she should marry the wrong brother. It was the most logical solution, several people opined and, they added, when they thought they were out of earshot, very gallant of him to step in and prevent Miss Langley being left a spinster.

Cal was quite certain she had heard those whispers. Sophia's chin was up, there was colour in her cheeks and her eyes were sparkling with what he strongly suspected was anger, not chagrin.

'Don't take any notice of them,' he said when they were at last free to walk across to the carriage.

'I do not like to be pitied,' Sophia said.

'Nonsense, they are jealous,' Cal retorted. 'At least, the ladies are. They all wish they could marry me.'

'Why, of all the conceited men!' She cut him a sideways glance. 'You are jesting? Aren't you?'

'Certainly not. You have only to eavesdrop a little. I'm a son of the Hall—and Will has not yet produced an heir; I must be as rich as Golden Ball if I am in the East India Company and, according to Mrs Whitely, I have powerful thighs. Now what do you think she means by that?'

'That your breeches are too tight,' Sophia flashed back. 'Mrs Whitely is a very foolish woman.'

'She is certainly an outrageous flirt.' The Whitelys had been amongst Will's dinner guests last night and Cal had enjoyed an interesting passage with her in the conservatory. The lady certainly exhibited both experience and a willingness to demonstrate it, but even with the lingering frustration of controlling himself with Sophia, he had felt disinclined to oblige her amongst his brother's potted palms.

While he was recalling Amanda Whitely's charms Sophia had fallen silent. 'Are we doing the right thing?' she asked him after a moment. 'Would Daniel really have wanted this?'

Cal did not pretend to misunderstand her. 'You marrying me? Yes.' It occurred to him as he said it that it was hardly tactful to be so certain. The more he thought about it, the more he was convinced that Dan had fallen out of his attack of calf-love. But his brother had proposed, been accepted. There had been no way back from that, not without dishonour. And he had inherited that obligation. 'He would have thought it for the best,' he added. 'I had promised him I would look after you. And I will.'

Despite his tiredness and his impatience with the whole palaver he found himself increasingly reconciled to this marriage, although he could not put a finger on quite why. Perhaps he was simply weary of being a bachelor. The prospect of a well-run home and not simply a house to lodge in was appealing.

Sophia slid her hand further into the crook of his arm. 'Sometimes it seems disloyal and then I look at you and think that twins are not the same as ordinary brothers and perhaps it is all right. For him, I mean.'

'Are we so alike to you, then?' Cal asked as he handed her into the carriage. Physically they had been, he knew that. There had been times when he had caught sight of himself in a mirror and had spoken, thinking it was Dan who stood there. But once people were with them for any length of time they never seemed to have any problem telling them apart.

'I have no idea,' Sophia said as she sat down, smoothing her sombre skirts into order. 'All I have are nine-year-old memories and drawings that are just as old. You will both have changed as you became men.'

'So what are those memories?' What had he got to live up to specifically? He had never been in love, only suffered the pains of adolescent calf-love years ago, so he had no idea what she was feeling still for his brother. But at least he could discover something about how she remembered him. He found he was eager to hear her speak of Daniel. Will had stopped halfway down the path to speak to a group of farmers; they would have their privacy for a few minutes more.

'You mean, not the ones of our childhood, but of his courtship? He was fun to be with, very relaxed. He never took anything seriously—except how we felt, of course. He was kind.' Her voice faltered and then gathered strength. 'He was very…romantic. And gentle. We used to creep away and sit in the summerhouse for hours, but he never tried to…to take advantage of the situation. And I always felt he was with *me* when we were together, not off thinking about anything else. Except you, of course. He was always with you in his head.'

'You noticed?' It had never occurred to him that anyone else would realise how it was with twins.

'Of course I noticed. I knew about it when we were children, but I realised more when I was in love with him,' Sophia said with a simplicity that jolted him. 'He would frown sometimes and say *What's the matter with Cal, I wonder?* Or his mood would change suddenly, in a way that was nothing to do with what we were doing or saying and I guessed that was you in his head. Was it the same for you—that constant awareness of your twin?' Callum nodded. 'Oh, I am so sorry. To have lost that intimate contact with another mind must be very painful. And lonely.'

'You understand that?' He swallowed, hard, fearing for a moment that the blurring of his vision was tears. No one, not even Will, had realised just how alone he had felt, how emotionally empty he still was. How cut off. It was gradually getting better, he was healing and he was not allowing himself to brood, but it would catch him unawares sometimes, like the stab of a knife. And the dreams… 'Yes, it was—is—lonely.'

She became a trifle pink and turned away from him to look out of the window, but he felt a touch on his fingers and glanced down. Sophia had taken his right hand in her left. 'I wish I knew how to help.' She gave a little squeeze and released him.

Cal stopped himself catching her hand again. It was pathetic that she should feel she must comfort him.

He saw the corner of her mouth move and realised she was biting the inside of her lip. 'Were you not jealous that I was taking him away from you?'

'No, I knew he would always be there when I needed him.' And he had never taken Dan's professions of love for Sophia seriously, he had thought it a mistake, right from the beginning. To be jealous of such foolishness never occurred to him. 'And my mind was on other things too,' Cal said.

Why should he not hold her hand? They were betrothed. He caught it in his, her small hand in its tight kid glove vanishing into his larger fist. She went very still, but gradually he felt her relax beside him. It was curiously pleasant and he found himself confiding more easily. 'I was in love, too—or I fancied myself in love. And I had not even had the temerity to approach the girl, let alone say anything to her.'

'Who was she, the girl you loved?' Sophia turned back, her expression now one of sympathy and an interest that his youthful emotions did not deserve. 'Did you miss her very much?'

'I recovered within weeks,' Cal recalled. 'She was a girl called Miranda who is now married to a worthy knight and the mother of a large brood of children, according to Will.'

'What's according to me?' The earl climbed in to join them.

'Village gossip,' Cal said.

'You can drop me at the end of the lane,' Sophia said as the carriage moved away towards the Hall. She had freed her hand. 'It is a fine day for a walk.'

'But you will dine with us tomorrow, of course,' Will said. 'Our relatives will wish to meet you before the wedding.'

'Oh. Of course.'

Sophia seemed a little daunted, Cal thought, managing to keep the frown off his face. He needed a wife who would be able to cope with dinner parties and entertaining. Now he was going to have to keep an eye on her and not give in to the thundering headache that was building up behind his eyes.

Chapter Six

Sophia saw the change in Callum's eyes, even though his face remained impassive. He was not pleased with her lack of enthusiasm, she realised. His change of mood, from confiding and almost gentle to irritated, brushed across her nerves like the touch of a cold finger. Talking of his twin had made her worry again that she was deceiving Callum, that he would not feel he should marry her if he discovered that her feelings for Daniel had altered.

Now that the die was cast and she had agreed to wed him she found that she had no wish to change her mind, although whether it was entirely relief that their money worries would be settled or a growing curiosity about this intelligent, controlled, wounded man, she could not decide. He was not going to be easy to live with, she suspected.

'Tell me who I will meet,' she asked, straightening her back. 'I will try to remember them all.'

'There are two aunts, their husbands and assorted

adult offspring with spouses, one widowed uncle, a brace of spinster cousins of our maternal grandmother and our father's two godsons,' Will explained. 'A motley crew,' he added when he had finished enumerating them. 'But Lady Atherton—Aunt Clarissa—is worth cultivating. You'll run into her in town once she goes up again and she's in with every hostess. She'll get you your vouchers for Almack's and see to your presentation next Season if my betrothed, Lady Julia Gray, cannot. The Misses Hibbert, the cousins, are an entertaining pair of bluestockings.'

He went on, patiently explaining each relative to her until Sophia's head spun. She was never going to remember them, she thought, and dragged her attention back to him as he concluded, '…godson, Donald Masterton. But that's probably exaggerated.'

'Oh, no doubt,' Sophia said brightly, wondering just what it was about Mr Masterton, or who he was, other than a godson, come to that.

It was not so bad as she feared when she and Mama arrived at the Hall the next evening. Sophia found herself surrounded by the younger relatives, who appeared most interested in her—or perhaps they were simply intrigued by her star-crossed romance.

William kept up a flow of conversation with the older men, the spinster cousins had vanished into the library and the matrons were soon immersed in family gossip. Callum stood alone by the fire under the portrait of the three brothers, almost as if he was deliberately pointing up the fact that one of them was missing.

Sophia wanted to go to him, slip her hand into his and stand with him, but the confiding man from the carriage outside the church had gone again and his aura of aloofness kept her away. She sighed, then straightened her shoulders—she had a duty to get to know this family who would soon be hers.

'Where is your town house?' one of the young women asked her.

Mrs Lambert, Sophia recalled. 'Half Moon Street. I do not know London at all, I'm afraid.'

'A very good address.' Mrs Lambert approved. 'And how many rooms does it have?'

'I have no idea.'

'Don't tease the poor girl, Felicity my angel.' That was the tall, rather saturnine young man who was the mysterious Mr Masterton. Or, rather, there was no mystery about him except in her lack of attention to Will's explanations on Sunday morning.

Sophia smiled warmly, feeling she should somehow make up for it. 'Things have all happened very quickly.'

'Still, I don't suppose it makes much difference to you, does it?' Mr Masterton remarked. Somehow he had detached her from the others and established a tête à tête in an alcove.

'Indeed it does! Really, Mr Masterton, Callum and Daniel might have been twins, but they were very different personalities.'

'So, Callum is second-best. How bravely you are facing marriage to a stranger, Miss Langley.'

'I did not say that. Callum is not… Comparisons are odious, Mr Masterton. One cannot go back to what might have been. We are very happy and I hope the family feels the same.' He was tactless and provocative, but somehow it was refreshing after the polite evasions and the poorly veiled speculation, like a mouthful of tart lemonade after too much cream cake.

He smiled at her heated response. 'I am not family, Miss Langley, only the most distant of connections and a godson of the late earl. But you certainly have *my* approval.' The emphasis was unsettling.

Sophia managed a tight smile as the butler appeared in the doorway. 'Excuse me. I believe we are going in.'

Callum came across the room and offered his arm and Masterton strolled off.

'It must be a comfort to have the family all here,' Sophia ventured.

'Not really.' Callum barely dropped his voice as they walked through to the dining room. 'Don't forget, I haven't seen most of them for nine years, except at the funeral. And we were never close in the past.'

That was disappointing. 'Oh. I had been hoping that these people would be visitors to the London house, that I was making a head start on knowing your London acquaintance.'

'No, these are the country mice on the whole, not the town ones. Are you daunted by the prospect?'

'A trifle,' she confessed. 'But you will introduce me to the town mice first, not the rats, won't you?'

That made him smile, but he soon sobered again. Dinner was a formal meal and she felt distanced from it and the other people around the table. Sophia made stilted conversation with Callum, wishing she could recapture the confiding intimacy of Sunday, and then turned with some relief to Lord Atherton, his uncle by marriage, on her other side.

'And what do you think of this new post of Chatterton's, then?' he enquired.

'I do not know, I am afraid,' Sophia had to confess. 'We have had no time to discuss it.' How little she did know! She knew her new address, but not a thing about its location, size or even the names of the servants. She knew Callum had a position which caused his relatives to nod gravely and with approval, but how he filled his days was a mystery. What would her role in his life be? She did not even have the slightest idea how they would be financially. A fashionable address argued wealth, but Callum might well be spending money on visible show to bolster his new position, and she couldn't forget that she had handed him a pile of debts to settle. She must be prudent with the housekeeping.

The conversation veered off to Lord Atherton's description of his recent trip to Edinburgh and there, at least, she was able to take an intelligent interest until Lady Atherton, acting as hostess, rose and led the ladies out.

The polite inquisition that followed was what she had expected. Sophia was able to maintain her poise while engaged in the chitchat that barely disguised questions about her family and her connections. She had been betrothed very young and her father had died soon after Daniel had left for India, plunging her into mourning. Somehow, as she emerged from that she had never begun to mingle with Daniel's wider family. If Will had been married it would probably have been different, but a bachelor earl kept a very different household from a married one and there were no house parties to be invited to.

Having dissected her connections, family and background to their satisfaction the ladies moved on to her ability as a housekeeper and—more difficult to cope with—her feelings about the Chatterton brothers. It felt like being pecked by a flock of starlings. She wished she had a pencil and paper to draw them with their sharp noses, nodding plumes and avid eyes. She had resisted the urge to tuck a pad and pencil into her reticule; this was hardly the kind of party where she could creep away and sketch from the shelter of a curtain as she so often did at dull receptions.

'Yes, I am sure we are doing the right thing,' she was saying through gritted teeth in answer to the rather more direct question put by one of the elderly Misses Hibbert as the gentlemen came in to join them.

'And where is Callum?' Lady Atherton asked. 'I want to know about this house he's taking his bride to. Poor dear Sophia knows nothing about it.'

'He has a headache,' William said. 'And begs to be excused.'

Sophia doubted he had any such thing. He had simply walked away from the stifling atmosphere of rampant curiosity disguised under banal socialising. But he might have said something to her, taken his leave, she thought with a flash of resentment when Mrs Lambert shot her a pitying look. She did not like being *poor, dear Sophia* who must be pitied; it was hard enough holding her own in this company as it was.

'The gardens are very fine here,' Mr Masterton remarked, taking the cup of tea she offered him. He seemed less brittle and dangerous now. Or perhaps resentment at Callum's abandonment of her made another man seem more attractive.

'Yes. The new terraces overlooking the South Lawn are delightful,' Sophia agreed.

'I was forgetting you will know the Hall a lot better

than I,' he said, putting down the cup and turning to the window. 'There is still a little light and it is intolerably stuffy in here. Perhaps you could show me what has been done?'

It was a tempting suggestion and she was tired of being dutiful. Sophia loved the gardens, and, although she had been careful never to presume on Will's invitation to use them as her own, she would often come and draw here when the stress of home and the debts became too much.

'Yes, of course.' She caught up her shawl from the back of the chair and went out through the door he held open for her.

'How fresh the air is. The summer is coming to an end, I fear!'

'You are not cold?' He took her arm and began to stroll along the broad terrace.

'Oh, no, Mr Masterton. There is hardly any breeze. Here is where the old terrace ended…'

'Donald, please. We are about to be family, after all.'

'Donald.' It seemed a little forward, but she did not care to seem stand-offish. 'The earl had this part extended so the view of the lake was improved.'

'And that charming structure?' He gestured to a small temple-like construction on the far corner of the paving. When he lowered his hand it came to rest over hers. Sophia stiffened, but he took no further liberties and she supposed she was being intolerably provincial.

'A little gazebo. It is the most charming spot to sit and read.' Somehow they were strolling that way. The wash of light from the windows receded and the dusk deepened. 'There will not be much to see now it is getting dark,' she added, pausing on the threshold.

But Donald kept walking until they stood in the centre under the dome, the curving seat with the wall behind blocking the view of the house. 'Delightful,' he said, and turned so they were almost toe to toe. 'And designed for flirtation.'

'Whereas I am not,' Sophia said, trying for a light touch while her heart pounded. No, she was not being provincial, but naïve. 'Really, Mr Masterton…Donald, we should be getting back.' If only Callum had tried to flirt, to court her, Sophia thought with an inward sigh. She would like to be courted.

'Don't you care for flirting, Miss Langley?' He was blocking her way back to the house, but he made no alarming move to touch her. If she had had a little town bronze she would know how to deal with this, turn his gallantry aside with a light, dismissive laugh.

She tried one and thought it quite successful. 'I do not. I have no idea how to flirt, Mr Masterton, and I have no intention of learning!'

'So Callum has found himself a good girl, then?' He was teasing her now, but there was an edge to it and she was beginning to think that her pique at Callum's neglect had led her out of her depth with this man.

'I hope so, indeed!'

'So I cannot wish for so much as a fleeting kiss in the twilight?' Donald murmured.

'You, sir, are a rogue!' That sounded quite confident; she was wary of sounding too alarmed for fear of arousing his hunting instincts.

'Just one touch of your lips?' He caught her hand and stood close, his dark eyes smiling down at her.

'Certainly not.' She gave her hand a little tug to try to free it. Masterton grinned, teeth white in the dim light, and stooped suddenly, his mouth planting a quick, impertinent caress on hers.

'Let her go.'

Oh, goodness. With her hand to her lips Sophia stepped back away from Donald Masterton, suddenly aware of how compromising this tête à tête must look. As she turned she could see Callum standing just within the doorway. His face was shadowed, but the anger radiated off him like heat from a fire. Either it was relief at being rescued that was making her breathless, or excitement at how masterful Callum sounded. Perhaps both.

'Just a little flirting between cousins,' Masterton said with a laugh, but the dark, mocking face was wary.

'But you are not a cousin,' Callum pointed out and stepped into the gazebo. Sophia looked at his face in the gloom and swallowed. He appeared quite calm—and quite murderous. 'I don't want to send you back in there with a bloody nose and cause talk.' He began to walk towards the other man.

'I'd like to see you try.'

'Callum, really, absolutely nothing of any consequence occurred—' Callum ignored her. He was over six foot, lean and broad shouldered, but Donald Masterton topped him by an inch.

Callum kept coming, his hands relaxed by his sides. Surely they were not going to fight, not over a minor indiscretion? And then, as the other man raised his fists into a posture of defence, Callum moved, slick and fast, and Masterton was tumbling through the air to land sprawling on his back on the marble mosaic.

'Get up.' Callum hauled him to his feet with one hand fisted into his neckcloth. Donald swung at him and Callum ducked, twisted and he fell again, this time harder. 'You do not flirt with Miss Langley. You do not go aside with Miss Langley. In fact, if I find you within six feet of Miss Langley again I will break your arm,' Callum said, dusting off his hands. He waited a moment, but Masterton simply closed his eyes and let his head fall back with a muttered oath. 'Sophia?'

'Yes. Yes, of course, but you cannot leave him like this.' She was babbling, she knew. 'What if he has a concussion?'

'I'll live,' Masterton said, opening one eye. 'Go on, leave me to recover what's left of my dignity.'

Sophia gathered up her skirts and almost ran from the little pavilion. She could feel Callum's presence close behind her, ominously quiet. 'Callum, I am sorry, I had no idea it was not wise to be alone with him. We were talking and it was so stuffy inside and... And it was just harmless flirtation.'

'Will told you quite clearly that he was a rake.' Callum took her by the arm and marched her back towards a side door.

'Yesterday in the carriage? I am sorry, but I lost concentration and missed that.' It sounded a ridiculous excuse, even though it was true. Callum's eyebrows lifted in what she was certain was disbelief. Sophia dug in her heels and they stopped. 'I have said I am sorry. I had no intention of flirting with him—or any other man, come to that—if you had not just abandoned me like that.'

'I had hardly abandoned you; you were in the middle of my family. Plenty of company, I would have thought. And what possessed you to go to that summer house in the dark with him?' Callum sounded every bit as sanctimoniously disapproving as her mother, she thought.

'Because I am not used to rakes,' she snapped. 'Or to flirtation.'

'And there I was thinking I was marrying a woman with a degree of *savoir-faire* and not a green girl,' he said, just as tartly.

'You know perfectly well that I have not had a great deal of experience in society. And, until you, not much with men, either!'

He narrowed his eyes. Sophia tried an olive branch. 'You were most effective back there.' It had been impressive, that controlled, skilled violence, and she realised with a pang of shame that she had found it arousing. She wanted to kiss Callum. No, she wanted him to kiss her, to take her in his arms with the same masculine energy he had fought with. She wanted to be swept away by him again. Or perhaps she just wanted him to show her some emotion other than possessiveness.

'It was neater than breaking his nose,' he said with a shrug. 'I'll send for the carriage to take you home. He'll be gone tomorrow.'

'It was pleasant to be flirted with,' Sophia said. He stopped and turned to her in the light from the lantern over the door. 'Until he kissed me, of course. I would prefer it if you flirted with me,' she added.

'You want me to flirt?' He sounded puzzled by the concept.

'I would like to be courted, not taken for granted. And I assume you do know how to flirt,' she said and saw him become as still as a heron poised above a pool, his eyes, glinting in the reflected light, as focused. He looked tired, she thought. There were shadows under his eyes, fine lines at the corners she had not noticed before.

'Is that wise?'

Was that sarcasm? 'I want to forget Mr Masterton. It is you I am betrothed to and this is rather a pleasant evening.' She wanted to add *I would never have flirted with him if you had been paying me any attention,* but that would sound peevish.

'I can't say I want to flirt with you just so you can forget your indiscretions,' Callum remarked. 'But if you insist… Wait there just one moment.'

Sophia stood and glared at the door as it swung to behind him. No one, it seemed, could accuse Mr Callum Chatterton of impulsive romantic gestures, or of being carried away by passion or even, she decided, of chivalrous behaviour. He had felled Masterton because he was dallying with his betrothed, not because he wanted to rescue a lady in distress or because he wished to be kissing her himself. She had thought, from what one read in sensation novels, or heard in whispers from one's friends, that violent action in defence of a lady would produce almost unconquerable passion in the male breast.

'Here.' Callum came out onto the terrace and offered her a champagne flute. 'Will's best vintage should banish any lingering thoughts of Donald. And I certainly don't want to taste him on your lips.'

'Thank you.' Sophia took it and tossed back the entire glass. 'What a practical solution, Mr Chatterton. No one could suspect you of hot-blooded passion, could they?' The shadowed garden seemed to be swaying slightly.

'I am sorry to be a disappointment to you, Sophia.

Perhaps you are forgetting the afternoon at Long Welling?'

'You mean your outrageous kisses? Those were simply designed to overwhelm me, sweep me into agreeing. I am talking about courtship, about getting to know each other.'

'Damn it, Sophia, it was not like that.' Callum emptied his own glass and set it down on the low wall that edged a formal knot garden. The scent of thyme and rosemary drifted up on the evening breeze.

'No? If you told me you were swept away on a tide of romantic desire I would, naturally, have to believe you.'

'It is a little late to rake over these coals, is it not? You have agreed to marry me, the die is cast.' Callum leaned against the door frame, the picture of careless masculinity confronted with irritating feminine nagging. He had not answered her question, of course. 'I told you not to expect a love match. If you want me to pretend this is a romance, then I must disappoint you.'

'I know that! But now I have to live with you for the rest of my life—and you have to live with me and I thought some closeness… On Sunday I thought…' Her voice trailed away in the face of his lack of reaction. 'Oh, never mind. I should not be out here, not even with you. Let me past, if you please.'

'No.' He stood upright and put a hand under her elbow. 'Come along.' He walked her along the terrace, around the edge of the house, across the end of the carriage drive and into the stable yard. 'The carriage to take Miss Langley home,' he said to the groom who came running at the sound of their footsteps.

'I cannot just walk away—I should say goodbye to the guests,' Sophia protested. 'And to your brother.'

'I will tell them you have a headache,' Callum said, bundling her into the carriage as it came to a stop. He climbed in after her and slammed the door. The groom had set a taper to the internal lantern and she searched his face for some clue to his feelings.

'Both of us? That was your excuse for disappearing earlier, was it not?'

'They will assume we are having a mutual headache,' Callum said as he settled himself on the seat next to her.

'A mutual—? You mean they will assume we are alone somewhere making love?' Sophia demanded on a wave of indignation.

'Probably. We had better make it so, don't you think?'

Chapter Seven

Callum turned and pulled her into his arms. 'We both taste pleasantly of champagne, I imagine.'

Sophia felt her body sway towards him. She could hardly complain about him not courting her and then object when he wanted to kiss her. The blinds were down. No one would be able to see.

Callum's mouth was firm and cool on hers and tasted, as he had predicted, of champagne. It also tasted of him, which was disturbing. She was coming to know that taste, to want it. But he did not repeat the all-consuming, passionate kisses that had so overwhelmed her before, but brushed her lips lightly with his in a whisper of a caress. Then he began to untie the ribbons that held up her long evening gloves and rolled the right-hand one down, almost to her wrist. He bent his head and touched his lips to the inside of her elbow, his tongue tracing the tendons, delving into the warm softness and then trailing down to her wrist where the pulse was pattering, faster it seemed than even her heartbeat.

'Callum,' she whispered as he began to pull off the glove, finger by finger. 'Callum?' The thin silk slid off and he raised her hand to his mouth.

'Isn't this what you wanted?' he asked, her hand so close to his lips that the breath warmed her knuckles.

'Yes. No—I do not know! Callum, I wanted you to *want* to flirt with me. But I should not have asked. Now I do not know whether you want it or if you are simply obliging me.'

'I am always ready to oblige you,' he said with a catch in his voice that might have been a rueful chuckle. 'I rather think I have forgotten how, though.'

'I doubt it.' It was her turn to be rueful now.

'No, I mean it.' In the silence she could not see his face, but their interlinked fingers gave her some hope that he would not close himself off from her again. 'At the risk of shocking you, Sophia, I could make love to you, bed you, very easily. That is instinct and technique. But I seem to have lost the ability to make love lightly, to tease. To flirt, if you want to call it that.'

'You appeared to be making a good job of it just now,' she said.

'Thank you,' Callum said drily. 'The truth is, I want to be married to you. I want you in my bed, I want you in my home. I want—I need—this state of limbo to be over. I do not want to be flirting with my betrothed.'

She could understand that; she felt much the same way, she supposed. Get this over with and they could settle down to their new life with the uncertainties out of the way. The undercurrent of bitterness in his voice warned her to be careful. She dare not say the wrong thing.

'Callum—' The carriage swayed as it rounded the

corner into the lane and jerked violently as one wheel hit the pothole that had grown steadily deeper all winter. Callum caught her hard against him and then sat her safely back on the seat. 'Callum, do you really have a headache? You look as though you have not been sleeping.' She stroked her fingertip beneath his eye and he flinched. 'Sorry.'

'I have a headache. I have suffered with them since the wreck, but I am getting them under control now. You need not fear you are marrying a man who will turn invalid on you.'

'I do not fear that,' Sophia said quietly. 'And you should not feel having headaches is a weakness, they will go with time.' He said nothing about his lack of sleep and she did not want to probe too deeply. He was doubtless very busy, that was all.

By the time the carriage stopped in front of the Langleys' garden gate Sophia had her glove safely secured and her voice calm. 'Thank you, Callum,' she said as he helped her down and opened the gate. 'No, please do not trouble yourself,' she added as he would have walked her up the path to the door. 'I am safe enough now. Goodnight.'

'Goodnight,' Cal said and watched his affianced bride disappear through her front door without a backward glance. 'That went well,' he snarled under his breath as he got back into the carriage and stuffed his cold hands into his pockets. Damn this country, was he never going to get warm?

He had not invented the pain that had built inexorably in his head during dinner to the point where his eyes had lost focus. The migraine headaches had attacked him relentlessly in the first few months after the shipwreck, but he had thought they had almost run their course. Perhaps they would not while the nightmares disturbed his sleep with such regularity.

The evening air on the terrace had been cool enough to revive him a little and the sight of Sophia vanishing into the gazebo with Donald Masterton had cleared his sight, even as it had fuelled his temper.

The pleasure of fighting Masterton was visceral, dark, elemental. It made him realise how therapeutic violent and uncivilised behaviour might be. He wanted to pound Masterton into a pulp and he wanted to drag Sophia into the nearest bedchamber and possess her to the point of mutual exhaustion.

Which was impossible. He could not behave like that to her. But he did not want the mild kisses that were acceptable for a betrothed couple, the sort of kiss they had exchanged in the carriage just now. He needed mindless passion, to lose himself utterly in a woman. Any woman, provided she was an abstraction and not a person he had to feel for, to love. It was too dangerous to love. The ladybirds he entertained provided sexual release, but you could not treat a wife in that way.

Sophia was confused and he did not blame her. It would be easier, surely, when they were wed? He would care for her, protect her. It was strangely comforting to imagine domesticity, a wife at home when he returned, a hostess at his table.

He would look after her materially, better than Dan could have done. He would, he hoped, get her with child soon and provide for his family too. He would try, very hard, not to hurt her, although he was not too certain how successful he would be in that. He suspected she wanted affection and he would do his best—she was easy to like. Despite her denials she might even expect to be loved, though she did not love him. But that was impossible because to love you had to lay open your soul and your mind for the other person and he did not think he could, not again. He had not even had to think about loving his twin. If either of them had been asked about their feelings they would have been embarrassed, very British and repressed about admitting such an emotion. How they felt had not depended on words, it had simply been the natural state of being.

But a woman needed the words. And Sophia deserved the truth, not hollow, comfortable lies.

Two days after being kissed by Donald Masterton in the gazebo Sophia sat next to her husband in the post chaise and tried to think about almost anything other than the fact she was now, irretrievably, married. That morning's service had been very quiet, very private. After an early luncheon they had set out for London and her new home. She had never felt so alone.

'This is positively luxurious. I have never travelled by post chaise before,' she said with determined brightness.

'It doesn't make you queasy, then?' Callum must have noticed that she was clutching tight to the leather loop that hung beside her. Better that he should think she found the action uneasy than that she was gripping it tight out of nerves.

'Not unless I stare at one fixed spot,' she said as the chaise swung round a tight bend. It threw her against his shoulder and he put out a hand to steady her, withdrawing it the moment she was upright again. 'Thank you.' Alone again.

Another mile passed in silence, then Callum said, 'You do not have to wear half-mourning, you know. I had no idea you would feel you must wear grey to your own wedding.'

'Not wear mourning?' She had thought he would expect it, insist upon it. 'I cannot leave it off; people would be shocked, they would think I did not care about Daniel.'

'When of course you do,' he said flatly. 'And you can leave it off. It won't bring Daniel back, it's depressing and it doesn't—' He broke off, the sentence unfinished.

'Suit me? No, it does not,' she agreed, perfectly aware that black and greys and mauve made her skin sallow and washed the colour out of her eyes. Callum noticed, of course. At that first traumatic meeting in March, when he had broken the news to her, he could hardly have been in any fit state to notice whether she wore sackcloth or full court dress. Since he had come back she had been wearing half-mourning whenever he had seen her.

Perhaps he thought that leaving it off would make a significant difference to her looks. If that was the case, then her husband was due a disappointment. She had catalogued her appearance in all honesty, that night when she had received Daniel's letter; she was not plain, but neither was she a beauty. Perhaps she could try for *interesting*, but she doubted it.

'Other than my mourning, I only have whites and pale pastels,' she said. 'Those would be quite unsuitable.'

'And not right for a married woman in any case,' he agreed. 'You must shop as soon as possible.' He shifted in his seat to look at her. 'Clear jewel colours,' he said. 'Deep blue, amber, ruby. Even violet.'

'Oh, yes,' she agreed, surprised to find Callum not only taking an interest in such things, but being so perceptive about what would suit her. 'You have a very good eye for colour.'

'I used to try to paint in watercolour,' he admitted. 'Not very well!'

'But no more?' He shook his head and she sensed it was not a good topic to pursue just now. 'Where should I shop?'

'I have no idea,' Callum said. 'London is a mystery that I am beginning to explore as I would an Indian jungle. I asked Will where to go for a tailor and hatter and bootmaker, and I am learning my way around masculine St James's, but it did not occur to me to ask about ladies' clothes. Aunt Clarissa will help, but she's not back in town for at least a month—her middle daughter is about to be confined with her first child.' He frowned at her, obviously taking in for the first time just how provincial she was.

'Never mind,' Sophia said, seized with a determination that she was not going to be a nuisance to him. Men were not interested in shopping, she understood. 'I am sure the lady's maid the butler has engaged for me will know.'

'A good idea.'

'What is his name? The butler?'

'Hawksley. Had I not told you?'

She shook her head. 'Perhaps if I know the details of

the house, it would help… I mean, I should be thinking about the housekeeping.'

'I told you none of this? I am sorry, Sophia.'

'You were preoccupied,' she said after a moment. 'Callum, I do want to make you a good wife, to make sure that things in your homes are as well run and comfortable as possible for you.'

'And you are not helped by a husband who does not brief you with the information you require?' he observed with more perception than she had hoped for. 'I am not used to having a wife—you must tell me when there is something you need.'

Some affection? More than a tenth of your attention?
'I will,' she promised. 'The house?'

'A drawing room and a dining room at street level, with the kitchens and domestic offices in the basement,' he said. 'I must admit I did not look at those. On the first floor there is the room I use as a study, a room you could have as a sitting room and a bedchamber. Above that, the main bedroom with a dressing room and a third chamber. The servants' rooms are in the attic.'

'That all sounds positively cosy.' For a moment Sophia toyed with a vision of domestic bliss. 'You will be busy in your study, I will be in my sitting room deciding menus or curled up with the latest novel. Then we will meet to exchange the news of the day in the dining room over a perfectly prepared dinner, or entertain modishly in the drawing room. Is that how it is done?'

'Absolutely. That seems to be the domestic model. And after dinner we will retire upstairs.'

At this point her desire to speculate aloud faltered. Would Callum expect them to share a bedchamber?

'Which bed do you…? I mean, which would…?' She could feel the colour heating her cheeks.

'I thought you would prefer the main bedchamber because of the dressing room,' Callum said as easily as if they were discussing the front hall. 'I can use the one on the first floor. It will be convenient for when I am working late; I would not wish to disturb you.'

'How considerate.' Sophia heard the edge in the words even as she said them.

Callum looked at her: a long, steady scrutiny from those enigmatic hazel eyes. He looked out of the window. 'I am not always an easy sleeper.'

Sophia cast around for another topic. 'We have not discussed housekeeping, or my dress allowance.'

'How much do you need?'

'I haven't the slightest idea,' Sophia said. 'I do not know the house, I do not know London prices, I have no idea how adequately equipped it is or how much entertaining you wish to do.'

'Then I suggest we wait until we see what a normal pattern of expenditure is and extrapolate from that.'

'I am not one of your counting-house clerks, Mr Chatterton. *Extrapolate* indeed!'

'If you can think of a better method, Mrs Chatterton, then please, let us employ it.' There was a long silence while he watched her face and then Callum remarked, 'You may not be one of the clerks, Sophia, but I would wager a significant sum that you are counting.'

'In French, backwards,' she agreed. His lips twitched, just a fraction, but the laughter he was suppressing was plain to see in his eyes. It was shocking in the lean, dark, controlled face. Shocking and irresistible. She smiled back. 'You are teasing me again.'

'I did not intend to. Really, there is no need to worry about such things yet.' Almost imperceptibly Callum relaxed into the corner and it was only as he did so that Sophia realised that he had been wound as tight as a spring, as tense as she was, if not more so. However many things there were in this marriage to worry about, for her it was the answer to a problem. For him it meant a profound change in his way of life, undertaken out of duty.

'I might be a spendthrift and squander all your money,' she warned him, keeping her tone light, but with serious intent.

'You would have to work quite hard at it and, in my estimation, you are too prudent for that.'

Sophia wrinkled her nose, not entirely certain she liked being described as *prudent*. There were so many other adjectives that one's husband of less than a day might more flatteringly apply. 'Are you wealthy, then?'

'Were you paying no attention to the settlements?'

'No.' The smile was still there, so she added, 'I did not marry you for your money.'

One eyebrow lifted and the smile became quizzical and less amused.

'Not like that. Yes, of course I was so grateful we could pay off the debts and that Mama will be comfortable. I did not want to become a governess! There were other things—it is a relief that Mark will have influential connections when he finishes his studies and is looking for a parish. If he can establish himself well, then he will be able to support Mama. But I did not seek a life of luxury.'

'Will your brother make a good clergyman, do you

think?' Callum asked. As he had when she told him about the debts, he did not refer to them again.

'I am sure he will,' Sophia said loyally, trying to repress the truth, which was that she thought Mark was becoming insufferably pompous. Her brother had descended for the wedding, patronised the amiable and unassuming vicar, lectured her on her own good fortune and announced his intention of pleasing their mother with a week's visit at no notice. Sophia, her nerves on edge, had never been so out of sympathy with him.

'He favoured me with a most enlightening lecture on the Christian duties of marriage yesterday evening,' Callum said, straight-faced.

'Oh no!' Sophia stared at him, aghast. 'Of all the preposterous things to do— Mark isn't even ordained yet, and he's so much younger than you and—'

But Callum was laughing now, a deep, wicked chuckle that made her smile back, even as she cringed at Mark's effrontery. 'What did you say? You snubbed him, I hope.'

'I listened with great attention and then asked him a number of very frank questions about a husband's duties in the marital bed. How I kept a straight face I will never know. It was very wrong of me, considering that I was about to marry his sister and I suspect he is a virgin.' Sophia clapped her hand over her mouth to suppress the gasp of shocked laughter. 'He became mired in the procreation of children, at which point I thanked him earnestly and told him he had given me a great deal to think about.'

'That was very wicked. I'm surprised at you.' But the reproof was ruined by the unladylike snort of laugher that escaped her. *Thank goodness, he does have a sense of humour after all.*

'Wicked? Oh, no, not me. I was always the responsible twin,' Callum remarked. For a moment she thought she had said the wrong thing, but he was still smiling. Then he turned from her; the moment of shared amusement was lost. 'Try to get some sleep. I will, if you do not object.'

'Of course not.' Sophia was not at all tired, but if Callum was not sleeping well then she should encourage him to get all the rest she could. She closed her eyes and waited until she heard his breathing become slow. After a cautious peek she pulled her small sketching block from her reticule and began to draw his profile. It was not easy as the chaise lurched and swayed, but it was engrossing and she soon lost consciousness of everything but the battle to translate her husband's face into lines and shading.

She had almost finished when he jerked, his eyes still closed. 'Sophia. No, don't—'

The pencil skidded across the page. She stuffed it and the block away and caught at his hands that had clenched into fists. 'Callum?

'What?' He came awake in an instant, his pupils wide as he stared at her. 'I'm sorry. A dream. Look—we have reached Kilburn Wells. Not long to London now.'

Chapter Eight

Cal pushed away the lingering traces of the nightmare, of Sophia vanishing into a dark mist, not looking back. He made himself think of her laughter as the chaise drew up in Half Moon Street. Her uninhibited snort of amusement, the transformation of her face at the shared joke, the naughty twinkle in her eye at his most improper teasing of her brother were all delightful. To share laughter like that, to share a joke without it having to be spelled out—a simple joy, but a precious one he thought he had lost.

He looked at her as he helped her down, but she was once more serious and slightly wan in her sombre grey carriage dress. Marriage had not brought colour to her cheeks. But why should it? Her family was secure, but at the price of her marrying the wrong man and being plunged into a strange new life.

'Another house to explore. It looks delightful,' she said politely. Cal took her arm as they went up the steps and through the door that Hawksley was holding open.

Under his fingers he felt her slenderness and measured the almost imperceptible distance she kept between them. How very ladylike, he thought, his body stirring at the thought of how unladylike he might be able to coax her to be that night. *She's a virgin who doesn't love you,* he reminded himself. *Take care.*

'Good afternoon, madam. Sir.'

'You must be Hawksley,' Sophia said. From somewhere she conjured up a warm smile.

'Yes, madam. Would you wish me to assemble the staff now or should I send for your maid, ma'am?'

Cal saw her cut him a fleeting glance, but she replied to the butler without waiting for his approval, 'It would be best to meet everyone now, if you please, Hawksley.'

They must have been waiting, poised behind the baize door under the curve of the steps, for it opened the moment Hawksley clapped his hands. 'Mrs Datchett, the cook-housekeeper, ma'am. Chivers, your maid. Andrew and Michael, the footmen, Prunella and Jane, the maids. Millie, kitchen maid.' There were bows and curtsies. Cal had worked hard to commit the names to memory in the same automatic way he had done when dealing with the dozens of clerks and servants and merchants who filled his working days, but Sophia smiled and exchanged a few words with each of the staff in turn, repeated names, made a little ceremony of it.

They beamed back at her. She obviously had the knack with staff, he thought as Michael took his hat and gloves and Sophia went towards the stairs with Chivers. 'Tea in the drawing room in fifteen minutes, please, Hawksley,' she said decisively. 'At what time would you wish dinner, Mr Chatterton? Or do you dine out this evening?'

He looked at her poised, one hand on the banister, her willowy figure half-turned to look back at him, expecting him to leave her alone on their wedding night and apparently quite composed about it. What did that say about her expectations of him? 'I shall dine at home. Seven-thirty, my dear, if that would suit.'

Sophia coloured a little at the endearment, but nodded to Mrs Datchett and Hawksley and followed the maid upstairs. Cal stood and watched until she vanished around the turn of the stair. His wife in his house. It was curiously, and unexpectedly, pleasant. And he would have neither, he realised, if it had not been for the shipwreck and Daniel's death. This charming, gentle young woman would be his sister-in-law.

'Sir?'

Cal hauled himself out of the deep pit of his thoughts. 'Yes, Hawksley?'

To his credit the other man did not flinch at the tone. 'Wilkins is above stairs, sir.'

His new English valet of a few months was a pernickety little man, much given to tutting under his breath at outrages such as a creased cuff or a loose button. Cal had not asked his body servant Ardash to leave his home and family to travel with him to England, and thank God he had not, or the poor devil would likely be dead by now. On the ship he had got used to looking after himself, but one of his first acts on arriving in London had been to find a man to maintain the standards of appearance and dress the Company's Court of Directors would expect.

'You moved my things down from the main bedroom and organised the room on the first floor for my use? Excellent. Then send hot water up, if you please.' He climbed the stairs to his new chamber, a safe one floor below the one that was now his wife's. He had every intention of visiting her bedchamber regularly, but he would choose his time, not succumb to the urge to make love to her just because she was next door. And with a floor between them there was no risk he would disturb her when the nightmares seized him.

Wilkins put down a pile of linens and bowed. He seemed to feel that his master's new status as a married man required some formality. Cal looked around the room to distract himself. It would do, although it seemed dark and rather bland.

'The valises are here, sir. I will have madam's heavy trunk carried up whilst you are at tea. Do you require a change of linen now?'

What he would like was a cold bath, Cal thought with an inward grimace. He shrugged out of his coat and surveyed the state of his cuffs. 'No, this will do until I change for dinner.' He rolled up his sleeves as Andrew the footman came in with a jug of water. 'For later, the swallowtail coat and evening breeches and the striped silk stockings.' He must signal the importance of their first dinner as man and wife with suitable attention. 'And I want flowers for the dining room and my wife's bedchamber. Andrew, will you organise that as soon as possible?'

'Sir. I'll go along to Shepherd's Market at once. Shall I get roses if I can? They may have some hothouse ones, sir.' Andrew looked as though he was bright enough to choose the right thing.

'Yes. Something pretty and elegant. Deep pink, if possible. Do not stint on quality or quantity.' Callum probed at his own motives as he tied a fresh neckcloth.

Was he attempting to woo his new bride? Or was this some sort of apology for that afternoon at Long Welling when he had so shocked her by his ardour? He caught his valet's eye in the mirror and smoothed the frown off his forehead. What did it matter, so long as Sophia was not unhappy and the household ran smoothly?

'Buy flowers regularly. Use your discretion unless Mrs Chatterton expresses a wish for anything in particular.' In India flowers and garlands were available in lavish abundance, for a few *paice.* Here they would be more of a luxury, an easy way to make Sophia feel that he was paying attention to her comfort.

She was sitting in the drawing room with tea pot and cups arrayed in front of her when he came down: a picture of domesticity. Cal thought she looked chilly, although he would have been hard pressed to explain why. He took the seat opposite and accepted a cup from her hands. 'Thank you. Is it me, or is this room dull? I never noticed it before.' He had bought the house from another bachelor.

Perhaps her presence in it, the little vignette of femininity she created, showed up the bland masculinity of the rest of the room. 'A trifle.' Sophia fished in her cup with the mote spoon to remove a stray tea leaf.

'Shall we move? I am sure we could find something else soon enough. You can choose somewhere you like.' He found he wanted to please her.

'One cannot simply pack up and shift houses just because one does not like the wallpaper, Callum!'

'Why ever not? It is commonplace in India to move house at the drop of a hat.'

'But I like the house itself,' she protested. 'It is just

that it isn't *ours* yet, not like Long Welling is. Will be.'
A soft pink colour tinged her cheeks. He liked the way
it made her look, and he liked, he discovered, the fact
that he was able to make her blush.

Best not to pursue that now. But it was strange how
attached she was to the old house even after it had been
the scene of their first falling-out. 'But we will come to
feel at home here, I am sure,' Sophia added hurriedly.

Cal crossed his legs to disguise the effect that
thoughts of Long Welling's master bedroom were
having on him. 'Redecorate as you wish. It needs to be
fit for entertaining.' Sophia brightened and he realised
that he had done something that gave her pleasure. It
was about time, he thought, mentally kicking himself.
His had hardly been a considerate courtship. Not a
courtship at all, just a demand. 'Do the whole house, if
you wish. My bedchamber is dull, too.'

'How much—?'

'Whatever it needs. I trust you not to indulge in
embossed Spanish leather wall hangings, Egyptian-
style chaises and full Meissen dinner services.'

'Oh, but I am so tempted,' Sophia said. 'Just think, I
will be able to obtain all the most fashionable journals
now I am in London. I can follow the latest style, the
most outrageous mode.' Her blue eyes danced as she
teased him and warmth stirred inside. Desire, certainly,
but something unfamiliar, comfortable and comforting
too. 'When shall we go and view the showrooms and
warehouses?'

She wanted him to come with her? No, surely not.
She was just checking that he did not wish to supervise
her expenditure. It had been fun to furnish a house
with Dan and they had haunted the auction houses and

the bazaars together. But now, without him? No, too many ghosts.

Dan would have loved it and would have indulged his peacock tendencies to the full. He would have chosen some outrageous and impractical wallpaper, teased Sophia into giggles with improper remarks about bed hangings and bought frivolous gadgets just for the fun of it. But there was so little between Sophia and himself to build upon, and he did not want to spoil her enjoyment in doing up the house just as she wanted it.

'Callum?' Sophia said, her head on one side, that smile curving her lips. It was only a shopping expedition, yet somehow he felt as though he was facing a test of real importance.

'You will have to do that yourself,' Callum said, bending forwards to put his cup down. 'I will be too busy for shopping and, besides, the house is your realm. Take one of the footmen and your maid.'

Sophie felt the pleasure at his generosity ebb a little. It seemed Callum did not attach any importance to them creating a home together, simply to her making a suitable framework for entertaining and the advancement of his career. Shopping would be delightful, of course, especially as she had both her wardrobe and the house to buy for, but it would be lonely too. How on earth did a new wife, with no contacts and a busy husband, make friends?

Sophia felt her smile slip and hastily adjusted her expression, but Callum was looking severe again. What to talk about now? He seemed dismissive of housekeeping and decorating, they had exhausted the matter of her clothing and, so far, they had not established any topics of mutual interest—always assuming any existed at all.

It would be rather a long time before there would be the children to discuss, she thought ruefully, and then remembered what must come first in the elegant French bed upstairs.

'What is wrong, Sophia?' Callum seemed uncannily perceptive. She must try harder to mask her thoughts from him.

'Nothing. Nothing at all.' That was too vehement and his brows drew together as though he suspected her of keeping secrets from him. 'I will go and oversee the unpacking.'

'I am not sure you should be spending your wedding day doing that sort of thing. If it had not been for that journey, which must have tired you, I would take you to the theatre. As it is—' Callum stood up and the room seemed subtly smaller, as though he had moved closer and was crowding her. Sophia found her eyes were at precisely the right level to notice what he was thinking of as suitable employment for a wedding day. She stood up with more haste than elegance.

She was blushing, she knew she was. Somehow, through the past few days, she had kept at bay the memory of what had happened at Long Welling, with the kind of desperation that a child applies to pretending it has not got toothache and does not need to visit the dentist. Not that being made love to by Callum would be like visiting the tooth-puller, exactly. She knew, in theory, what to expect, and surely it would not be so bad? Embarrassing, of course.

Even thinking about it made her tremble. Was that desire? Ladies did not take pleasure in the marriage bed, Mama had explained. It was a duty that led to the reward of children. With a man one loved it would be easier, but with Callum she felt desperately shy and worried about disappointing him.

'I must… I mean, there are things I need to have today, and Chivers does not know what I want. There's my dressing case and my nightgown and…'

Callum's mouth curved as she stumbled to a halt. 'I am sure Chivers will realise that you will require a nightgown.' That smile. He was a younger, much more approachable man when he looked like that.

'No…but, I mean she will not know which one.' *Oh, for goodness' sake, Sophia, you are in a deep enough hole. Just stop digging!*

'A special nightgown for your wedding night?' He was teasing her now and the embarrassment began to give way to something else. Something more than liking. The desire to be friends, to share that amusement.

'Um…yes. Well, I thought I ought… I enjoy embroidery.' The laughter was still there, so she ventured, 'A young lady is not supposed to think about wedding nights, but sewing roses around one's nightgown gives one time to contemplate…' Now she really had mired herself into the hole. In a moment he was going to enquire acidly who she had been imagining in her bed with her. How tactless of her. No doubt she was crimson. He must think her completely gauche.

'I will be very careful with it, then, if you have made it yourself,' Callum said and the hint of a smile in his voice somehow made her confusion even greater.

'Thank you. Anyway…' she began to edge towards

the door '…I really need to make sure she knows what she is doing…'

Callum opened the door for her and Sophia escaped into the hall. She had to be pleased that Callum wanted to come to her bed—at least that aspect of their marriage would be close. As she climbed slowly up to her bedchamber she wondered how much he minded that she had been betrothed to Daniel. How would she have felt if the positions had been reversed and she had had a sister who had been betrothed to Callum and who had then died?

Jealous, she decided and stopped on the landing to consider that. She would have been jealous because, frankly, Callum Chatterton was a very attractive man. Or would she have felt that way if her imaginary sister… 'Oh, for goodness' sake,' she muttered under her breath. Men did not have the same sensibilities over such matters as women, she was certain. Callum was a man, and she was a woman, so he wanted to sleep with her. And he wanted an heir. For the rest, she was sure he regarded her, at best, tolerantly and, at worst as a constant reminder of his twin.

Which probably explained his coolness most of the time. *It isn't my fault,* she thought resentfully as she pushed open her bedroom door. *I never expected him to marry me. I did not ask him to. But men know best. Or they think they do…*

'Ma'am?' Chivers looked up from the trunk she was bending over, her expression wary.

Sophia realised she must have been frowning and smiled. 'I came up so we could discuss what needs unpacking first.'

'It is all done, ma'am.'

And so it was. The pretty lawn nightgown with the roses around the neckline was laid out on the bed, her brushes and jars were arranged on the dressing table and a glimpse through the open door into the dressing room showed open drawers and presses. The trunk that Chivers was emptying was the last of the luggage.

'You are very efficient,' Sophia said, sensing that the maid was a trifle put out to be supervised.

'I hope to give satisfaction, ma'am. I thought the black silk with the beading for this evening? I have it downstairs in the washhouse to steam out the creases.'

'That will be perfect, thank you, Chivers.' It was her only suitable evening gown so the maid was being tactful by implying there was a choice. 'I need to shop for just about everything,' she admitted. 'Mr Chatterton will be entertaining a great deal, so I will need a number of evening gowns.'

'And morning and walking dresses and lingerie, ma'am. And hats, pelisses, spencers, shawls, shoes, gloves, reticules…'

'Oh dear. Is all of my wardrobe that unsuitable for town, Chivers?'

'It is very suitable for an unmarried lady who has been in mourning, ma'am,' she said with tact. 'But not for a married one. Will you be shopping soon?'

'We will start tomorrow and I hope you will be able to tell me where we should go.'

'Me, ma'am?' Chivers closed the lid of the trunk and stared at Sophia. 'Surely the ladies of your family and your friends…'

'I have none. Not in London. And I have never been to town before; I have no idea where to go.'

The maid's face showed a hint of pity and Sophia

realised just how lonely she felt. Mama, her friends and acquaintances, were all miles away and here she was with no one to confide in and a husband who was virtually a stranger. *Husband. Oh dear, I wish I had a married friend I could talk to.*

'My last lady was very fashionable, ma'am. I know the fashionable shops and the best *modistes*, never fear.' Chivers was all practicality again as she bustled into the dressing room and began to tidy up in there. 'Will you be having a lie down before dinner, ma'am? And then a bath before I dress your hair?' The answer required was, she made clear, *Yes*.

Of course, Sophia realized; the maid knew it was her wedding night and was expecting her to be devoting the time before dinner to resting and then primping. Probably she should be in a flutter of romantic and maidenly excitement, not torn between unladylike desire, resentment, excitement and downright nerves. 'Yes, Chivers,' she said with every outward sign of confidence. 'That is exactly what I shall be doing.'

Chapter Nine

The clock struck eight and Cal laid down the newspaper he had been reading. It was pointless; he was not absorbing a word of it. It was beginning to dawn on him that marriage was going to turn his life upside down. The shock of the shipwreck, the grief of losing Daniel, the strangeness of life in England after so long away, had been a huge upheaval. He had got through that, largely by sheer hard work and a refusal to wallow in self-pity. Dan had gone and with him boyhood dreams and illusions about love. He did not think himself a coward, but he knew with a deep certainty that he was never again going to lay himself open to the pain of loss such as he had just experienced.

He loved Will, his other brother. If anything happened to him, he would mourn and grieve deeply, but he would not lose a part of himself, part of his heart and soul, as he had with the death of his twin. It was good that he had married Sophia out of duty and not out of love because he did not think he could risk making himself so vulnerable ever again.

But marriage, even a marriage of convenience, was an intimate thing. For better or worse he was tied to Sophia now. He had been tied to Dan by love and affection and the mental link that others found so uncanny but which, for a twin, was perfectly normal. Now he must live with a woman with whom he did not share any kind of mental closeness.

The door opened and Sophia entered. For a moment he was still, so lost in his thoughts that he just stared at her. Then, as she came further into the room, he got to his feet with a murmur of apology and pleasure. His wife—he really must get used to that word—was glowing.

'Sophia.' He took her hand and bent to kiss her cheek. 'You look lovely. And you like the roses, I think?'

'Pink roses in my hair and corsage with a black gown is unconventional, I know,' she murmured, but he could see he had pleased her. She was wearing a modest string of pearls at her throat and studs in her ears and pale pink long kid gloves, and the effect with the sheen of the black silk gown was surprisingly sophisticated and dashing. 'It was a lovely surprise. I came out of the dressing room after my bath and there they were.'

Cal's imagination seized on the image of Sophia, flushed pink from her bath, emerging into a room full of pink roses. 'I find I can take pleasure in pleasing my bride, even if I was not very good at it as an engaged man,' he admitted. She glanced up at him and blushed and he could tell she knew what he was thinking about. Not all of it, he hoped, not an innocent like Sophia. She could have absolutely no idea what he would like to do with her, to her.

Neither of them seemed to know what to say next. What did he converse about with a wife who had no idea about his life? They had nothing in common except Dan, and that was not something they could talk about; it would be too painful for her, he was sure. Should he risk boring her by talking about the Company? Or life in India?

As though she read his mind she asked, 'Will you be attending the East India Company offices tomorrow?' Sophia sat down in the exact middle of the chaise and spread her skirts elegantly around her. Was that deliberate to stop him sitting next to her? She had recovered her poise faster than he had, it seemed.

'I am afraid so.' Callum took the chair opposite.

'Afraid? Is something wrong?' She caught her lower lip between her teeth for a moment. 'I am sorry, I do not mean to pry into your business.'

'Not at all, you have every reason to ask. I can always tell you if something is confidential. No, I meant I was sorry I could not be with you.'

'Oh, I will not need you—you know I must be shopping for clothes.' Sophia laughed. 'It would be worse than the things for the house; I am sure you would be bored to tears. Chivers knows just where to go. But I must ask you to tell me what my dress allowance will be before I catch a glimpse of all the temptations in the shops.'

Callum relaxed. She seemed happy at the prospect of shopping. He had feared sulks because he was leaving her alone, but this was excellent; the maid was obviously competent and shopping appeared to keep females occupied for hours on end. He was not going to have to dance attendance on her all day.

'I had given that some thought and I have jotted down these figures,' he said and reached into the breast of his coat for his notebook. He extracted a slip of paper and passed it to her. 'That is what I thought for your dress allowance, your pin money and the housekeeping.'

Sophia stared at it. 'For the year?' she asked after a moment.

'No, quarterly. The redecorations will be extra. I suggest you take notes of what you think would be suitable and we can discuss it. Sophia?'

She stared at him. 'This is very generous. I had no wish to be such an expense to you. You paid off our debts.'

He shrugged. 'Any wife would cost as much. I cannot expect to be married on a bachelor's budget.'

'No, of course,' she agreed, once more the polite lady, all the animation she had shown at the prospect of a shopping expedition banished.

Once she had found her feet she would be an excellent hostess, he thought. Her natural grace, good breeding and restraint easily outweighed the sheltered country life she had lived. It was a pity that those flashes of vivacity were so few and far between.

'Dinner is served, madam.' Hawksley stood by the open door.

'My dear.' Cal rose, extended a hand and escorted his wife into the dining room to sit at the foot of the table. She seemed rather distant when he took his own place, but perhaps that was the length of the table, the exuberant display of flowers halfway down—he really must remember to thank the footman—and her reserve in front of the servants.

As the meal progressed it was obvious that his anxiety about finding topics of conversation was misplaced. Sophia progressed smoothly through remarks on the weather, speculation about the latest news on the royal family, some amusing anecdotes about their country neighbours and solicitous enquiries about the hour at which he preferred to take breakfast.

It was pleasant, easy and just a trifle dull. He rather suspected that he was being managed. Cal dragged his thoughts away from their uncomfortably jumbled wanderings between Company business and erotic fantasies, and exerted himself to take an active part.

When the merits of the almond tartlets had been adequately discussed Sophia nodded to Andrew to assist with her chair and rose. 'I will leave you to your port, Mr Chatterton.'

'I will be with you directly, Mrs Chatterton,' Cal countered, getting to his feet as she left the room. One glass, that was all. A man's wedding night was no time to be lingering over the port.

But he did linger, twisting the stem of the glass round and round as he watched the candlelight shine through the blood-red liquid and the wine sloshed against the sides like waves on a miniature sea. Blood-red waves. Chance and the power of nature meant he was alive and here and Dan was gone. And the woman in the room beyond who was behaving with such impeccable good manners had lost the man she loved and had got him in his place.

Cal tossed back the wine and reached for the decanter. His wedding night. Well, at least he felt confident about that aspect of this marriage. When he had kissed her at Long Welling Sophia had trembled in his arms—and it had been with desire, not fear. But she was an innocent and a sheltered one at that. He would just have one more glass while he considered how best to go about it.

Sophia decided that Callum's idea of 'directly' was not hers. She sat and waited in the elegant, dull drawing room for half an hour, then allowed herself to feel annoyed. That did have the benefit of giving her something to think about beyond her nerves and wondering if she was going to enjoy Callum's lovemaking.

It was all well and good if she did, but he would not be *expecting* her to enjoy it, would he? She had been, he believed, in love with his brother. She could hardly confess to a man mourning Daniel that until she had seen Callum she had had to look at his brother's portrait to remind herself what he had looked like and that she had fallen out of love with him years ago. To experience raptures in Callum's arms would make her seem either improperly wanton or lacking in respect to his brother. He would know she had married him under false pretences.

The clock chimed. Not that she would be experiencing anything at all, let alone rapture, if he did not emerge from the dining room soon. Was it normal for a new husband to sit alone drinking port at such a time? Sophia got to her feet, crossed the hallway to the dining-room door and applied her ear to the panel. There was the distinct *ching* of a decanter stopper being carelessly replaced.

Sophia lifted one hand, touched the door handle and then withdrew it. No, she would not go in and ask when he was joining her, she was going to bed. That would demonstrate either a suitable reticence or her irritation at being kept waiting, however he chose to take it.

She did not have to ring for Chivers. She was in the bedchamber when she reached it. Sophia thought the maid was exhibiting considerably more excitement about the occasion than the mistress, judging by the young woman's smile and the way she fussed around undressing Sophia. She submitted to a spray of scent, to a fetching ribbon in her hair and to having the bowls of roses set either side of the bed because it would have seemed strange not to expect the attention, tonight of all nights. She had no desire to start rumours about her marriage in the Servants' Hall.

'Such a pretty nightgown,' Chivers murmured, giving the sleeves a final tweak as Sophia settled back against the heaped pillows. 'I'll wait until you ring in the morning, ma'am, before I bring up your chocolate. Goodnight, ma'am.'

Presumably she was now expected to recline here, every ringlet in place, a shy smile on her lips, until her husband deigned to arrive. That paled after ten minutes. Defiantly Sophia picked up a novel from the bedside table and began to read.

'My dear?' Callum stood in the doorway clad in a red robe. Something about his stance warned her that he had been there some time.

'Callum.' Her breathing was suddenly all over the place. Sophia wriggled back up from her comfortable huddle and pulled off the dangling ribbon that had slid down to the end of its lock of hair. She made rather a business of re-tying it. 'Have you been there long?'

'Long enough to see you are engrossed. What are you reading?' He closed the door and began to snuff out the candles on the dressing table and mantelshelf, leaving the branches on either side of the bed burning. The shadows flickered and the darkness closed around them, stranding the bed in an intimate island of light, cut off from the rest of the world.

'A novel.' Sophia put it back on the table and dropped a handkerchief over it. 'Just nonsense.'

Callum sat on the edge of the bed, right against her hip, and picked it up the book. His robe gaped at the neck to reveal bare skin and dark hair. Sophia swallowed. Her apprehension flooded back.

'*The Husband and Wife, or, the Matrimonial Martyr* by Mrs Bridget Bluemantle,' he read out. 'Engrossing nonsense, apparently—you are halfway through volume three.'

'You object to novel reading?' Sophia sat up straighter, prepared to do battle to defend her books.

'Not at all, and I am not the kind of husband who insists on regulating his wife's reading. But the title does not argue much optimism about the married state, which is lowering, considering why I am here.' She could not decide whether he was serious or teasing her. His profile as he looked down at the book gave nothing away.

'I had decided you were not coming,' she retorted, remembering her grievance.

'And that was a relief?' Callum stood up and shrugged off the robe with his back towards her. She had been right: he was wearing nothing beneath it. Her gaze slid over broad shoulders, narrow waist, smooth skin marked by small scars on his left shoulder and a sickle-shaped mole on his right hip. She had never seen a naked adult male before. The classical statues at the Hall looked like this, but they were not moving, nor did their muscles shift intriguingly under skin that was a pale gold in the candlelight. Sophia clenched her hands on the edge of the coverlet to stop herself reaching out and caressing the taut curve of his buttocks. He would think her beyond all modesty if she did that.

Then he began to turn and she shut her eyes as well. There was only so much she could cope with, she thought, biting her lip against a gasp of nervous laughter. And the statues had fig leaves.

The edge of the bed dipped. She moved over to the right-hand side to give him room and took the bedspread with her before she remembered to loosen her grip on the edge. She had to say something; he had asked her a question. 'A relief? No, of course not. After all, the worst is soon over, isn't it?' Perhaps that was not the most tactful way to put it.

There was silence from the other side of the bed, then Callum said drily, 'I would hope so. I have never slept with a virgin before.'

'Good. I mean, I am sure you have not.'

There was the sound of breathing, close to her ear. How had Callum moved without her realising? Sophia opened her eyes just in time to see the heat and intent in his eyes as he bent to kiss her and then she was swept up in the kiss, just as she had been at Long Welling.

He expects me to enjoy his lovemaking, she told herself. *It is hopeless to pretend I do not wish to.* Her arms went around Callum's neck and she found herself shifting to cradle his weight over her. Through the thin silk his aroused body was explicit against hers.

'This delightful nightgown is very much in the way,' he murmured in her ear, accompanying the words with tiny flicks of his tongue.

Sophia stifled a moan. 'I'll take it off if you'll just...' Move... Stop that... She must open her eyes and sit up.

Callum rolled off and lay there on his side watching her, his head propped on one hand, while she wriggled and finally emerged, the nightgown clutched to her front. They stared at each other for a while. Sophia felt herself grow pinker and the curve of Callum's lips grew more pronounced. 'You are laughing at me,' she accused.

'I am enjoying you,' he said. 'You are enchanting.' With a little gasp, like a bather jumping into cold water, she let go of the fabric and closed her eyes tight.

The sound he made as he took her in his arms again and settled himself was a very satisfactory growl. *I please him, at least so far. He won't expect me to know what to do next...* His body was strange and exciting under her hands, sleek with muscle, rough with hair. She could smell his skin, spicy and hot and faintly musky, and then he found her mouth again and after that Sophia gave up on thought and simply clung to the lean body over hers and surrendered to the feelings that were so much more than she had ever imagined.

The pressure of his mouth over hers, open, hot, demanding, created an ache, low down, and the urge to mould herself tightly against him *there* as though that would ease it. She realised that his body was hard against her belly and that was frightening, but exciting too. It made the ache worse and so did pressing against him. Then Callum's hand cupped her breast and he began to play with the nipple and the ache turned into a stab of sensation that had her whimpering into his mouth.

Then the kiss deepened, became more demanding, and Sophia lost awareness of everything except the sensation that was singing through her, the strength of Callum's hold, the urgency of their bodies. But Callum's mouth never left hers and his hands were stroking and exploring and she was so dizzy that it was impossible to think about where she was, what was happening beyond the silken slide of his mouth over hers, the torture of his hand on her breast, the demanding throbbing ache so low down.

Then his hand slid between them and he touched her, intimately, parting the folds that felt wet and swollen and the delicious shock had her arching up against him, her gasps swallowed by his kiss. He shifted, lifted away a little and she whimpered in protest until his weight came back.

'Best to be fast, I think,' he murmured. Then something hard was pressing into the hot, wet core of her and she gasped, tried to shift, but it was too late. There was pressure, a yielding, a sensation of exquisite fullness and then a stab of pain that had her recoiling, struggling, shocked out of delight and into reality. She had cried out, she realised as she emerged out of the sensual delirium he had plunged her into, back to alarming reality.

'Shh,' he murmured, lodged impossibly deep inside her. 'Shh. That's the worst over, I promise. Trust me, Sophia.'

And, after a shuddering moment while her body

fought to accept his, she found she could, after all, accommodate him. But the magic had gone. This man, intimately joined to her, moving within her, was a virtual stranger. She did not love him, she hardly knew him any more. And she was no longer herself.

Sophia opened her eyes and saw that Callum's were closed, his face stark as though he was in pain, his breath coming in deep, effortful inhalations as he thrust into her. *A stranger.* Her body tightened as though responding to her frantic thoughts. She felt him within her as muscles she had not known she possessed clenched around him and the pleasure flooded back, and with it a feeling of tenderness for her husband who had rescued her.

Callum gasped, thrust and then hung, shuddering, over her as she felt his heat gush and spill into her. Sophia tightened her arms around him and felt a confusion of emotions, a sense that there was still something her body needed, the thrill of intimacy, shyness. And guilt.

Chapter Ten

Callum rolled onto his back and lay staring up at the ceiling while his breathing got back into some sort of order. That had been good. Sophia had been so responsive—way beyond his hopes. Not perfect, of course, for either of them, but that would come.

She was naturally sensual and she would learn fast how to pleasure him. His body felt heavy and utterly relaxed. Sated, he thought, hauling his eyelids open as they threatened to descend. Not *quite* sated, perhaps. It would be good to do that again in a little while. He had never felt that close to a woman while he was making love to her. Perhaps there was more than the usual sense of responsibility to make it good when the woman was one's wife and that was all it was. Yet somehow he had sensed her desire and her nervousness, her pain and her yielding almost as if they had been his own.

He found he was smiling and turned his head to look at Sophia. He had given her some pleasure, of that he was certain. As he moved, so did she, to turn her head away, but not before he saw the fat tear running down her cheek.

'Sophia!' He sat bolt upright and she curled away from him defensively. 'What is it?'

She said something in a low mumble. He bent over her, but all he could make out was '...Daniel.'

'What?' he snapped. For several seconds he thought she was not going to answer him, then Sophia sat up and rubbed the back of her hand across her eyes. They were wide, almost bemused.

'I...'

'What is wrong?' he asked again, trying to keep his voice down. 'Did I hurt you?'

'No.' She shook her head. 'Well, yes, but I expected it. It did not matter.'

'You enjoyed it? I gave you pleasure?' It was the first time in his life that he had needed to ask that question and it was not doing his temper much good to have to ask it now, of his wife.

Sophia ducked her head so he could not see her face. 'Yes. Yes, you did. Of course.'

'You said Daniel's name.'

She took a deep, shuddering breath. 'I have a confession to make,' she said, her face still stubbornly hidden from him.

'What?' He made his voice gentle with an effort. To be jerked out of that post-coital, sensual happiness was a shock. But what secrets could she possibly have that could provoke this reaction?

'I did not love Daniel,' Sophia blurted out.

Callum found he was staring at her hands, twisted together in distress. 'Of all the things I might have expected you to say, that one would never have occurred to me,' he said after a moment.

'I know. I swore I would love him. I meant to. But I fell out of love, I suppose.'

'My God.'

Sophia looked up, her eyes swimming with tears she was somehow holding in check. They were very lovely, blue and wide in the candlelight. 'You are disgusted with me for being so fickle, I realise that.'

'No, I am not. Of course not. I always thought the betrothal was wrong—you were both too young.'

'You told me I would fall in love again, properly, when I was grown up. How angry that made me!' She managed a smile. 'I thought you were pompous and condescending.'

'I probably was, pontificating on the subject of marriage at that age,' he admitted. *Hell, all those years of nagging Dan to write, feeling guilty about not making him come back and marry and all the time...*

'Why didn't you write and break it off?' he asked.

'And jilt Daniel? After the promises I had made? But I didn't realise, not for years, that was the trouble. If I had, early on, I would have written. Instead I settled down into being comfortably betrothed, I suppose. It gave me a little freedom that other girls did not have. I had my art and that absorbed me.'

'Art?' She was surely not still spending her time with those endless scribbles and daubs, was she?

'Oh, yes.' Sophia's mouth curved into a smile and the tears were gone. 'That is the most important thing in my life. Except my family. And you now, of course,' she added. He hoped that was not an afterthought.

'And there was no other man?' Callum could have

laughed at the surprise on her face at the question, but he kept his own straight. Deep down he had no idea how he felt about this revelation, other than a fixed resolve not to reveal his suspicions that Dan had fallen out of love even faster.

'No. Honestly, I was faithful to him,' Sophia said with an earnestness that shook him. Dan had not been faithful, not at all. But then, no one expected the man to be under those circumstances. The idea of Dan embracing almost ten years of celibacy was impossible to contemplate.

'I am sure you were.' Callum discovered that he had put one hand over hers. The twisting fingers stilled and after a moment threaded confidingly into his. 'But you have grown into an attractive woman. Other men must have noticed.'

'Which other men? We could not afford for me to have a Season—and anyway, why should we? I was betrothed. Local society, with the exception of William at the Hall, is very confined. My friends are in St Albans, but that is also a small society; people knew I was spoken for. And I never saw anyone I was tempted by,' she added with a shy glance from under her lashes.

'Hmm, very virtuous.' Did that look mean that *he* would have tempted her? No, if she had fallen out of love with one twin, she was not going to fall for the other. 'When did you realise?'

'When I got the letter telling me that you were both coming home. It came the day the wreck happened, I calculated afterwards. Daniel sent it by a faster, smaller ship that had left Calcutta a few days before yours.'

Callum looked back over almost a year and remembered the conversation at a party in Government House when he realised that Dan had not warned Sophia of his return. He had nagged and his brother had gone off guiltily to scrawl a note.

'That night, with his return so close, I realised that I did not want to marry him, that I had fallen out of love.'

'Would you have told him?'

She looked appalled. 'I do not know! How awful, I never thought of that. I just knew that I had left it far, far too late to break it off and that anyway, we were so desperate for the money I did not dare.'

'It was that bad even then? I did not realise.'

'Oh, yes. It was bad, although our creditors were holding off because of the betrothal, they knew they would be paid eventually.'

'So when you realised what had happened you knew it would plunge you into serious financial difficulties?'

No wonder she had been so distressed even though she had not loved Daniel. She had behaved with great control and dignity, but the stricken look in her eyes had penetrated even his own black grief.

'Yes. I felt—I *feel*—so guilty about worrying over that at such a moment. I tell myself there is no value in fretting over what might have been, regretting what I did not do—that helps no one.'

'You should have asked William for help. We would have done something,' Cal protested. The slender fingers interlaced with his tightened. 'Pride?' he asked.

Sophia nodded. 'And guilt, I suppose.'

'Then what were you going to do? What would you have done if I had not come back and asked you to marry me?'

'I told you. Find paid employment,' she said. 'I think we would have had to sell the house as well. Mama would have lived with Mark when he was ordained and had a parish.'

'In your shoes I would have bitten the hand off anyone offering to rescue me from those straits,' Cal said. 'Not resisted as long as you did.'

'No, you would not,' she contradicted. 'You would have stuck out that stubborn chin and refused. Can you imagine yourself accepting a marriage of convenience to a wealthy woman because you needed money?'

'It is different for a woman,' he said.

'Yes,' Sophia agreed with a somewhat watery attempt at a smile. 'I discovered that. But this is all beside the point. Callum, do you not see? I let you believe I still loved Daniel and you felt you had to marry me out of duty to him. But all the while I should have been honest with both myself, and with him, and released him from the engagement years ago.'

'It was not easy, was it?' he asked her, wondering why anger was not stirring inside him. She had broken her word, failed to love his twin, done nothing to release either of them and then married him to save herself from penury. He *should* be angry. 'You had to struggle to bring yourself to do it.' Perhaps that was why? She had not snatched at his offer lightly, greedily.

'I could do my duty by my family, which was to marry well, or be honest with you.'

'And you do not know me, let alone love me, so your course of action was plain—do the best for your family.'

'Yes. I should not have told you, I can see that now,' she added, her expression miserable. 'I should have been strong enough not to ease my conscience by admitting it. At least then you would not have known that you had married me for nothing.'

'Nonsense,' Callum said briskly. 'I needed a wife and I have found one without delay. We will deal well together, never mind how we happened to come to this point. I do not regard it and neither should you.' Did he mean it? He had no idea, but he had to say it. Anything else would be cruel. Sophia was his wife now, for better or worse.

He gave her hand a squeeze and released it, slid out of bed. 'I'll leave you, you must be tired now.'

She sat and watched him as he walked around the bed to pick up his robe, the sheet clutched to her breasts, her eyes still dark. Like this, she was beautiful. Desire surged back and Callum tied the sash tightly around his waist. He might want her, but he would not make love to her again tonight, not while he had this new reality to come to terms with. And, strangely, the one question that was beating at his brain was, *Why don't I mind about Daniel?*

'Callum?'

'Yes?'

'Nothing. Sleep well.'

There was little chance of that, he thought as he closed the door quietly behind him.

Callum was in the dining room, addressing himself to a large steak when Sophia came downstairs the next morning. She had to confess to herself that she was grateful for the presence of Hawksley to open the door for her and Michael to hold her chair so that she was occupied with thanking them and seating herself and did not have to meet her new husband's gaze until he had resumed his own seat.

'Good morning, Sophia.' There was a newspaper

folded beside his place and a pile of letters at his other hand, but he seemed content to neglect them for conversation.

Sophia managed a composed smile and pushed to the back of her mind the embarrassing realisation that the staff knew what they had been doing last night and that Callum was probably thinking about it too. Soon she would get used to it, she supposed, but for now, the more she thought about what had happened in bed, the more blush-provoking it seemed. She had screamed. What if anyone had heard her?

Or perhaps all Callum was thinking about was her disloyalty to his twin and the fact that she had deceived him by allowing him to think she had still been in love with Daniel.

'Good morning. It seems to be a very pleasant day. Yes, coffee, please, Michael.'

'There is post for you.' She blinked and came back to the present as Callum lifted the top three letters from the pile and passed them to her. She recognised her mother's hand on one; the others were from friends in St Alban's. 'Hawksley, please see that Mrs Chatterton's post is handed to her directly in future.'

'Sir.'

This was, Sophia knew, a considerable concession. Most husbands would expect to have all the incoming post pass through their hands as a matter of course. She smiled her thanks, met a heavy-lidded look and glanced away, blushing. Callum had not stayed with her last night, or come to her room this morning. He had been gentle when she had confessed, but doubtless he was displeased with her.

Her tongue had certainly seemed to freeze. She had

wanted to tell him that she would do her best to please him in bed, that she felt very grateful that he had taken her in Daniel's place, but the words had sounded gauche and foolish even as she began to whisper them, and her voice had been choked with the tears that had welled up in shock at the sensual pleasure, the discomfort, the confusing way Callum had made her feel.

Instead her confession had tumbled out, proving to him that he could not trust her to do the right thing.

If she had tried to explain her feelings, she would probably only have embarrassed him. Mama had warned her that men did not like to speak about emotions or deep personal matters once the first courtship was over. Besides, he might think she was trying to tell him that she had fallen out of love with Daniel and into love with him. She cringed inwardly at the thought. The wonderful intimacy that she had felt with Callum for a few minutes, skin to skin, heart to heart, was something for the bedroom. Perhaps she would feel it again. For the rest of the time well-bred restraint was obviously appropriate.

Michael put a plate of eggs and ham in front of her and she began to eat, surprised at how hungry she felt. Callum pushed away his own empty plate. 'I must go to Leadenhall Street today and I expect to be away until dinner time, I am afraid.'

'Leadenhall Street is where East India House is, is it not?' Sophia recalled. 'You will have a great deal of business, I quite understand.' It was a relief, in fact. She would have the opportunity to explore and talk to the servants and start to feel less like a guest and more like the mistress of the house. 'I will need to discuss menus with Mrs Datchett. Will you dine at home every night this week?'

'I have no idea. I ate out most of the time before—bachelors do. Now I am married it would be more fitting for me to entertain here. I may need to bring colleagues home to work in the evening. Surely the woman can improvise? My Indian cooks always did.'

'She would not want to serve an inferior meal to your guests. Indian cuisine is different, I am sure.' Sophia felt herself bristling at the implied criticism of one of her staff.

'It certainly is. Tell her that if I do bring guests without warning we will not expect a formal dinner party. Will that help?'

'I am sure it will.' Sophia gestured to the footman to pour more coffee for both of them. Callum had been used to a bachelor existence with Daniel. No doubt their servants had improvised to cope with whatever their young masters wanted and the brothers would not stand on too much ceremony. England was quite another matter and no doubt his comments would find their way back to Mrs Datchett's ears before long. Diplomacy would be called for.

'Madam's cards have arrived, sir.' Hawksley proffered a salver and Callum picked up the rectangle of pasteboard on it, nodded his approval and passed it to Sophia.

'There you are. We must be married, it says so there.'

Mrs Callum Chatterton
Half Moon Street and Long Welling Manor, Hertfordshire

The card was stiff, gilt edged and elegant. 'Oh. Thank you.' How daunting. These were for when she made calls without her husband. At home her name had been on Mama's card, so this was the first time she had had her own. But who on earth was she to call upon? She knew no one in London.

'Right. I'll be off, if you will excuse me. I'll leave you to get on with your letters.' Callum rose and came to bend over her shoulder. Sophia turned to say goodbye and was surprised by a kiss on the cheek. Against her skin his was smooth, with just the faintest hint of bristle after his morning shave. Castile soap, a trace of sandalwood, virtually no trace of the warm smell of heated male skin. Even so there was a tug, low in her belly, as her newly awakened body responded to the closeness of his.

'Goodbye,' she said, with an attempt at cool composure and hoped her thoughts did not show in her voice. 'Have a good day in the City.'

His grimace made her smile and then he was gone, leaving her alone in her own house, with her own servants. Her first day as a married woman.

Sophia finished her coffee and bread and butter as she listened to the sounds of her new home. Carriages in the street, snatches of conversation as people passed, the clatter of booted feet running down the stone steps into the narrow area at the front of the house and then more voices as someone in the kitchen opened the lower door. Callum's voice talking to Hawksley in the hall, the bang of the front door, the slight sound of Michael shifting his stance as he stood by the buffet waiting for her next order.

All she had to do was to make this household run like clockwork. Her husband was a hard-working man with a lot on his mind; he must come home to domestic perfection, a home that ran so smoothly he never even noticed. That was not so hard, she told herself, even if she had no idea what Callum's likes or dislikes were yet. And by the time she had managed that, then perhaps she would have made some acquaintances, begun to create a new life for herself. 'Michael, please give my compliments to Mrs Datchett and ask her to join me in my sitting room in half an hour.'

That had sounded confident enough; she only hoped the woman was easy to deal with. She had rehearsed everything they needed to settle in her head and was waiting, a list to hand, when the cook-housekeeper entered. She seemed a pleasant, competent woman, Sophia decided after a few minutes. She suggested things that needed to be bought for the kitchen and scullery, announced that the staff quarters and service area were most satisfactory, nodded agreement to the housekeeping allowance that Sophia proposed and then asked, 'And will you be entertaining much, ma'am?'

'I expect so. In the meantime my husband may well bring colleagues home to dine at very short notice. He does not expect a formal dinner on those occasions. Is that likely to be a problem?'

'No, ma'am. If we agree the menus for the week I'll make sure we have enough food in the larder to add extra dishes as required.'

That was a relief. 'Can you cook Indian food, Mrs Datchett?'

'No, ma'am!' She frowned. 'No, but there's a receipt for a curry in one of my cook books. That's Indian, I think.'

Mrs Datchett bustled off back downstairs and Sophia

set herself to explore her new domain. Her bedchamber and dressing room were well appointed; they just needed a fresh coat of paint and some new hangings, as did the rooms on the ground floor and the hall, stairs and landings.

Which just left Callum's study and bedroom. The doors were unlocked and he had not said he did not want them disturbed. Even so, it was with the sensation that she was entering Bluebeard's chamber that she turned the handle on the bedroom door.

Chapter Eleven

H<small>is</small> valet had unpacked and tidied the room, but Callum had somehow managed to imprint his personality on the space far more than Sophia felt she had in her own chamber. Wilkins had gone out on an errand to the bootmaker so she could explore without fear of interruption.

There were silver-backed brushes on the dresser, a silver dish with tie pins in it, a few small boxes, everything with the cat's mask from the family crest. He must have taken things from the Hall, she guessed, to replace those lost at sea.

In her room was the trunk filled with the trousseau she had embroidered with this very crest. Fortunately she had not followed her mother's suggestion of adding an entwined *D* and *S* to the cat's mask, so everything was usable and if she did not draw attention to it perhaps Callum would not think about who they had originally been intended for.

She moved around the room, touching the books

heaped on the dresser, on the floor beside the bed, uneasy about picking them up. There was a pencil and a pile of paper on the nightstand as though thoughts might come to him in the middle of the night and have to be recorded immediately. An oil painting of the Hall hung on one wall, on the other a smaller version of the triple portrait of the brothers that hung over the fireplace in William's study.

Daniel's charming, boyish smile was vivid, even in this copy, contrasting with Callum's steady, thoughtful gaze. That was the Daniel she remembered, but was it the man he had grown into? The adult Callum she could see clearly in the youth, but he had a harder edge now that this serious boy had been lacking. Sophia reached up and touched Daniel's painted cheek. 'I'm sorry, Daniel. Sorry I fell out of love with you, sorry you are gone.'

There were Indian objects too, she found as she wandered around the room. Callum must have sent them home over the years. She picked up a small soapstone carving of a god with the head of an elephant, an ivory panel carved deeply with swirling vines, fruit, birds and a tiny lizard, then a set of boxes, vivid with enamelled colours, so light that they must be *papier maché.*

The slippers by the bed were backless embroidered leather with curling toes, the robe at the foot of the bed was not the plain red one she had seen last night, but a gorgeous weave of blues and black in heavy cotton. Callum would look like an exotic Eastern prince wearing those, she thought with a sensual shiver.

On impulse she turned back the covers and ran her hand into the bed. No folded nightshirt: he must sleep naked. Feeling as though she had been caught watching through a spy hole, Sophia jerked back her hand and straightened the bed.

Still, she couldn't drag herself away. It was as though this exploration would reveal the man she had married, answer questions she dare not ask. The bottles on the dresser were coloured glass and each, when she removed the stopper and sniffed, held a different perfumed oil. Sandalwood in one, a musky, disturbing fragrance in another, a third filled with something that teased her nostrils with the warm scent of spice.

The clothes press held the sombre coats and waistcoats of a gentleman who had been in mourning. The woollen cloth was of the highest quality, the dark waistcoats were silk. What was his normal taste? Would he buy more flamboyant waistcoats now, more dashing coats?

Drawers revealed piles of white shirts in fine linen, muslin neckcloths, handkerchiefs. All new and good quality. She touched things, ran her fingers over them, inhaling the scent of starched linen and masculine leather. There was a pile of hat boxes from Lock's and more boxes revealed gleaming boots and evening slippers. Callum had not been averse to shopping for himself, she realised.

Sophia scanned the room. Had she left everything as it had been? Yes, she was sure of it, he would never know she had been in here.

Next door the study was quite incredibly untidy in contrast to the bedchamber. Obviously Wilkins had no control here. Books had been unpacked from chests and were stacked all around and in piles on the shelves. A drawing slope had been set up and boxes on it revealed pens and rulers, inks, chalks, a box of watercolours, the squares of paint dry and brittle.

Sophia stood for a while looking at the pristine white sheet pinned to the board, her fingers itching for a pencil, a stick of pastel, anything to draw with. She turned away before the urge to mark the clean surface overcame discretion.

A pile of papers was on one end of the desk under a piece of marble with a carving of a tiger on it. Folders were heaped at the other end, bristling with markers. There were letters, too, stacked on the leather desktop, already annotated on their wrappers.

She stood by the desk and looked around. Here she did not dare touch anything. The desk needed a blotter. She must add checking the inkwells and the blotting paper to the footmen's routine.

Callum knew people, many people, here in London, she realised, looking at the amount of correspondence. His work would bring him into contact with them, every day. He would not be lonely and he would doubtless soon make friends, and so would she.

Now she would have luncheon and go out shopping with a dress allowance beyond her wildest fantasies, and in shops that she had dreamed of visiting. It would be feeble of her indeed to feel sorry for herself with that prospect in view.

Cal sat back in the hackney carriage and willed himself to relax for however long it took to negotiate the evening traffic between the City and Mayfair. Strange that a musty, battered carriage represented the peaceful neutral ground between two battlefields—the East India Company headquarters and his own household.

The Company he could deal with, given hard work and careful tactics. Already he could see his path clearly there. They had sized him up in the first weeks, considered the reports he had worked on, the way he had reconstructed what he could of the information lost in the wreck, both his work and Daniel's. They would have listened to the senior company officials who had survived and, eventually they made him the offer of a post that was all he had hoped and more.

It had been a strain, focusing on the work, the discussions, while he was still physically and mentally wounded from the wreck. Perhaps his sombre demeanour and total focus had been what had convinced them. He would probably never know.

But now he had a shared office, a clerk and a challenge to reform an area of the business that was very much to his taste and he knew he would find it, quite legitimately, highly profitable. It would be pleasant to be rich. He smiled, amused at himself. He was not badly off now—it would take a foolish or unlucky servant of the Company not to make money—but to be in the position to develop the two estates into something fine, buy all the bloodstock he fancied… Perhaps exert enough influence that a title came his way. Yes, tempting.

The other campaign was his marriage and that promised to hold far more damaging skirmishes. Sophia's confession coming so soon after the culmination of their lovemaking had left him almost dizzy. She had not loved Daniel. Part of him resented that on his twin's behalf, but he knew it was unjust. He had healed enough to be able to see Dan again just as clearly as he ever had. His brother had fallen out of love with Sophia—it would be hypocritical to blame her for doing exactly the same thing.

Except for one small detail—of the two of them, she was the one who could have broken the engagement with honour. And she had not. If she had, he would never have thought to offer for her, let alone press the matter. He should be angry with her, but he was not and a small glow of satisfaction that he could not analyse kept disturbing him. Surely he was not glad that she had fallen out of love with Daniel? That would be absurd, it was not as though he was in love with her himself.

This morning she had been poised and pleasant, apparently happy to be with him. But she had not seemed in the slightest bit concerned that he was leaving her alone all day, and when he had kissed her cheek she had stiffened. For a mad moment he had been tempted to pull her from the chair, kiss her hard and possessively on the mouth, there and then in front of the watching servants.

It occurred to him that perhaps he had been too demonstrative in his lovemaking last night. She was very innocent and shy. Now the memory of that little shiver when he had touched her was lodged in his mind as well. Last night had been the first time for her and he knew he must have hurt her. It would be his duty, and his pleasure, to make certain that every time from now on was better.

Never had the contemplation of duty been so arousing. The images his brain was conjuring up stirred his body to the point of discomfort. Grimly Callum began to calculate compound interest in his head. By the time he was delivered to his own front door his unruly body was under control, but he was still achingly aware of it. It did not help that he recognised it was entirely his own fault. *She is almost a virgin,* he reminded himself.

'Madam is in the drawing room, sir.' Hawksley took hat, gloves and cane. 'Dinner is at eight, if that is satisfactory.'

'Whatever Mrs Chatterton says. Please send up hot water and Wilkins. I will bathe and shave.'

Callum paused on the threshold of his room. It looked just as it had when he'd left it that morning and yet he had the feeling that someone had been there. One of the maids, no doubt, dusting. And Wilkins would have tidied up, too. Yet he could not quite shake off the sensation of a presence that lingered on the edge of his perception.

He turned and opened the door to his study. Again, just as he had left it. He closed his eyes and inhaled deeply. England smelt strange after years of the dust and strong scents of India. Ah, yes, just the faint hint of the rose perfume that Sophia wore. How strange that he had sensed her presence so quickly. That teasing hint of perfume must have been what had alerted him—he had no idea his sense of smell was that acute. And there, in the rug about three feet from the desk, were the prints of two small heels. She had stood, and looked, for several minutes to leave those deep little dents.

Unaccountably disturbed, Callum began to prowl around. Nothing was touched. The heel marks were indented beside his drawing slope, too; she had studied that also. What had she said last night about her art? That it was the most important thing to her? He had forgotten all about the way she had been smudged with charcoal and chalks as a girl.

He went to his room and bathed and changed with his

mind only half on what he was doing. 'I must speak to the maids,' Wilkins said, tight-lipped as Cal considered the neckcloths he was proffering, draped over his arm. 'They have been rummaging.'

'Rummaging? Where?' Cal selected a length of muslin and began the intricate business of tying a knot of his own invention.

'Amongst your shirts and other things, sir. I know to a fraction just how I leave them. And every drawer is always left completely closed. Someone has been touching them and replacing them with care, if not total precision.'

'Nothing is missing, I hope.' The valet shook his head. 'Then I would not mention it. Mrs Chatterton may well have been checking over my linen.'

Wilkins appeared to be restraining himself with an effort. His thoughts on wives interfering in his domain were quite obvious, but training held and he said nothing.

How very intriguing. Cal inserted a diamond tiepin and gave his cuffs a final twitch. Sophia was curious about him, it seemed. It made him realise that he had hardly given her, as a person, a thought except insofar as her thoughts and actions affected him and his plans. There was the woman he had made love to and the well-behaved young lady whom he had married and the woman who had fallen in and out of love and lost his twin—but what was going on in her head? What was important to her now in this marriage?

What, he wondered with a frown, did she think of him?

It was an hour since she had heard Callum come in. Sophia unpicked the last dozen stitches that she had set in her embroidery, pricked her finger, said 'Rats!' in a most unladylike fashion and stuck it in her mouth before the blood got on to the linen.

'What on earth is the matter?'

And now her careful pose of sweet domesticity for her returning husband was shattered. She took her finger out of her mouth and held it away from her gown while she fumbled in her reticule for a handkerchief. 'I was sewing and I pricked my finger and I do not want to get blood on the cloth or my new gown—oh, thank you.' Callum shook out a large clean linen square and handed it to her. 'Have you had a good day?' He did not look as though he had spent a tiring day bent over paperwork or in stuffy meetings or whatever it was that he did. She realised that she had no idea.

'Interesting and quite positive, I think. That is a very handsome gown.'

Was that warmth in his eyes as he studied the amber silk with its coffee-brown ribbons? She felt a definite warming herself as she studied the lean figure in the dark elegance of evening dress. There were muscles under that smooth tailoring; she had felt them shift under her hands as he drove into her body.

'You do not think it is too bright in colour? I was a trifle unsure, but it had been returned to the *modiste* and it happened to fit and I thought that while I waited for the other gowns I had ordered to be finished...' She was prattling with nerves. Sophia stopped and reminded herself to breathe.

'I think it is very suitable. The ribbons are a trifle sombre, perhaps. Could they be replaced with ruffles or something?' Callum grinned, transforming his expression. 'Or am I completely adrift—will it quite ruin the style if you do that?'

That smile. *Oh, my goodness.* That was all she needed on top of her overheated thoughts. Sophia smiled back, her heart lifting. She had not realised just how tense she was. 'Of course it will! Have you no experience of ladies' fashions, sir?' It was meant as a joke, but then she remembered that he had no sisters, had not been in England for years, so the only ladies' fashions he would have encountered would have been in India and the ones he would have taken an interest in were probably on the backs of his mistresses.

She knew she had blushed and that her smile had frozen on her lips. She could tell he understood why she was so suddenly out of countenance; the wretched man seemed to read her like a book. Sophia subsided into embarrassed silence.

'Very little, beyond admiring them at social events. And, of course, society fashions in India are always a good season or two behind the mode here. If you are enquiring if I bought my mistresses fashionable gowns, no, I did not.' He waited a beat, then added, 'They always preferred silks.'

The image of Callum reclining on heaped cushions like an Eastern potentate surrounded by exquisite golden-skinned beauties with long black hair and dark eyes swam vividly into her mind. She recalled the robe and slippers in his room and how she had found the idea of him wearing them unsettling. She had heard that the East India Company encouraged liaisons, and marriages, between their officers and Indian women, but somehow she had never related that to Daniel or Callum.

Pride came to her rescue. 'I can well believe it,' Sophia said with a smile that felt tight on her lips. 'Why should they want to be enveloped in tight lacing and layers of petticoats and silly frills in that heat when there are those beautiful fabrics and flowing costumes?'

Callum narrowed his eyes at her response. So, he had been trying to shock her, had he? 'Did you bring her with you?' she asked. 'Your current mistress at the time? Was the poor soul drowned?' Even as she said it she winced inwardly at how her temper had betrayed her into cruelty—he would have felt affection for the woman at the very least.

'No, I did not. We should not be discussing such things.' He strode into the room and poured wine into a glass.

'Why not? I am not a sheltered little virgin any more and you brought the subject up.' Callum lifted the glass to his lips, his profile turned to her, revealing nothing except a complete absence of humour. 'And I would like a glass of wine, if you please.'

He put down his glass and poured another. 'I paid off my mistress when I returned to Calcutta. And I have not taken one since. Are you satisfied? May we drop the subject now?'

'Certainly, if it makes you uncomfortable.' She took the proffered glass and pointedly avoided touching his hand as she did so. 'Thank you.'

'It does not make me uncomfortable,' he snapped, 'if by that you mean I have a guilty conscience. It is simply not a suitable subject for discussion with one's wife.' Sophia merely arched one eyebrow in what she hoped was elegant disbelief. 'Do you think Daniel and I were living like monks?'

'Of course I do not! I suppose I always knew that is how men behave, whilst unmarried women must maintain an aura of virgin purity and wait for them to decide to stop their raking and come home.'

But that was a lie. She had never once thought about Daniel and other women because the truth was, by the time she had come to understand about such matters, she must have fallen out of love with him and it did not matter to her. But whether Callum kept a mistress did matter somehow, even though she knew many married men thought nothing of it. 'Not that coming home and marrying is any guarantee of fidelity, I quite understand that, too.'

'Indeed?' Callum demanded. He had taken up position before the empty fireplace beneath a large mirror that reflected his back to her. The rigid set of his shoulders appeared as furious as his front view. Sophia quaked inwardly and took a gulp of wine. 'You expect me to set up a mistress in London, do you?'

'Well…not immediately. You have a lot to deal with just now and I expect it is not a matter of impulse. It must be like choosing a quality horse, I suppose—an investment.'

'Let us be clear, Mrs Chatterton. I am married to you. I took vows. That means I am faithful to you. If I had made arrangements before, then those are now over. Is there anything in that statement that is open to misinterpretation? Because if so, let us deal with any further questions you might have about my morals here and now.'

She had made him very, very angry, she realised. What on earth had made her think she could tease him? It must have been that grin, that sudden flash of humour.

Sophia said the first thing that came into her head. 'I am sincerely glad that I am not one of your clerks, or some poor soul up before you as magistrate.' His expression of cold displeasure darkened and she added, 'That was very clear, thank you.'

'Excellent. And I hope the same goes for you. I will not tolerate unfaithfulness.'

'How dare you! If you think for one moment that I would take a lover—'

'Dinner is served, madam,' Hawksley said behind her.

Chapter Twelve

Callum would not come to her tonight, not after that ghastly scene in the drawing room. Sophia sat bolt upright in bed, her hands knotted in the sheet. How much had Hawksley heard? She had not been aware of the door opening behind her—had it been ajar? The entire staff could have overheard.

She felt sick. Callum was obviously furious—how could he be anything else? Her foolish teasing had turned into a display that he could characterise as vulgar or jealous or immodest, or all three. And she could not blame him. Why had she reacted so badly to the thought that he might take a mistress? It was what men did. And she could hardly delude herself that hers was a love match.

He had been so polite throughout dinner afterwards that it had cut like a knife. Of course he was well bred and so much in control that he could preserve a perfect front before the servants. From somewhere she had conjured up equally polite responses with the result that they must have sounded like complete strangers who did not take to each other very much, gamely making conversation during some interminable dinner party.

Hawksley had looked as though he was stuffed. So had Michael and Andrew. But then good servants always did when they were trying to be inconspicuous during meals.

He won't come tonight. He won't come until he forgives me—and how am I ever going to make him do that when I dare not mention the subject to apologise?

The door opened and the candles flickered wildly. 'Callum?' It came out as a squeak.

'Who else were you expecting, pray?' There was an edge to the question that she supposed she deserved. Her husband was still in evening breeches and tailcoat. As she watched, wide-eyed with apprehension, he began to undress, each garment placed on the chair with a deliberation that only tightened her trepidation, notch by notch.

'No one, of course. I was not expecting you. I thought after we had quarrelled that you would not want to come to me.'

'That was not a quarrel,' Callum said as he sat down and rolled off his stockings. 'That was a clarification of expectations.'

He stood up and draped his shirt over the back of the chair. Sophia's eyes followed his hands to the waistband of his breeches. The thin silk hid nothing, which was something that young ladies were expected to ignore. One averted one's eyes from this insight into male anatomy, although as one outrageous dowager had said within Sophia's hearing at a party, it was interesting to see what the young men were thinking about.

Callum was not, apparently, thinking about making love to her. Then why had he come? Perhaps she was going to get another lecture about her behaviour, although she could not think of anything else she had done wrong. Not yet. A sin of omission, then. Sophia swallowed a sigh.

He stood there, hands at his waist for a moment, then turned and began to systematically snuff out the candles, as he had done the night before, only this time he did not stop when he reached the bedside table, but extended a hand to the wicks of those too.

'Would you prefer it if the room was dark?'

Perhaps he wanted it? Uncertain, she nodded and the final flames vanished, leaving only the smell of hot wax.

Wide-eyed in the gloom, Sophia heard the whisper of falling material and then the covers were moved as Callum slid into bed beside her. He turned and pressed her back against the pillows and she became aware that he did, after all, want to make love. Had she been forgiven, or had he blown out the candles because he preferred not to look at her while he was still angry over her tactlessness?

His hands were not unkind as they moved on her body, nor was his kiss careless, but then she had never feared that he was a man who would hurt her physically. Sophia tried to recapture the sensual feelings she had experienced the previous night and found, although exactly the same things appeared to be happening, there was none of the pleasure as his hands cupped and caressed her breast, teased her nipples, stroked down her hip.

Was it the darkness? But the strong body over hers

was the same to touch, to smell, as it had been before: she felt no fear of him. His hands were as skilful, as bold, as they had been before. But something was missing, some magic that had been there on their wedding night, despite the discomfort and all her fears.

Sophia made herself relax, tried to recall what she had done with her own hands, how she had held Callum, encouraged him, caressed him, but her body seemed as numb as her mind. He was pushing her thighs apart now and she opened to him, obedient and passive.

She felt him lift his head as he braced himself over her. 'Sophia.'

'Callum,' she whispered. 'Callum.' And he thrust and filled her and began to move and still she felt nothing at all except the strength of the man possessing her and a kind of desperate loneliness.

Had it taken so long before? He seemed to be waiting for something else to happen. She clung to him, moved with him as best she could and bit back the sigh of relief when Callum shuddered and went limp in her arms.

His heart thudded against her breast. After a moment he turned his head on her shoulder and she felt his breath on her cheek. 'You… That was not good for you.'

'Yes, yes, it was,' she lied, forcing a smile because she knew he would hear it in her voice and believe her satisfied. 'It was just…I am a little tired and perhaps upset because of our… The discussion before dinner.'

'I will help you.' Callum shifted and she felt his hand between her thighs, parting the slick swollen folds.

'No, no, really, it is all right.' She did not understand what he meant to do, but she did not think she could cope with the embarrassment of finding out. She tightened her muscles to hold her legs together and after a moment he withdrew his hand.

'I will let you sleep, then.' He got out of bed, pulled the covers back over her and she heard him moving about in the darkness, gathering up his clothes.

'Goodnight, Callum,' she said as the door opened and she saw him silhouetted against the landing candle-glow.

'Goodnight.' The door closed and left her in the darkness, confused and uncomfortable and bitterly disappointed.

She had hoped to spend the next day quietly drawing, which never failed to calm and cheer her, but instead, at two in the afternoon, she found herself sitting stiffly in a hired carriage, her new calling cards in her reticule and Chivers in her best outfit perched opposite.

'I forgot to tell you, I had callers yesterday when I was out,' she had said at breakfast. 'Five cards—and none of them people I have heard of.' She patted the oblongs of stiff pasteboard with their gilt edges and black printing into a pile and passed them to Callum as he pushed back his breakfast plate.

'Mrs Sommerson, Lady Archbold, Lady Randolph, Mrs Hickson and the Dowager Countess of Milverley,' Callum read. 'An impressive haul, and all in person too.' He indicated the turned-down corners. 'You had best pay some return visits speedily—and let it be known on which days you will be at home for morning calls yourself. Sommerson, Archbold and Randolph are Directors of the Company, Mrs Hickson is a distant cousin of mine and Lady Milverley was a friend of my mother. I let it be known at the office that we were receiving and doubtless the family have been writing to all their acquaintances in town and mentioning that we were coming up.'

'You will come with me this afternoon?' It was a plea, not a question, and she felt ashamed of her cowardice. 'I did not think we would receive calls, not at this time of year. Why are they all in London? It is almost October.'

'Not everyone flees to the country during the summer and, in any case, people are drifting back now. We will receive some invitations, too. It is good,' Callum added encouragingly. 'There won't be too many people—no great crushes. You will be up to snuff by the time the Season starts.'

'The ladies called on you by themselves.' Callum turned over the little pile of cards. 'It will be expected that you return the call without me. I'll have a carriage sent round from the stables this afternoon, you won't want to use a hackney.'

'No,' Sophia agreed. 'Thank you.' She managed a brave smile. 'What a good thing my new afternoon gown has been delivered.'

The knowledge that her gown was in the mode was a help now. At least she did not feel dowdy. And even if the ladies were at home, it would only be half an hour at most with each of them. It would be just as it had been in the country, only this time she was not with Mama and the ladies would be total strangers. Callum had said nothing about the need to make a good impression, but he had not needed to; she was acutely aware that four of them would be reporting back to men who held great sway in the Company. If they told their husbands that Callum Chatterton had made a mistake and married a gauche, socially inept young woman, it would damage his career.

'Lady Randolph's house, ma'am.' Andrew, who had been riding with the coachman, opened the door, took the card she handed him and went up the steps to give an impressive 'London knock' on the dark green door. It opened, Sophia crossed her fingers in the hope that no one was in, but Andrew was coming back and the door stayed open. In she must go.

'Mrs Chatterton, my lady.'

'My dear Mrs Chatterton.' A willowy lady rose and came forwards. 'How kind of you to call.'

'Lady Randolph.' Sophia managed the slight curtsy that was required. There were three other women, all middle aged, all regarding her from the circle of chairs around the tea tray. 'I am so sorry I was away from home yesterday.'

'Not at all. You young things are all so busy these days,' she said languidly. 'Let me introduce you. Mrs Sommerson.' Plump with a tight, mean mouth that seemed reluctant to smile. 'Lady Archbold.' Grey hair, grey eyes, large teeth. 'Mrs Hickson.' Snapping black eyes, a small terrier of a woman.

Sophia shook hands, slightly overwhelmed, but also grateful that this was the first house she had come to. It had cut the calls she needed to make to two. 'Ladies, I had intended to call upon all of you. Thank you for calling yesterday.'

'Not at all.' Lady Archbold fixed her with a beady stare while her hostess poured tea. 'We naturally wanted to make sure that Mr Chatterton's new bride had every attention. Such a promising young man.' It sounded like a threat or a warning of what she must live up to.

Sophia cast around for a neutral topic of conversation, then saw the picture that hung over the fireplace, a portrait of two young girls sitting on a bench in a flowery garden, a basket of puppies at their feet. The paint looked fresh and glistening and very new.

'What a delightful double portrait, Lady Randolph.'

It was obviously the right thing to say. Her hostess beamed. 'My granddaughters by Joshua Robertson.'

'He must be very talented. He has caught their personalities, it seems. There are so many artists to select from, it must have been hard to choose.'

'Well, we picked a coming man,' Lady Randolph said. 'I wished not to simply follow the fashion. These celebrity artists get above themselves, one feels.'

And charge so much more, too, Sophia thought wickedly. 'And they are all men, I suppose?' she said. 'There are no Angelica Kauffmanns to be found in London these days?'

'Certainly not! One could not patronise such a female even if there was.'

'But she was very good—a fine artist?'

'That has nothing to do with it,' Mrs Hickson said with a sniff. 'These famous men might pretend otherwise, but it is a *trade*, after all. A woman might as well take up cabinet making! And, of course, the environment is hardly decent—all those unclad models and *hours* spent in studios. One knows what goes on! Wild parties, louche behaviour—no female artist could be anything but one step from being a common harlot.'

'She might as well go on the stage,' Sophia said with a smile and gritted teeth. She had suspected that would be the attitude, but she had hoped that in the sophisticated climate of the capital the conservative attitudes of a country town would not prevail. She had been wrong.

Two hours later Sophia emerged from Lady Milverley's Mayfair house, feeling she had spent the afternoon being pummelled and rung out in a box mangle. She had done her duty, she thought she had made a good impression and not let Callum down, but this collection of new acquaintances made her feel lonelier than ever. Certainly none of them was of an age to become a friend and all of them seemed to have been inspecting and assessing her. She only hoped she had passed muster.

As soon as she reached home she ran up to her sitting room and found her sketch book.

By the time Callum came home the five ladies had been consigned to paper along with the host of other portraits she scribbled down, almost compulsively. But it only partly soothed the knowledge that her work must remain unseen outside her circle of acquaintances, a mere genteel pastime.

There on the page were all the servants, the guests at the dinner party when Masterton had kissed her, people seen on their journey to London, shoppers and shop assistants. The likenesses seemed to flow from her pencil, taking with them all the little jabs at her nerves, her irritation over the curiosity, her fears about making the right impression, even her loneliness.

'There were more calls this afternoon.' She made a mental note to speak to Cook—the soup had too much pepper. 'Two more ladies with Company connections, a Mrs Hooper with her daughters—she tells me she is a connection of Papa's, although I cannot quite work it out—and Lady Constable, who says she was Daniel's godmother.'

'Excellent.' Callum seemed to find the soup acceptable. 'You see, I said you would manage perfectly well. We will be receiving invitations soon. The ladies have taken to you. Tell me, what have you done for the rest of the time?'

Every evening he would take an interest in the mild excitements of her day—what she had read, where she had shopped, the problems with the kitchen maid and the discovery of mice in the drawing-room skirting. Sophia felt she was being judged, kindly, against an unspoken standard of Suitable Wife and, on the whole, being found acceptable. But she did not mention her drawings, or tell Callum about them; *that*, she sensed, would not be considered acceptable. Still lives and landscapes, yes. Sharp, unflattering little portraits of his acquaintance, no.

She did her best to reciprocate in these conversations. She studied the newspapers carefully, borrowed books from the circulating library on trade and India and China and asked about his work. It seemed a very responsible one, forming the medium-term strategy for the luxury goods that the company handled.

'It is an uphill struggle to convince some of the members of the Company to make any changes, though,' Callum confessed with a wry smile. 'They have a pet supplier or a favourite kind of produce and that is that— to try to convince them that to load their ships with tea rather than silk at a particular time or to hold back on a certain product because the market will soon be amply supplied and the price will fall, is like pushing against a door that is jammed shut.'

'So how do you do it?' Sophia asked, her embroidery left untouched in her lap. This, to her, was far more interesting than what was in the newspapers, not for itself exactly, but for the way it gave her an insight into Callum's thinking.

'Like a military campaign. I plot the weakest points, see where the tactical advantage lies, decide where it is prudent to retreat—I seem to be doing a lot of tactical retreating just at the moment.' But he smiled as he said it and she laughed and there was a moment when she wanted to reach out and touch his hand, link her fingers into his long brown ones and tease him a little and just be friends.

Then she saw Callum's eyes darken and the amusement faded from his face and was replaced by something else that made her breath catch in her throat. Her mouth went dry and all she was conscious of was the urge to cross the narrow space between them, curl up on to his lap and kiss him. But he never kissed her, never caressed her, during the day. Would he think her wanton if she did? Would she be gauche and clumsy? 'Callum?'

But the moment had passed. He was reaching for his glass of port and his face was once again back to its pleasant, neutral mask. 'Nothing. Sorry, I must not bore you with this stuff, it can be of no interest to you.'

'I asked because I *am* interested,' Sophia said and bent to bundle her untouched embroidery into the basket at her feet. 'But it must be tiresome for you to have to explain it to me after you have been immersed in it all day.'

She stood up and Callum got to his feet too. He moved, as always, with the ease that so attracted her and she felt that familiar tug of desire.

'I think I will go to bed now. Thank you.' He opened the door for her and she passed through with the sensation of having lost a precious moment of intimacy.

Chapter Thirteen

'**Y**ou are looking a trifle peaky, if I might say so, ma'am,' Chivers remarked as Sophia got out of bed the next morning.

'That is exactly how I feel, Chivers,' she admitted as she rubbed the small of her back. 'Oh, how foolish of me—it is the usual cause!' She did some rapid mental arithmetic: yes, more or less on time.

At first, as she washed and dressed, she simply registered it as the routine discomfort, then the fact struck her that she was married now and her husband would want to know whether or not she was with child.

It was not a topic for discussion over the breakfast table. Sophia waited until Callum went to his study to gather his papers for work and followed him upstairs, straightening her back against the miserable low ache. He was standing at his desk, bent over the documents spread between his braced hands, but at the sound of the door closing behind her he looked up.

'Sophia? Is something wrong?' He was at her side in

two long strides and caught her by the shoulders. 'You are ill?'

She wondered what he saw to make him so concerned; she thought she had schooled her face not to show any discomfort and he had not noticed anything at breakfast, but then he had been engrossed in *The Times* for most of it. 'Nothing—except nature taking its course. I thought I should tell you that I am not with child this month.'

'Not—? Oh, I see. It is of no matter.'

'Is it not? I thought you were anxious for children, for an heir. It is my duty—'

'Duty?' His brows drew together in a sharp, level line. 'I hope it is more than that—no child deserves to be merely the product of *duty*.'

'I did not say that! I would never look upon a child in that way—but I am your wife and you made it clear that you expected me to give you heirs.'

'I am sorry if I put it so baldly.' Callum swept the papers together and stuffed them into a folder. 'I will, naturally, not trouble you until you tell me that it is… convenient for me to visit your chamber again.'

Convenient? Oh, yes, our marital relations are a matter of convenience for you now, not of passion. I suppose I am cheaper than a mistress.

'How very considerate,' she said, more sharply than she had intended, and turned to go.

Damn. He had blundered. He was disappointed that Sophia was not with child, but so, no doubt, was she. Cal came round and stood before her, blocking the door. He studied her set face. 'Are you in discomfort? In pain? You are very pale.'

'I am sorry, I had not meant to trouble you with it. It is just the usual cramps and backache.'

'Usual?' Of course, that feminine mystery that was simply an inconvenience for the men in their lives must be most uncomfortable. He had never thought of it. 'You must remember I have no experience of these feminine matters—no sisters to grow up with,' he offered in mitigation. Sophia visibly bit back a comment and Callum could not help but smile. 'And, no, my mistresses would vanish discreetly for however long it took.' He took her arm and gently urged her into a comfortable chair. He wanted to help her, but this was an intimate secret and he had done nothing to make such confidences easy, he knew that. He kept hold of her hand. 'Tell me how it hurts.'

Blushing, she described the symptoms.

'So how do you treat it?'

She shrugged. 'Just put up with it. It will be better tomorrow.'

'Nonsense.' He hated the thought that she would uncomplainingly drag herself through the day if there was something to be done. 'Why should you put up with that? It sounds most unpleasant.' He began to shepherd her towards his bedchamber.

'Callum? You will be late to the office.'

'I can work from home. Wilkins!'

'Sir?' The valet emerged from the bedchamber, a hat in one hand, the brush in the other.

'Please send a message to Leadenhall Street to say I am detained at home for the day. Then have Cook send up a hot brick from the kitchen when I ring. And we are not to be disturbed—Mrs Chatterton needs to rest.'

'*Callum!* Whatever will he think?' They were in the

room now and the door was shut. He found he was anxious, as if she was ill or injured. He reminded himself that this was normal, that she was used to it. But it was strange having someone so intimately close to him to care about, to worry over. He had worried about Dan, but at least his twin had been a large, strong male.

His wife looked almost fragile today. He had tried to keep her at a distance, emotionally, it felt safer that way. But he couldn't do it if she was hurting. He'd had no idea that marriage would be so…consuming.

'I do not pay my valet to think,' he said briskly. 'Now then, let us get you comfortable.' He began to unlace her gown, then her corset, then peeled her chemise and petticoat down to her waist as she stood there, passive under his hands. He had never undressed her, he realised. He had wanted to, often. Wanted to catch her in his arms and kiss her, fondle her, undress her slowly and see if he could break through the polite yielding with which she tolerated his lovemaking. But you did not behave like that with a wife, as though she must be ready for you whenever you demanded it.

But if she wanted it too… Callum got a grip on his wandering thoughts and found Sophia's skin cool under his hands that lay on her shoulders. 'Off with your shoes and lie down on the bed. On your side with your back to me will be best, I imagine.'

He had stripped off his coat and was rolling up his shirtsleeves by the time she curled herself up on the bed. 'What are you doing?' she asked, her voice wary.

'In India one learns to doctor almost everything from snake bite to fever. I refuse to believe that this cannot be alleviated.' He sorted through bottles until he found the one he wanted. There was a clink of glass as he pulled out the stopper and the room filled with a warm, spicy smell that transported him straight back to the spice market in Calcutta.

Callum sat on the edge of the bed, his hip against the curve of her buttocks and poured oil into his right palm, letting it take the warmth from his skin. 'Just relax. Is this the spot?' He pressed his hand, warm and slippery with oil, gently into the small of her back, and let the other stroke lightly over the slight swell of her belly above the edge of her turned-down petticoats.

She sighed. 'Oh, yes. Oh, Callum, that is bliss.' He kept his hands gentle, kneading and stroking with just enough pressure to relax the knotted muscles. Sophia breathed deeply and closed her eyes. He knew how relaxing the smell was, he used this oil when he had a headache. He worked quietly, letting the scent fill her senses.

'You are purring,' he said, after perhaps five minutes.

'You could make a tiger purr,' she murmured, and he felt Sophia relax as she drifted into sleep.

When she woke Sophia found herself curled up on Callum's bed, a cover over her and something bulky and warm snuggled into the small of her back. Cautious investigation revealed a hot brick, well wrapped in towels. She turned over and found that her aches and pains had almost gone and that the bedchamber door was open, as was the study door opposite.

Callum was sitting at his desk, his head bent over some papers, one hand raking through his hair. He seemed completely engrossed, but as she watched him he looked up, straight into her eyes, as though she had called his name. He got up and crossed to the bedchamber, tugging the bell pull as he came in. 'Better?'

'Much better, thank you.' She pulled the covers around her like a shawl, sat up and swung her legs off the bed. 'You have magic in your hands.'

He shrugged, but he seemed pleased with the compliment, she thought. 'I have rung for Chivers. If you want to get up, I wondered if you would keep me company in the study.'

'Will I not distract you?' The idea was intriguing.

'No. You could read. Or draw if you like. Use my things.'

'I would like that, thank you. I saw the slope in your study.' She stumbled to a halt. He would know she had been in there looking around. Then she recovered herself. It was her house and she was in charge of it. Of course she would check all the rooms.

'I used to have one in India and I brought that one up from the Hall without thinking. My sketchbooks went down with the ship.' He turned away abruptly. 'Somehow I don't feel much like taking it up again.'

'Did you draw landscapes?'

'Some. And people.' He became very still, his attention apparently fixed on the bed post. 'I drew Dan. I wish now I had sent some home before we sailed, but I never did and now—' He shrugged. 'I do not expect I will start again.'

'You painted in watercolours, did you not?' Sophia asked. He looked puzzled. 'You told me when we were driving to London. Would you teach me, Callum? I have never been able to master it.'

'I don't know. Perhaps. I might not be good enough.'

'Then we can struggle with it together,' Sophia said.

Best perhaps not to push him, there were some painful memories involved. 'Here comes Chivers, I'll order luncheon to be sent up.'

She had thought Callum healed after Daniel's death. But it seemed the scars were still tender and the hurt lurked close to the surface. Then she recalled the look in his eyes when he had raised his head and seen her watching him. Perhaps, after all, she was helping him, just a little.

'I will just read, I think,' Sophia said. 'I don't want to bend over a drawing book at the moment.' The truth was, she was itching to pick up a pencil, but how could she, in his own study, after what Callum had just told her?

'You are not bored, I hope?' He laid aside his pen. 'I thought of having a dinner party next week. And now you are making calls we will start to receive any number of invitations.'

'No, I am not bored,' she promised him. If truth be told, despite her longing to make friends, the thought of plunging into London society was just a little daunting. So long as she could draw, then she would not be bored.

Callum was scrupulous in avoiding her bed. At first Sophia told herself that she was glad to have her bedchamber to herself and that it was delightful to be able to curl up in bed and read for as long as she wanted to, just as she had before she had married.

After four days these protestations were wearing somewhat thin. The truth was, she knew that she wanted the closeness that lovemaking brought even more than she wanted the frustrating pleasures that her husband's touch brought her. There was something more, she knew that, but somehow she could not reach it, nor could she bring herself to abandon all reserve and allow him to completely overwhelm her.

For that was what it would be, she suspected. If she once yielded utterly to Callum, then she would no longer be herself, the woman she had been. She would feel for him more than she wanted. Certainly more than a man who had married out of duty would want.

But she needed to hold Callum and to be held and she needed the nearness that she had experienced when he had soothed her pain and allowed her to sit quietly in his study while he worked.

In an effort to fill the void she drew with an almost feverish urgency, tearing off pages and throwing them on the fire in frustration at their inadequacy to express what she saw and felt.

The sketches she had drawn of the imaginary, adult Daniel almost followed the still lives, the portraits of the servants and views from the windows onto the fire, but something held her back from destroying them. At first she thought it was because they were rather better than she had thought when she was creating them, then she had to admit that she kept them because they were uncannily like Callum. With a sigh she tucked them under the cover of her portfolio. What she really wanted was to draw her husband, but he was hardly at home these days and when he came back in the evening it was always with a pile of papers and work to be done after dinner.

'Madam?'

She glanced up. There was Andrew with a salver. 'The second post, madam.'

And there they were, the first of the expected invitations. Sophia spread them all out and looked at the dates. None of them were on the same night, all of them could be, and doubtless Callum would say, must be, accepted. A musicale, a soirée, a reception and a dinner party. She reviewed her wardrobe and decided that she was adequately gowned for all these. There was nothing for it but to put on her best behaviour and do Callum credit.

Andrew moved around the room, quietly, efficiently repairing the small untidinesses she had created, then whisked out. The house ran like clockwork. Callum's house, Callum's servants who hardly needed to refer to her, although, of course, they did. Callum's contacts and friends and superiors who she must cultivate for the sake of Callum's career.

Stop it! she thought. He had rescued her from spinsterhood and paid drudgery and given her a life of ease and security. He had saved Mama from genteel poverty and, as soon as Mark was ordained, he would make sure that Will found her brother a good parish, even if Mark had bored and patronised him on their wedding eve.

But, ungrateful as it was, she missed her old life. In Hertfordshire she had managed the house, the budget. She had contrived and schemed and kept them going, somehow. She could see who she wanted of her friends and she could draw whenever the mood took her. She had been free and her mind had been exercised to its utmost.

There was a snap and Sophia looked down to see the pencil held tight in her fingers was broken. But she still had this, still had her art. She opened the portfolio again. It was good, wasn't it? Or was she deluding herself? Was she simply a moderately talented young lady? If her art sold, then she would know she had talent, know there was something that remained of the old Sophia. Dare she put it to the test?

'I am working at home this morning,' Callum said as Sophia poured him a second cup of coffee at breakfast, six days after she had told him that she was not yet with child. 'I thought perhaps you would like to go for a walk in Green Park this afternoon. Unless you have more shopping to do.'

'Oh, yes, thank you. I would like that very much.' Sophia heard the excitement in her own voice and wondered at herself. Her husband—the husband to whom she had been married for two weeks and two days, she reminded herself—had suggested a walk and she was so pathetically grateful for the simple treat that she sounded as though he had offered her a box at the opera for a year or a carriage and pair for her own use.

'It would be pleasant to stretch my legs,' she added in a more moderate tone. 'I had thought to go to Hatchard's, and I have some trifling shopping, but I can do that this morning, it is nothing of importance. I must buy more silk stockings, I laddered a pair at Mrs Sommerson's musicale last night.'

'Very well. I will see you at luncheon at one o'clock.' Callum folded his newspaper, picked up his coffee cup and went out, leaving her to finish a mental shopping list. It proved remarkably difficult. *Tooth powder, a nice big bath sponge... I should tell him that he can come back to my bed. Stockings. Better get silk ones and some cotton ones. Shall I go and tell him now? But it will make it sound as though I am lusting after him. But I miss him... Don't think about it. Tooth powder...*

Chapter Fourteen

Sophia was still brooding on the best way to convey that she was ready to welcome Callum back to her bed as they walked the short distance down Half Moon Street to cross Piccadilly and enter Green Park. Callum certainly appeared to be in an amiable enough mood. He had complimented her on the luncheon, admired the moss-green walking dress with darker green pelisse and matching bonnet with grosgrain ribbons.

Now there was nothing for it but to meet his eyes when he guided her across the road and turned back from flipping a coin to the crossing sweeper. 'I—'

'I think perhaps we should discuss the…disagreement we had on the subject of mistresses,' Callum said. Sophia was so taken aback that she stumbled on the kerb and he had to catch her hand to steady her. 'I rather lost sight of my sense of humour,' Callum continued. He kept hold of her hand, which was rather pleasant. 'Or perhaps I should say that you touched my conscience on a sore spot. You have not mentioned it again, but I sense it is not forgotten.'

'Forgotten? No, I have not forgotten. I was…tactless and naïve. Why should you have a guilty conscience about having a mistress in India when you had no obligations elsewhere?' Sophia freed her hand, slid it into the crook of his arm and let him guide her down the diagonal pathway.

'I did not say it was logical.'

'I thought you were—logical, I mean. The organised brother, the sensible one.'

'Sensible?' Callum snorted, but he did not explain his amusement and his expression, when she glanced up at his profile, was rueful. 'Yes, I suppose I am. Most of the time.'

'And Daniel was not?'

For a moment she wondered if she was wrong to ask him to talk of his twin, then he shrugged. 'Daniel was not… Daniel was impulsive. He let himself feel and then acted on those feelings without, sometimes, thinking it through.'

'Such as the time he proposed to me?'

'Perhaps. He was spontaneous and open and generous.'

'You are generous,' she offered.

'But not spontaneous and open.'

'That does not mean you do not feel, that you do not care. That you do not have as much emotion inside, even if you do not show it on the outside.'

'Would you wish me to be more open about my feelings, Sophia?'

She looked up from under the brim of her bonnet and caught a glimpse of heat that made her heart skip a beat. Did he mean physically? 'Yes,' she said. 'Yes, I would.' He said nothing, simply tucked her hand more firmly into the crook of his arm. 'I like it here,' Sophia remarked a few minutes later when it seemed that the subjects of mistresses and feelings were to be put behind them without further discussion. In the distance she could see the towers of Westminster Abbey floating like a mirage above the trees. *I really am in London,* she thought. *This is my new life.*

'London?'

'Green Park. I do not feel ready to face the fashionable throng in Hyde Park, even if it were proper that I should.'

'Because you are shy?'

'I am afraid so!' She laughed at her own nervousness. It was absurd that she, who only weeks before had been resolved upon making her own way in the world by finding employment, should become anxious when she had a gentleman to protect her. Or perhaps that was the problem: Callum would tell her what to do, provide for her, and she would become a grateful, obedient puppet.

There was that uncomfortable thought about independence again. Well-bred ladies observed certain constraints on their behaviour, of course, but she had as good an education as a girl could hope for, she had ideas in her head, some talents to her name. She wanted to spread her wings, to be herself.

'You have no need to be shy,' Callum said when she did not expand on her admission. 'You are personable, you have all the social arts. You were a great success at the party last night. You enjoyed it, did you not?'

'Thank you. Yes, I did find it entertaining.' And

she had. How foolish to have accepted a marriage of convenience and then wish for more.

Callum pointed out some of the fine buildings overlooking the park and they stopped to admire the elegance of Spencer House. 'Rather more splendid than our little dwelling,' he said. 'A house in Half Moon Street is hardly up to what you might expect after Flamborough Hall.'

'But it is a very fashionable street and well located. What on earth would I do rattling around all day in something the size of the Hall?' she asked. 'I never expected a large town house.'

'When I am able to sort out my affairs, and can see how I am placed now I am settled in England with this new post, then we will find something larger. Half Moon Street is too small for a family, in any case.'

Startled, Sophia looked up at him and realised her free hand had gone to her belly in an instinctive gesture. 'Well, that will not be for nine months at the very least,' she said. 'If you want… I mean, it is convenient again…' Her voice trailed off.

Was he thinking about lovemaking too, or her failure to conceive yet? His arm tensed, pressing her hand tighter to his side and he shot her a dark, smouldering glance that made her toes curl in her kid half-boots and sent a shaft of heat into the pit of her stomach. Goodness, that answered that question! When he looked like that he disturbed her too much for her own peace of mind. She still hoped that when they made love she could overcome whatever it was that seemed to stop her giving way to the feelings she knew hovered just out of reach. But she had told him to be more open, she had invited this.

'Shall we walk on?' Callum changed direction, back into the centre of the park, and Sophia struggled to find a safe topic of conversation. *Do you mean to take me home and make love to me in daylight?* was probably an inadmissible question.

'Would it be considered fast if I were to come here to sketch?' she asked as they approached a small stand of trees ringed by shrubs. 'I would bring Chivers, of course. Or should it be a footman?'

'A footman might be wise, just in case some park saunterer takes a fancy to annoy you,' Callum said. 'That looks a pleasant spot.' He strolled towards a bench that stood in a green glade almost surrounded by bushes. Sophia's pulse gave a little kick of anticipation, but all he said as they seated themselves was, 'Tell me more about your art. You said it was the most important thing to you after your family.'

'Mainly I draw in pencil or in chalks and pastels. I draw anything and everything,' she added. 'Portraits, landscapes, still life… But I am only an amateur.' Even as she said that she felt uncomfortable to be belittling such an important part of her life, her creative expression. She knew many gentlemen would consider it unsuitable for their wives to have an almost professional interest in what should be a lady's genteel diversion. If Callum knew she was contemplating selling her drawings he could not approve, she was certain. A dutiful wife would not even contemplate it.

'I suspect it will be better than that.' Callum shifted on the bench and laid his arm along the back of it behind her shoulders. 'I can recall when Daniel was courting you that you were always smudged with charcoal or leaving white fingerprints from chalk. And there were attempts at portraiture that Daniel bore very patiently.'

'They were very bad,' Sophia admitted, recalling the best of them, the miniature that she kept with his letters. Those had stayed behind in her old room in Hertfordshire.

'But I cannot believe you have not improved with practice,' Callum said.

'I hope so, or I am seriously deluded!'

'This is a good spot. We will come here one day and I will try again with watercolours and you can sketch—or perhaps learn from my daubs.'

'I would like that. Thank you.' It felt as though a barrier had been breached between them.

Callum set his high-crowned hat on the seat beside him and leaned closer, his attention fixed on her right cheekbone.

'What is it? Do I have an insect on my face?'

'No. Speaking of art has made me study the nearest lovely thing more closely.' She shook her head at the arrant flattery, but he continued to look at her face. 'Only the faintest little heart-shaped freckle. Just…there below your lashes.' His fingertip touched her skin, then trailed a quivering trace of sensation along the top of her cheek. 'Are there any others? I haven't noticed any, but by candlelight they may not be so easy to find as in the daylight.'

'I don't know. I used to have freckles, but Mama made me use Denmark lotion and I thought they had all gone.' Her voice was shaking and she tried to steady it, but to do that she must control her breathing and that was all over the place and he was leaning closer now. It was the first time he had ever caressed her during the day and they were in the open, in public.

'A pity. Poor little orphaned freckle.' Callum's lips pressed against the place where his finger had touched. His hair, almost as dark as hers, tickled her face and she put up a hand to steady herself against his chest.

'It might not be the only one. You could look,' Sophia suggested, greatly daring.

'I could. What a provoking suggestion, my dear.' His voice was growing husky and he moved, just enough to bring his mouth to hers, so close his breath brushed her lips and made her laugh. 'I have missed you.'

'That tickles!' He laughed too and her wariness was gone, replaced by a new, strange sensation that was making her tense, but in the most delightful manner. Was this desire? 'I missed you too,' Sophia ventured. If only she had the courage to reach out to him, not to make love, but for closeness and companionship. But if she did, and he found that intrusively familiar, it would hurt too much. She must wait for him, it seemed. Married couples were not supposed to be demonstrative, Mama had warned her about that. *Coward*, she told herself.

Behind Callum's head she saw movement and pulled back. 'Someone is coming.'

'Damn. I had hoped to kiss my wife in sylvan solitude for a while.' He sat back a little, just enough for propriety, but he did not turn and his expression held wicked promises for when they could be alone. 'Who is it? A picnic party or a governess with a swarm of infants?'

'Neither, just another couple, strolling. I expect they will pass us soon enough.' They looked a very happy pair, about the same age as Callum and her. They walked arm in arm, his head bent close, she looking up into his face and smiling. 'No, they are stopping, she is adjusting the ribbons on her villager hat. I do like that style.'

'Then you must buy one.'

Sophia dimpled a smile at him. 'I had one and you knocked it off in the lane.' She went back to studying the other couple. The breeze was getting up and the woman was having trouble setting the wide, flat hat with its low crown back on her head. Her companion reached to help her. 'Oh, no! She has accidentally stabbed him with a hat pin—she's dropped it—now the breeze has caught the hat—he is giving chase.'

With one hand holding his own hat in place the man set off at a run after the disc of straw plait as it tumbled over the cropped grass. The woman watched for a moment, smiling, and then walked on. She was aiming, it seemed to Sophia, for a bench just past the one she and Callum occupied. 'Oh, now he has lost his own hat.'

The hatless lady laughed, a clear, bright peal of laughter and Callum froze. *'Averil?'* He turned on the seat and stared. 'Averil!' Then he was up and running to her. He caught her in his arms and she flung her own around his neck, clinging as he bent his head and kissed her.

Sophia stumbled to her feet and stared. There was passion in the way the two figures held each other. This was no peck on the cheek between close friends, this was something more, a lot more. A sickening jolt went through her and she almost moaned aloud with the pain of it. Jealousy, anger, loss all jumbled together.

He had forgotten her, had not even troubled to pretend to her—*his wife*—that he did not know this woman.

She stood rooted to the spot in a paralysis of unhappiness, her hands fisted at her side. To stay? To leave? But her feet would not move. There was a shout and something—someone—hurtled past her. The other man, she realised, as he fell on the entwined couple and took Callum by the shoulder.

He was going to hit him. *Good,* she thought, furious and shaken that he could kiss another woman like that, minutes after those intimate caresses. The other man was taller, broader and utterly menacing. *Excellent.*

'Chatterton!'

'D'Aunay!' No, they were not about to fight, they were embracing and the lady Callum had kissed was beaming with pleasure. 'When did you get back to town?'

'Just yesterday.' The other man was striking. Not good-looking, not with that aggressive beak of a nose and stubborn chin, but he had a commanding presence. 'Our honeymoon was interrupted by the demands of their Lordships at the Admiralty a couple of times, but it served its purpose: Bradon has recovered from his fit of chagrin over losing his betrothed to a half-French adventurer—his words—and we can mingle in society without risk of gossip distressing Averil.'

'I am sorry, we burst in on your private conversation. I am the Countess d'Aunay. Miss—?' Sophia turned to find the woman at her side.

'Mrs Chatterton,' she said icily. 'You were kissing my husband.'

'Your husband? You are married to Callum? But he was not betrothed, Daniel was.'

'Daniel is dead,' Sophia said, staring at the stranger. This was a madhouse. 'I am Sophia Langley.'

'*You* are Daniel's betrothed?' Averil Heydon stared at Sophia, her face stiff with what must be disapproval.

'Yes.' Sophia felt her chin lift; she was not going to be criticised, not by a stranger.

'Oh, I am so sorry for your loss. But you and Callum have each other now—Daniel would have been glad.' No, it was not condemnation on the countess's face, but the effort to hold back tears.

'I hope so.' Sophia felt a lump forming in her throat and swallowed hard, embarrassed by their shared emotion. There was a pause, then both women looked towards their men.

'Sophia,' Callum said, 'this is Averil Heydon who was on the *Bengal Queen*. She was swept ashore and rescued by Captain d'Aunay and now they are married.'

'Captain?' She turned to the other woman. 'Forgive me, I thought you said you were a countess?' And who was this Bradon?

'Luc is a French *comte*, an *émigré* and in the Royal Navy,' Averil explained. She tucked her hand confidingly into Sophia's elbow. 'I was coming back from India to marry a man I had never met. He was not best pleased to discover I had thoroughly compromised myself and, what's more, was delighted to marry Luc rather than him. It was all hushed up, but we thought it better to stay out of town while he got over it.'

'Chatterton was my best man at a very small wedding,' d'Aunay said with a grin.

'How lovely,' Sophia said with a smile, but something twisted painfully inside. Averil d'Aunay had known Callum's twin, she could speak of Daniel with real knowledge and true grief as a friend. She should be glad for it, but she felt shut out and knowing that was wrong did not help. Sophia turned away from the look on Callum's face; he seemed happier and more relaxed than she had seen him since he had returned home. 'You must come to tea. We do not live far away—Half Moon Street.'

'But we have just moved there too! We must be neighbours,' Lady d'Aunay said. 'What fun.'

Sophia told herself not to be foolish. Averil d'Aunay appeared to be a delightful, warm person. Someone who she would welcome as a friend. 'Let us go back then,' she said, turning to the path. 'We will go ahead and Mrs Datchett will have tea ready by the time the men catch us up.'

'You have not been married long then?' d'Aunay asked as he and Callum emerged from the glade. Sophia and Averil were already well ahead, making their way at a brisk walk uphill towards the distant gate.

'Two weeks, just over,' Callum said after a moment's frantic mental arithmetic. It was not the thing to forget how long one had been wed—not this early in the marriage. But was it really more than fourteen days? Not sleeping with one's wife did not help. She had said it was *convenient* for him to visit her bedchamber again; it was encouraging that he had not had to ask.

'It was very quiet, and in the country,' he said. 'Although not as quiet as yours. We did not care to make a great to-do about it, given that Sophia had been betrothed to Daniel.'

Sophia had seemed not at all averse to being kissed in the park, although she had not liked him embracing a strange woman! Had she thought he had been lying about mistresses? Or was her frown simply jealousy? The thought that Sophia might be jealous was rather pleasing.

'It seems a very good solution for the two of you to wed,' d'Aunay said. 'I am sure your brother would have approved. You will have a helpmeet for your career and she is looked after.'

'Yes, indeed,' Callum said and changed the subject to d'Aunay's latest commission. For some reason his friend's easy acceptance that this was a cold-blooded marriage of convenience jarred. *But that is what it is,* he thought, frowning at the two young women who walked ahead, their skirts fluttering in the breeze. They seemed deep in animated conversation, their hands moving expressively. Sophia had found a friend, it seemed.

Chapter Fifteen

Sophia found she was riveted by Averil d'Aunay's story. Beside its own intrinsic drama, at last she was hearing more about the wreck. She could never expect Callum to speak of it.

'The day after the shipwreck I was washed up on St Helen's, one of the uninhabited islands in the Scillies. Luc was based there on a secret mission. He found me on the beach. We became…close,' Averil explained. From the way her cheeks coloured, *close* was a euphemism.

'But you were still going ahead with the arranged marriage?' Sophia asked, confused.

Averil nodded. 'I had given my word. Papa had agreed all the financial details. But I had to do my duty. And then I found out something truly horrible about Lord Bradon's character. He thought I had lost my virginity to Luc—which I had not,' she added. 'But he was prepared to marry me anyway and if I was pregnant with Luc's child he would have got rid of the baby, as though it was an unwanted kitten. I ran away to Luc.'

Averil hesitated then said, 'I hope you do not disapprove too much of the fact that Luc and I lived together for a time before we married.'

'Why, no! From what you say it was the only possible thing to do. How dreadful that Lord Bradon should behave in such a disgusting manner, especially after your awful ordeal during the shipwreck.'

'Thank you.' Averil took her hand and squeezed it. 'It is so good to have another woman to confide in—there is only one other I dare tell the truth to.'

'Of course.' Sophia returned the pressure of her new friend's hand. A friend. A London friend. How wonderful.

'Look, There is our house with the dark blue door,' Sophia said.

Averil followed her up the steps. 'Our house is the next but two. Such a coincidence that we should be neighbours. I do like these little houses, even though I know Luc always kept his mistresses here. Still, he will not be having another one after me—I would rather be the last than the first,' she said. Her amusement put the last nagging thoughts about Callum's past into proportion and Sophia found they were both laughing as Hawksley opened the door.

Rather be the last than the first. Averil's words kept echoing around Sophia's head long after she and Luc had left. *I was jealous of her when I saw her in Callum's arms,* she thought. *Jealous? I could have scratched her eyes out!*

She looked across at her husband and forced herself to think what that emotion meant. Had it simply been hurt pride and surprise? He looked up from the journal he was scanning and smiled, a slow curving of his lips, but the warmth was there in his eyes before he went back to his reading.

I love him. Oh, Callum. How had that happened? She had thought she was beginning to be fond of him, she knew she admired him, she almost feared that she desired him. But this, this was a disaster, was it not, to love a man who did not love her?

'A penny for your thoughts, Mrs Chatterton.' The journal was folded on the chaise beside him now and he had shifted position. How long had she sat there trying to absorb this revelation?

'I was just thinking about what to wear tomorrow,' Sophia improvised. 'It is Lady Archbold's musicale.'

'What should you wear? The pale blue silk,' he said promptly, surprising her that he had any idea of what was in her wardrobe. She had not worn that gown yet.

'How do you know I have a pale blue gown?'

'I must have seen Chivers taking it downstairs to press it, I suppose. Do you need to rush out and buy anything to go with it?'

Not only seen it, but taken notice and considered how she would look in it. She had thought all he was interested in was her more flimsy nightgowns and the fact that she did not spoil her looks by wearing black.

'Indeed not, that would be extravagant. I have just the thing—a dark blue reticule and matching slippers.'

'We should discuss our dinner party,' Callum said. 'If that goes well, then we can plan a larger party. This house may not be large enough for a musicale or a soirée, but I think we can seat a dozen. Of course, we ought to think about a reception: we can use the Flamborough town house for that. We'll fix a date.

'Which reminds me—where are our wedding gifts? I felt certain we now owned about six fish slices and a quantity of soup tureens, but last night's soup was in the china one I bought when I moved here.'

'They are downstairs. I wrote and thanked everyone,' Sophia said. 'William's secretary kindly made me a list.' She stared around the room, half-expecting that crystal and silver and porcelain would appear. 'I am sorry, I haven't had them unpacked yet. It was all such a rush, and then we did not actually need any of it and there was so much else to think about.' Her voice trailed away. There was really no excuse. She had very little to do that would justify forgetting vital household tasks. Hours spent sketching were no excuse.

'You must be the only lady of my acquaintance who would not fall upon boxes full of gifts at the earliest opportunity.'

'I know.' It must seem bizarre to him, that she could write thank-you notes and not want to enjoy the objects themselves. 'It just did not seem real somehow,' she admitted truthfully.

'What didn't?' Callum's brows drew together.

'Being married. After all this time. To you,' she added, then bit her lip before she made it any worse.

For a moment she thought Callum would be angry with her—it had been the most tactless thing to say. But instead he snorted with laughter. 'And it will take the appearance of a set of fish knives and some fancy dinner plates to convince you that you *have* married me?'

'No.' She found herself laughing too. 'No, *you* convinced me of that.' *I am married and in love with my husband.*

'Interesting. And do you feel married now?' If he found that amusing he was keeping a perfectly straight face, but she was coming to learn that she could not always read Callum's moods by his expressions.

'Very married, thank you,' Sophia said primly, pretending not to notice the very wicked twinkle in his eyes. 'How could I fail to after dealing with a crisis in the kitchen over my husband's dislike of every variety of tea that is put in front of him, the housemaids complaining that he never uses the waste bin in his study and the laundry maid in tears because most of his handkerchiefs were put in with a red kerchief and are now pink.'

'What a very unsatisfactory husband I must be. Send to Twining's in the Strand for teas; I will write you a list. As for the others, I cannot help the handkerchiefs and I will try to remember not to screw up papers and lob them inaccurately at the fireplace.' He studied her face and she began to wonder if her emotions were plain on her face. 'Are those truly the highlights of married life to date?'

'No. those are just the low points.' It was very pleasant teasing him, seeing him smile. Now, if only she could manage not to blush… 'Other things have convinced me more pleasurably that I am a married woman.'

'Indeed?' Callum leaned back on the chaise and she contrived to tear her mind from how elegantly his long body lounged there and concentrate on what felt perilously like a flirtation.

'Certainly.' She began to count things off on her fingers. 'My generous dress allowance, my pin money, living in London—they are all delightful.' Perhaps he would come over and do some of the other, much more intimate things, teach her to enjoy them with him.

'And you do not pine for what might have been?' he asked, cutting through the relaxed atmosphere as effectively as if he had slammed a door.

'No! You know I did not love Daniel. How awful it would have been to have married him and have had to pretend.'

'Whereas with me you do not have to pretend.' Callum said it so smoothly that Sophia had no idea whether it was a barbed comment or not. *But I have to pretend the opposite,* she thought, her thoughts and emotions tangling.

'But…' Sophia closed her eyes, trying to cut out the sight of the darkness in his as she struggled to find the right words. Callum would see his dead brother every time he looked in a mirror. It must be so hard for him to forget, to heal. 'You do not look like the Daniel I remember—or the Callum either, come to that.' She looked at him, struggling for the right words. 'You have changed since you went away, grown into a man, as I'm sure he also did. But I would have had to learn what he was like, all over again, just as I have had to learn with you.'

Callum did not reply immediately, but it seemed to her that some of the darkness lifted, as though she had said something he wanted to hear. The clock on the mantel struck the half-hour and he got to his feet. 'I must go and change for dinner. Now we know they are back in town, we could invite our new neighbours to dine, don't you think?'

'Oh, yes.' She rose too. 'I will come up with you.' Callum opened the door, then offered her his arm as they climbed the stairs. Sophia felt a surge of happiness. Callum might not love her, but he seemed much more in sympathy with her now. And she had made a new friend. And she rather hoped her husband would come to her room tonight.

Callum did come, so soon after she had retired that Chivers had scarcely time to gather up her discarded clothes and take herself off. The moment he came in Sophia dropped the book she was glancing through.

'Would my company tonight be welcome?' he asked. 'I gathered from what you said in the park that it might be.'

'Certainly,' she said, watching him through her lashes, her heart pounding with anticipation. As was his habit he snuffed the candles on the tallboy and the dressing table, but when he approached those on the far side of the bed she said, 'No, please leave them.'

'On both sides?' Callum hesitated, his hand still out-stretched to the first wick, but when she nodded he said, 'I thought it would be easier for you.'

'Easier?' He must think her embarrassed to see his body, to have him look at hers. She bit her lip; she had not realised he had sought darkness out of consideration for her modesty. 'No. I like to see… I mean, it is very impersonal in the darkness. You sound like you in the dark, of course, and you smell like you—' his eyebrows shot up '—in a good way! But I prefer to be able to see you as well.'

That seemed to please him. He was certainly aroused, she thought with a tiny wriggle of nervous anticipation, but still he stood there. Not so much hesitating, she thought, but thinking something through.

'Please, Callum.'

He did smile at her then. *He is a different man when he smiles,* Sophia decided. *No more or less attractive, but younger somehow, more open.* 'Light them all again,' she said, greatly daring, and he did as she asked until the room was glowing and the warmth reflected off his tanned skin as he took off coat and waistcoat and shirt. And this time he let them fall to the floor, unheeded, his eyes on her.

'Your skin has held the sun,' she said, finding her voice catch. 'I am surprised, after so many months away from India.'

'I was very tanned when we left. We always swam, year round, where it was safe,' Callum said. He sat on the edge of the bed, still in evening breeches and stockings and Sophia studied his muscles sidelong through her lashes. 'And bachelors are careless about lounging around in the heat in shockingly little clothing in their own compounds. Even in the shade the sun is so intense in India that one colours easily.

'Then on the ship it was hot for much of the voyage and the men were casual in their dress during the day. You see?' He lifted her hand and traced with her fingertips the darker vee of skin where his shirt must have lain open.

'And here.' There was another line just below his elbows. The hair on his forearm felt rough and she turned his hand so she could trace the smooth, paler skin on the inside of his arm. He gave a little shiver, so she tickled the inside of his elbow and made him laugh.

'Be careful—I might retaliate.' She stopped and he smiled. 'Keep touching me, I like it.'

Greatly daring, Sophia transferred her explorations

to his chest. The miracle that Callum was relaxing with her, opening himself to her just as she realised she had fallen in love with him, was still too fresh; she felt too insecure to trust it would last.

She flattened her palm against his flat belly and ran it upwards, fingers spread so they raked through the dusting of dark hair to his nipples. They crinkled and tightened as she scratched lightly with her nails, delighted by his sharply indrawn breath.

'We both have altogether too many clothes on,' Callum said and stood up, reluctant, it seemed to her, to leave her caressing hands. He unfastened his breeches, pushed them down, taking stockings and garters with them.

'You swam naked,' she said as he twisted to toss them onto a chair and she could look at the tight curve of his buttocks, the length of hard-muscled thighs.

'Of course,' he said and turned back to her.

Sophia swallowed. Now they were more relaxed together she was looking at him properly for the first time and the reality of aroused manhood so close she could reach out and touch was more disturbing than it had been on their wedding night, somehow. She lifted one hand and hesitated.

'Touch me,' Callum said, so she did, stroking down the surprisingly soft skin over the pulsing hardness. When she dared look up into his face his eyes were closed and his jaw taut. A pulse leapt in his cheek as though he was holding himself still with enormous effort and, before she could think about it, tell herself it was wanton and lewd, Sophia leaned forwards and kissed him, her lips lingering. It was shocking, she wanted to take him in her mouth, to lick to—

'Oh, my God.' He moved too fast for her to protest. One moment she had been bent over him, her hand hesitating just at his hip, wanting to hold him still, and the next she was on her back, her nightgown bunched around her waist as Callum plunged into her.

'Sophia, I—' With what seemed a superhuman effort he stilled, dropped his head until his forehead rested on hers, his breath warm on her face. 'I'm sorry. Did I hurt you?'

'No. Don't stop. Please don't stop, Callum.' She tipped her head back so that his mouth came down on hers and held him hard and close as he moved within her and the tension that had been inside her since that first night built to a swirling knot and then broke apart into shuddering delight and she lost all sense of where she was, only that she was with Callum and she loved him.

The fog was swallowing her up. Dark, grey like cold smoke. He had needed her, reached for her and now he was being punished for it. 'Come back!' *She turned, held out her hands to him, but the fog seemed to pull her, the long tendrils like tentacles around her waist, her throat, dragging her into its depths. And he was in water, his limbs leaden, his shoulders burning with the effort to stay afloat, his vision blurred and he could not reach her.* 'Sophia!' *She was gone.*

Cal whistled as he rode up Cornhill to Leadenhall Street. After the first few days in London he had grown tired of rattling to and from the office in a musty hackney carriage and had sought out a livery stables in a nearby mews that provided him with the daily use of a neat bay gelding. With a change of formal clothing kept in his office it meant he could ride when the weather held fair.

Today riding suited his mood perfectly. Sophia had made love last night with a warmth and a responsiveness that had, for a while, chased away the shadows that had been haunting him. But he had dreamed last night, even so, woken in a muck sweat, the bedclothes tangled round his legs, his throat sore as though he had been shouting. Another nightmare, although he could not recall the details, the old one about the wreck and Dan merging into a new one about losing Sophia.

But that was worth it, even if it was the price of their lovemaking. Sophia's gaze had been clear and open as she had lain in his arms and looked at him. She said his name as it was dragged from her at the height of her pleasure. In the days since their marriage he had done everything in what he knew was a considerable repertoire of technique to make her feel comfortable with him, to relax enough to allow him to pleasure her and, after all, it had simply taken light and openness and giving in to his own rush of desire for her to respond with innocent passion.

There was still something, a reserve that he could not identify, but perhaps he was expecting too much, too soon. All he could ask was that she was happy and content married to him.

For himself, he was very well pleased with his wife, he thought as he reached the East India Company offices and swung down to the pavement. The house ran to perfection, Sophia was a pleasant and intelligent companion and the nights were going to be satisfying. He had not looked for any of that in this marriage of duty, but then it seemed to him that he had hardly been thinking clearly at all.

He had thought he was. He had believed himself healed after Dan's death, ready and able to move on with his life. One thing had nagged at his conscience—Sophia—and doing the right thing for her chimed exactly with his growing awareness that he needed a wife for his career and to give him his heirs.

It had seemed very simple then. Now he was actually married he was discovering nuances of emotion and feeling he had not considered for a moment. Sophia made him think of Dan and he realised that once the first raw grief had subsided he had avoided doing that. It was painful, but it was also strangely soothing. People avoided speaking of his twin, but Sophia did not, although he could tell she was still distressed over her realisation that she had not loved him.

It was more difficult than he had imagined it would be to have someone living so close, so intimately. When he stayed at Flamborough Hall the place was so big that he and Will virtually had to make an appointment to meet. In their succession of bungalows in India life with Dan had been so normal, so relaxed, he had hardly thought of it. They had each gone their own way, known how the other was feeling.

But in the little Mayfair house he was forced into domestic intimacy with his wife at every turn. And that was both pleasant and, when he suspected that he had upset her, uncomfortable. He had not wanted to become close to her and yet he was, day by day, finding her entangled more and more in his life. And on the whole that was oddly pleasant. But the danger was always there. It was one thing to enjoy the company of his wife, another to give over his heart to be broken. It was all right, he told himself, he had his feelings under control.

A porter sent out a messenger boy to hold his horse while he unbuckled the saddlebags with the day's papers and then led it away, a big smile on his face at the size of the tip Callum had tossed him. Yes, he was feeling good today, better than at any time since that moment when the *Bengal Queen* had struck the rocks and his world had shattered.

'Morning, Pettigrew,' he said as he walked into the office he shared.

'Morning.' The Honourable George Pettigrew glanced up from his desk as Callum strolled into their shared office and tossed the saddlebags on to a chair. 'You sound on good form, Chatterton.'

Callum grinned. He felt it. Staggeringly good sex, Averil and Luc d'Aunay back in town and the house in Half Moon Street beginning to feel like home.

'I've got the latest China trade figures for that report you're doing for Arbuthnott. I need to go down to the counting house, but I'll hang on until you've checked them through in case there are any queries.' He unbuckled one of the bags, passed over a fat budget of papers and watched the other man skim through the summary and conclusions. He was impressed by Pettigrew. The man was intelligent, steady, but not stodgy, and worked hard. He'd invite him for dinner, he thought. Sophia would like him.

'Thanks, this is just what I need.' The other man tapped the papers back into a tidy pile and pulled some folded sheets from his portfolio. 'Don't want to buy a ship, do you?'

'A what?' Arrested, Callum stopped checking through the morning's post and stared at the other man.

'Big thing with sails, takes cargo back and forth. Makes money.'

'Oh, that kind. Sinks occasionally.' His stomach knotted even as he made the wry joke.

'That's what insurance is for. I've got a chance at a quarter-share in an East Indiaman, but that's far too rich for me. Wondered if you'd like to come in with me and split it? I've got the details here.'

Callum pushed aside the post and reached out a hand for the report. 'I'm interested. Tell me more.'

Chapter Sixteen

H<small>e</small> was not a bachelor any longer, Callum reminded himself that evening as he watched Averil and Sophia sitting with their heads together in companionable discussion. He had a wife now. And yet now he woke at night in a cold sweat, dreaming that something had happened to her, that he had grown to love her, that she would break his heart. It was almost as bad as the old nightmare, the one about the wreck.

'No doubt discussing their unsatisfactory husbands,' d'Aunay said with a chuckle as he poured more wine into Callum's glass.

'No doubt,' he agreed. 'I have been found wanting only this evening—arriving just in time to change when we had been invited here for supper is obviously unacceptable behaviour.' Instinct told him to keep Sophia at a distance, not to let her into every aspect of his life. And when she objected he felt guilty and then he wanted to resent her and somehow he could not.

The other man grinned. 'You have responsibilities. Sophia will learn that and learn to forgive you for them.'

'I suppose so; at least I did not have a vase thrown at my head.'

'In my experience that is mistress behaviour,' d'Aunay said with a chuckle. 'I think wives are too aware of the value of their household objects and are more likely to punish us in more subtle ways.'

'True.' But this had not been a tantrum. Sophia was hurt that he had not remembered to let her know. He did not want to hurt her. His resolution not to care was melting away.

Callum watched one ringlet slide free of its pins and fall to Sophia's shoulder. The skin was very soft there, silken under his lips, and her hair smelled of rosemary and lemon and… There were sure to be many enjoyable ways to make up a domestic tiff. Too many ways to become closer and closer to the stranger he had married, too many ways to lay his heart open to the knife again.

He turned to the man beside him. 'When do you go back to sea? Or is that confidential information?'

'Not in general terms. It will be a month, perhaps. I must go down to the dockyards at Chatham in a few days to inspect my new command. They are refitting and I have learned not to trust the quality of work to chance—not after the time we unfolded the spare sails at the bottom of the sail hold and found a damn great cannon hole through one.'

'I wonder if you would be willing to look at a ship on my behalf,' Callum said, thinking aloud. 'I've been offered a share in an Indiaman. The reports look good, but I'd appreciate a professional eye on it. She's in the East India docks now.'

'Yes, of course. That's an interesting investment.' D'Aunay sat back and crossed his long legs, very much at ease, except that the assessing look in his eyes was not lost on Callum. 'Any more shares going?'

'There might be,' Callum said. 'Are you free on Monday? We could go and look at it with Pettigrew—he's the colleague who put me on to it.'

'Are you working at home today?' Sophia asked on Monday morning. Callum had spent much of Sunday closeted in his study, emerging only for meals and to escort her to the Chapel Royal at St James's Palace for morning service. Now he lingered far longer over his coffee and newspaper than he usually did.

'Hmm? No, I'm going down to the docks with d'Aunay and a colleague from Leadenhall Street in about half an hour to look at a ship. I'll be out of your way.' He went back to his newspaper.

'I was going to go to Ackermann's in the Strand to buy more drawing materials,' Sophia said. She did not want him *out of her way.* Last night had been very harmonious. She smiled a little at her choice of word.

'Yes? You must show me your drawings.'

'Oh, no. Not yet. Not until I practise some more,' she prevaricated. The more she had drawn since her marriage the more she felt there was an improvement. She had looked at them only the day before and thought they were of a publishable standard. But she could be deluding herself. The only way to find out was to submit her work to a professional for his judgement and the easiest way she could think of to do that was to show her best sketches to Mr Ackermann and ask his opinion.

'Do ladies ever sell their art?' she asked on a sudden

impulse to test his reactions. 'There must be many very talented artists—so many girls are taught young. It would be encouraging to see the work of other women.'

'Ladies sell their art? Of course not! At least, they may do, but it is certainly done anonymously. It would cause more scandal if it were known than that wretched Lamb female's capering about on the stage. Nude models and orgies and loose living—you can just hear the old tabbies yapping about it. It doesn't matter how much of a nonsense that is, that is the way such things are looked at. I'll take you to the Royal Academy, but you will not see any ladies exhibiting there.'

'I see.' Anonymously. It did not sound as though he disapproved as such, only recognised the scandal that would happen if something leaked out.

Callum pushed back his chair and got up. 'I'll go and collect d'Aunay.'

'Will you invite your colleague to join us this evening?' Sophia asked on impulse. They had invited Averil and Luc for dinner, her first formal party. She knew Callum had made the party that small to give her confidence as a hostess, but it would be pleasant to show him that she could manage more.

'All right, if that would please you. Pettigrew is pretty sure to say *yes*, even at short notice. He's a bachelor and always complaining that he never gets a decent dinner.'

'We must convert him to the delights of married life in that case,' Sophia said and twisted round for the expected peck on her cheek. Instead she received a kiss full on the mouth.

'I don't expect you to demonstrate all of them to him,' Callum growled, then nuzzled her cheek and walked out. She heard him laugh at something Hawksley said in the hall and her heart lifted.

Mrs Datchett was delighted at the prospect of a larger dinner party and threw herself into finalising the menu with gusto. Once it was agreed she bustled off, leaving Sophia with the realisation that she still needed to unpack the wedding presents to create a table setting worthy of guests.

She had been avoiding the wedding gifts because the memory of the day itself, the anxiety and indecision that had led up to it, had clouded the memory for her. Perhaps it was because her marriage was giving her more happiness than she had ever expected, but the morning passed pleasantly as she unwrapped and looked carefully for the first time at fine china and crystal, silverware and linen. Despite the short notice, and the surprise of the Chatterton family and their friends, they had rallied round and given generous, thoughtful presents. For the first time Sophia felt herself part of that wider circle: she was a Chatterton now.

Over a light luncheon she decided that all the preparations were made for the evening. Now she could go and buy the drawing supplies and perhaps, if she felt brave enough, ask for an appointment with Mr Ackermann.

'Ma'am, Mr Ackermann says he has looked at the drawings and can see you now if that is convenient.' The young assistant smiled happily at her, neat in his greenbaize apron and sleeve protectors, his hair slicked down, his face shining with enthusiasm. He looked about fifteen. Sophia's stomach contracted with nerves. What had she let herself in for?

She followed him and waited for the door to the inner sanctum to be opened for her. She should have brought her maid, she realised. But she had not wanted to involve Chivers in what she could not help but feel was deceiving Callum. She should have discussed this with him first, she knew that. And she knew, perfectly well, that he would object in no uncertain terms to his wife offering her art for sale. Better to prove that she could do it, without scandal, and then confess when he could see his opposition was quite unnecessary.

'These would be suitable for one of our series of memorandum books.' Half an hour later Rudolph Ackermann spread a dozen small sketches of flowers, trees and fragments of landscape on the desk. 'Charming. We could put *Illustrated by a Lady of Quality* on the title page.'

'Oh, yes, I would not wish for my name to appear.' He liked them! The majority of her sketches lay in the portfolio, but even so, to have any singled out as suitable for publication was both a shock and a delight.

'Indeed.' He named a sum of money and Sophia repressed a gasp of pleasure. She did not need it, but it was proof, at last, that her work was good enough. 'I will have an agreement drawn up for your perusal if you would care to call again in a few days,' Mr Ackermann continued. He glanced at the portfolio. 'Your figure drawing is also interesting, although all these examples are too personal to be of use to me. However, if you were to work on some classical studies, or figures in a landscape, I would be interested in seeing them.'

'You think my figure drawing is adequate?'

'More than that.' He touched a sketch she had made

of Chivers. 'The portraiture is charming and appears to be most revealing of character.'

Sophia emerged clutching her parcel and portfolio, dazed and delighted and with an appointment for three days' time to finalise terms. Now she knew her drawings were of saleable quality, the urge to do more was almost overwhelming. She wondered if Callum would allow her to draw him, for the only sketch she had made was the one in the chaise on their wedding day and that was marred by a pencil slash across it from when he had startled her. The thought made her shy for some reason. Perhaps, because she knew now that she loved him, it would be too intimate, too revealing of the way she felt.

She was about to hail a cab when she noticed another shop, its window filled with colour and a small crowd standing outside laughing. The multi-paned bow window was full of prints pinned in rows along strings. Cartoons, she realised, caricatures of public figures and international events. They were cruel, perceptive, vigorous. She blinked at one of the Prince Regent, his mistress and a chamber pot—and crude. These were definitely not the sort of popular images she had seen at home, but she could not resist them. Sophia opened the door and went in.

On impulse, when she arrived back in Half Moon Street Sophia went straight to Averil's door and knocked.

'Yes, Mrs Chatterton, my lady is at home.' The butler stepped back to give her access into the hall and, as Sophia stepped on to the marble floor, a voice came clearly through the half-open drawing-room door.

'I cannot like it, Averil! How could she forget Daniel

and marry a man she hardly knows within months of the wreck? It seems heartless. And poor Callum—what was he thinking about to let himself be trapped like that?'

The butler, his hands full of Sophia's parcels, froze; it was quite clear he knew who they were discussing, but it was too late to deny her entrance now.

'Well, I like her,' Averil's voice was equally forth-right and just as clear. 'And so will you, Dita. I have no doubt Callum thought it was the right thing to do—and you know what he is like: Sophia probably had no choice in the matter once he had made up his mind!'

The butler dumped the packages unceremoniously on the hall table, flung the door wide and announced, 'Mrs Chatterton, my lady,' with an air of desperation, presumably in the hope of forestalling any further *faux pas*.

Sophia walked in, her mouth dry and her stomach in knots. Averil stared at her from the chaise, her face a picture of embarrassment and alarm as the other woman in the room, an elegant creature with dark hair and wide green eyes, sprang to her feet.

'Oh, my dreadful tongue! You must be Callum's wife,' she said and came forwards with impetuous con-fidence, both hands held out. 'I am Perdita Lyndon and I do apologise—I had no right to leap to conclusions. Averil is quite correct, of *course* Callum would have left you no choice in the matter. The man is an unmovable object when he decides upon something.'

'Lady Iwerne.' Sophia took her hand and managed a stiff little nod. Despite the frank apology she felt quite sick. She knew who the outspoken lady was. She had heard her name several times—another of Averil and Callum's friends from the *Bengal Queen*. She had survived the wreck and, so Averil had told them, was now married to her rescuer, the Marquess of Iwerne. And not, it seemed, moved to like her, or trust her motives, however open her apology had been. She swallowed the lump in her throat and turned to Averil. 'I am sorry, Lady d'Aunay, I have called at an inconvenient time.'

'No, of course you have not! I so wanted you to meet Dita,' Averil said remorsefully. 'Oh dear, and now I have become *Lady d'Aunay* to you, just when I thought I had made a new friend. Please, Sophia, come and sit down by me and let Dita retrieve matters. Benson!' The butler reappeared. 'Bring tea and the very nicest biscuits.'

Sophia sat, her stomach still in a miserable knot.

'I am tactless and outspoken but, please believe me, I am not usually given to attacking people I do not know behind their backs,' Lady Iwerne said, sitting down again in a swirl of expensively tailored skirts. 'My only excuse can be that I feel defensive for both Daniel and Callum because of what happened—and that is most unfair to you. I cannot imagine what it must have been like to lose your betrothed. It was so brave to marry Callum.'

Sophia knew she could nod, dab at a tear, accept all the sympathy and they would believe her. But it would be a lie and she could not accept credit for courage from Callum's friends. 'It was very much to my own benefit,' she said stiffly. 'Callum could have married anyone and I would have been left a spinster.'

'But he felt it was his responsibility to look after you,' Averil said, leaning across to squeeze Sophia's hand.

The ready sympathy dissolved the miserable knot inside, made her want to explain. 'Yes, he did. And I said *no*, of course. But he would not listen and Mama wanted it, and my brother is training for Holy Orders and it would have made such a difference… I still said no, even though I was tempted, so tempted. I want children, a family. But I wasn't sure it was right and then he…we—' She broke off, blushing.

'He made you want him? Callum's tactical skills are just what one would expect,' Lady Iwerne said with a wry smile as the butler brought in the tea tray. 'How very clever of him,' she added as the door closed again and Averil began to pour. 'He is most attractive,' she added slyly.

'And now, here I am, indeed, Lady Iwerne,' Sophia said, trying to pretend she had not heard that last remark. 'I only hope I can make Callum a good wife.'

'Call me Dita, please. We will be friends, I know it.' And looking into her intelligent, vivid face, Sophia believed it. Dita smiled. 'I, being far less dutiful than you, can only hope Callum will make *you* happy. You are very modest, but it is not as though he gains nothing from this marriage—an attractive, intelligent wife, support at home as he starts his career in England, someone who knows and understands his family. Do you love him?'

'Yes—oh!' With a hand that shook, Sophia took the tea cup Averil was offering. 'I did not mean to say that. He doesn't know how I feel.'

'And it is such a difficult thing to say, isn't it? Only three words, but when one has no idea what the reply will be, they just seem to freeze on your lips,' Averil said with a smile. 'And men are even worse than we are—sometimes it takes them a while to understand how they feel.'

Dita rolled her eyes. 'Quite. Well, you have us now.

How can we help? Let me think. Is everything all right in the bedroom? Does he need seducing?'

Averil gave a snort of laughter. 'No!' Sophia knew she had gone crimson. 'Everything is just wond— I mean, that is not the problem.' As she recovered her composure she realised that Dita's assured manner of speaking of such things probably meant that she and the marquess had been lovers, just as Averil and Luc had been before their marriage. It was shocking, but it was also reassuring to know that feeling about lovemaking as she did was not something unusual or wicked. She had wished for married friends her own age to confide in, and here they were.

'Callum is very cool,' she added with some haste. Dita's exquisitely groomed eyebrows rose. 'I mean, out of the bedchamber. Very pleasant, very kind and amiable. Sometimes it is like living with a man who is on the other side of a sheet of glass. Sometimes I think that making...er...the bedroom, is the only thing that really warms him.'

'He was always the controlled one, the ambitious, hard-working twin,' Averil said, frowning. 'But I would never have called him cool or distant. He was witty and a good friend.'

Dita nodded in agreement. 'I've seen him in fits of laughter and engaging with other people's enjoyments.'

'He still misses Daniel dreadfully, I think. It has hurt him very much to lose him,' Sophia said. 'They were in each other's heads, somehow. I can remember that. It must be like losing part of yourself. I don't know how to fill that void for him, or even if I should try. I had fallen out of love with Daniel, you see. Callum knows that. I felt, I *still* feel, so guilty about it—but how could

I feel the same? We had grown up. I was different, he must have been too.'

The words seemed to spill from her mouth and the relief at saying it, at being honest with friends, and not just with Callum, was intense. The other women were silent as her impulsive words died away into silence. Were they shocked? Disgusted? She braced herself for their reaction.

'I can quite see that. Ten years apart—of course you had changed,' Dita stated. There was a sympathetic silence, then she added, 'Well, at least you are out of mourning, by the look of things. That will help both of you.'

'We have begun to go out in society now. In fact, we are having our first dinner party tonight.' A thought struck her. 'I know it is dreadfully short notice, but would you—?'

'Come to dinner? We would love to—I was hoping you would ask. Now I know I am forgiven. We must have another cup of tea, and then we will catch up on all the news.'

Chapter Seventeen

Sophia returned home at seven in the evening fizzing with excitement. She swept through the front door just as Callum came down the stairs, suavely elegant in evening dress, his golden skin and dark hair the perfect foil for white linen and deep blue cloth. 'My dear, I was about to send out a search party.'

'Oh, Callum, I am late, I am so sorry—and after I was so cross when you were late the other day, too! Did you have a good day at the docks?'

'Thank you, yes.' He eyed her portfolio and the brown paper parcel. 'You have been shopping at this time in the evening?'

'Oh, no. I mean…yes, I went shopping and then I called on Averil and Lady Iwerne was there so I have invited her and Lord Iwerne for dinner tonight as well. They've just got back to town from their honeymoon, too, just like Averil and Luc. I do like her, very much. Only, we fell to talking and I quite forgot the time. But I remembered to send a message to the staff about the two extra guests, and the wedding presents have been unpacked,' she finished, breathless.

'I shall be delighted to see both the presents and our guests.' And he did look pleased, Sophia thought with relief. She had not been sure it was quite the thing to invite a marquess to dinner at such short notice.

'I must run and get changed.'

Callum stood aside courteously to allow her to mount the stairs. 'Perhaps I can look through your drawings while I am waiting.' He reached for the portfolio.

'No!' Sophia whirled round and snatched it back. 'Not those dreadful scrawls, I would be mortified to have them looked at. I'll…I'll find something better than these to show you.'

She whisked upstairs and into her sitting room. Her old folder was on the side and she shuffled some of her better drawings into it, then, with a guilty pang, pushed the portfolio with Mr Ackermann's card and notes and the caricatures she had bought in it under the sofa. Sooner or later she must confess what she had done, but not quite yet. She wanted to savour the triumph of actually selling her work before she had to defend her actions.

Andrew came at the tug of the bell pull. 'Please give this to Mr Chatterton.' She handed him the folder and ran up to her room to dress for her first dinner party as a married lady.

Cal checked with Hawksley that all was ready for the evening, then settled himself in the drawing room with Sophia's folder of drawings. He had no very great expectations after her reluctance to show them to him. Just because she had been drawing for many years did not mean she had any talent; he only hoped he did not have to struggle to find some kind words to say. It was strange how living with Sophia had made him so sensitive to her feelings. Or perhaps that would have happened with any woman: he was just not used to domestic closeness.

The drawing that lay on top was of a woman, her head bent over sewing. She was obviously utterly focused on her work and yet the pose was one of tranquillity and grace. He stared at it, recognising Chivers despite the fact that her face was not visible. He turned the sheet over and found a minutely detailed flower study, then a sweeping sketch of Green Park followed by another portrait, this time of a small child staring solemnly at a cow. Green Park again, he thought, arrested by the way Sophia had caught the mixture of fear and curiosity on the toddler's face.

She wanted children, he recalled. So did he, of course. An heir and, he supposed, the proverbial spare. That was unpleasantly close to the bone—life was dangerous and unpredictable and the thought of losing a child made his blood run cold. It would be even worse than losing Daniel. As bad as losing Sophia. He pushed the idea away and thought of a little girl. Yes, that was ideal, three children. At least. As he looked at the sketch in his hand Callum found the abstract wish for children had become something else, a definite desire to have children with Sophia.

Where had that come from? The realisation that she would make a good mother, he supposed, although it was more than that, somehow.

He was still sitting there, daydreaming, the folder

open on his knee, when Sophia came down, a trifle pink from hurrying.

'You look very fine, my dear,' Cal remarked. She had gained a little weight, a little colour in her cheeks, since they had married. It was hard to remember why he had ever thought her plain.

'I do?' She patted at her piled curls, frowning into the overmantel mirror.

'Indeed. The pink in your cheeks suits you and running down the stairs has produced a most alluring effect around the neckline.'

Sophia looked down at the rapid rise and fall of her bosom and became pinker. 'Wretch!'

'Which reminds me, I have a present for you.'

'For me?'

How intriguing, he thought. Her reaction was a polite query, not an instant demand to know what it was. But then, this was his wife, not his mistress. And, although Sophia had married him for security and position, she was not at all grasping. In fact, he rather wished she would ask him for something, anything. 'It occurred to me that I had bought you no jewellery and that we are entertaining formally for the first time tonight.'

'You gave me my wedding ring and your grandmother's lovely sapphire.' Sophia held up her hand, the gems winking in the candlelight.

'And now this.' He picked up the long dark-blue leather case from the table beside him as he got to his feet.

'Oh.' She seemed reluctant to take it and then, when she did, she held it, unopened, in her hand. 'I have done nothing to deserve it.'

'You are my wife. You do not have to earn such things—it is my pleasure to give them to you.'

Sophia shook her head. 'I cannot help but feel this is an unequal relationship.'

'It is marriage.' Cal took the box and opened it, wondering what made him such an expert on the subject. Marriage to Sophia was not proving to be quite what he had imagined, a polite, harmonious domestic arrangement with privacy and restraint on both sides and no need for any awkward emotion.

White fire flashed along the length of the case, a line of brilliance against the dark velvet lining. He lifted the necklace and put it around Sophia's neck, lingering a little as he fastened it, letting his fingers stir the dark tendrils of hair her maid had so cunningly left to caress her skin. 'And I do not think that marriage is a matter of an accountant's books, a debit-and-credit balance. It is, I hope, a matter of trust and partnership.'

It was a pleasure to touch her, a pleasure to adorn her with what was, ultimately, the fruits of his hard work. These were not inherited gems. But one day, perhaps they would be. One day Sophia might give them to their daughter on her wedding day. Something swelled in his chest, a mixture of pride and apprehension and a tenderness that made him catch his breath.

Sophia stood and looked at their reflections in the glass, the diamonds pulsing with the rhythm of her breathing, his hands lying possessively on her shoulders. 'It is *lovely*. Trust and partnership. I hope that, too,' she said slowly and then, with sudden vehemence, she turned and caught his hands in hers. 'I want that. I want to share my thoughts with you and to have you share yours with me. To be part of your life, even though you never wanted me there.'

'I never saw you there, but now you are here, my wife, I am glad of it,' Cal said, surprised to find he meant it. 'Trust, then, and understanding and sharing?'

'Yes.' Her eyes were clear and dark and happy as she looked into his and Cal felt a jolt of some emotion he hardly recognised displace the sensation of apprehension in his heart. Happiness. Such a perilous emotion. 'Yes, please, Callum. And the necklace is beautiful, thank you. I am sorry if I seemed ungrateful.'

'I do not want gratitude,' he said, meaning it and wondering as he spoke what he did want. 'But a kiss would be very acceptable.'

Her arms went around his neck and she smiled up at him. 'But that is as much a pleasure for me as for you, Mr Chatterton,' she said as he lowered his mouth slowly to hers, savouring the anticipation.

'The Marquess and Marchioness of Iwerne, Captain the Count d'Aunay, Lady d'Aunay, ma'am,' Hawksley pronounced with the air of a butler who felt he was loftily above such circumstances as discovering his master and mistress locked in a passionate embrace in the middle of their drawing room.

Callum took absolutely no notice of the butler, or of the four guests who entered on his words, until he had finished the kiss, apparently to his satisfaction.

Sophia emerged blushing and laughing to meet the sardonic amber gaze of a tall, black-haired stranger. Instinct alone would have told her that this was not Callum's bachelor colleague from East India House, even if he did not have Perdita at his side: he had a tangible air of confidence and privilege that warned her that this was the Marquess of Iwerne. *Warned* was the apt word, too, she was certain. A good man to have on your side, a dangerous enemy.

'My lord.' She was not certain how low one had to curtsy to a marquess—he was one step below a duke, after all—but she had hardly begun to bend her knees when he stepped forwards and took her hand.

'Alistair,' he said and smiled. Really, if she was not already in love with Callum, Sophia thought, managing somehow to keep her composure, she would not know where to look, his friends were such attractive men.

He released her hand and held his out to Callum, pulling him into a hard, rapid embrace that seemed to communicate more than words would have done. It hit Sophia suddenly that perhaps the last time Callum had sat down to eat with three of the people here Daniel had been with them too. Had she been extraordinarily insensitive to invite the Lyndons?

Then she saw that Callum had relaxed and was smiling and realised that she had not understood. He did not have to explain anything to his friends, they did not have to say anything out loud for him to know he had their support. It was only she, his wife, who was uncertain and who risked blundering with everything she said, or left unsaid.

'The Honourable Mr George Pettigrew, ma'am.' Mr Pettigrew's arrival released some of the tension she was feeling; he had never known Daniel, presumably had no idea of the circumstances of his colleague's marriage and his presence forced everyone to talk of more general subjects.

* * *

Dinner had gone well, Sophia decided two hours later, looking down the length of the table with some satisfaction as the guests finished sampling the selection of sweet fritters that flanked the orange-cream cups. Callum met her gaze and she took a breath to ask the ladies to retire. Instead he said, 'Would you like to own a ship, my dear?'

'A *ship*? You mean a yacht?'

'No, an East Indiaman. That is where we have been today, looking at one for sale in the docks.'

'A whole ship?' She managed not to gulp. One could not ask one's husband if he could afford to buy something vastly expensive, not in the middle of a dinner party.

Callum grinned. 'A share. Pettigrew and d'Aunay and Lyndon are joining me. Together we will own one quarter.'

'It sounds wonderful. What is she called?'

'The *Morning Star,*' Mr Pettigrew said. 'I think it ought to be changed, there are at least three others of that name that I can think of.'

'Wouldn't the other owners object?'

'I cannot see why, not if we can suggest something acceptable and unique,' Alistair said.

'I know.' Callum looked round the table, then his gaze came back to fix on Sophia. 'There is inspiration enough sitting here.' He raised his glass. 'Gentlemen, I give you *The Three Belles.*'

'Three—? Ah, a pun.' Luc smiled. 'It will make a marvellous figurehead.' He lifted his glass to his own wife and then to Averil and Sophia. 'Three belles, indeed.'

Sophia waited until the laughter and toasts had subsided, then nodded to Andrew who came to pull back her chair. 'Ladies. Shall we?' As they left the room the men resumed their seats and she heard George Pettigrew say, 'I reckon she'll do us proud.'

'Perhaps we should start our own shipping—' Luc's voice was cut off by the door closing.

'This is delicious,' Averil said happily. 'A ship named after us.'

'If the other owners will allow the change.' Sophia still could not quite take it in.

'I don't know who they are, but we do have the fact that Alistair is a marquess on our side,' Dita pointed out. 'I would guess he outranks most of them.'

'And the fact that we have our Mr Chatterton,' Averil put in. 'Luc tells me that the rumours are that he is *very* well thought of at Leadenhall Street.'

'He is?' Of course, she had every confidence in Callum's ability and hard work, but it was early days yet, surely?

'Apparently he is spoken of as likely to be the youngest-ever member of the Court of Directors in a few years,' Averil said. 'Luc picks up all the Company gossip along with the naval talk.'

'Oh.' How wonderful. And how like him that he had not boasted to her of his successes. Or perhaps he thought she would not be interested. That was lowering, although not as bad as the worry that he simply did not think it necessary to confide in his wife. She pulled herself together to find the other two were discussing Dita and Alistair's travels after the wedding.

'Well, Alistair has inherited a very small castle in the Scottish Highlands so we went there first. Then we travelled back by way of all the relatives who needed visiting,' Dita said. 'Between us we have dozens—or so it seemed!'

'I heard it always rains in Scotland,' India-bred Averil said with a shiver. 'And it is cold, isn't it?'

'It was, I am glad to say,' Dita retorted with a wicked grin. 'It was a horrid draughty castle, the rain kept pouring down and there was nothing to do but keep warm in bed in the intervals of inspecting the state of the place and resolving to sell it at the first opportunity.'

Averil giggled. 'We had a wonderful time in Herefordshire and it hardly rained at all. Now we will be here until Luc's ship is ready to leave: the Admiralty require him.'

'What will you do when he is at sea?'

'Learn French,' Averil said with a grimace. 'I must become fit to be the wife of a French count. Luc says—'

But what Luc said was lost as the men came in from the dining room. Somehow Sophia kept smiling and chatting and making small talk over the tea cups until the last of their guests left. Callum returned from seeing George Pettigrew off and collapsed on to the sofa next to her. 'That went very well, Mrs Chatterton. You are obviously destined to be a great society hostess.'

'Were you not tired? You have had a long day.'

'No, not at all. I had an interesting day and it was good to see old friends again.'

'I am excited about the ship.'

'Good, I thought you might be.' Callum stretched out his legs and draped one arm around her shoulders, his fingers playing with the necklace at her nape.

'And proud that you and the others want to rename it after your wives. I worried that the majority owners might refuse, but Dita and Averil say that with the influence that Alistair and you can exert there will be no problem.'

'A marquess is always a good card to play.'

'And a man tipped to be a very young Director?' she asked.

'Hell.' Callum sat up and pushed his fingers through his hair, destroying an elegant Brutus style. 'Where did you hear that?'

'Luc apparently hears all the Company gossip.'

'Ah. It is exaggerated, of course.'

'Is it?' Sophia twisted round on the sofa to look at him. 'I am very proud of you.'

'Proud?' Callum seemed utterly surprised by her words.

'Of course! I was proud that you had secured a good post, I am proud that you work so hard and I am not in the slightest bit surprised that your reputation is so good—' She broke off, confused by the shuttered look on his face. 'Callum, I wish you had told me of this. Boasted a little.'

'I am not used to discussing such things,' he said, his face bleak. 'If there was something to be proud about I did not need to mention it, Dan knew…'

She waited, something, love perhaps, giving her the patience to let him find his way through this.

'I thought marriage would be something I could put in a box,' he said slowly as though working it out as he spoke. 'I would look after you, you would create a well-run home for me, entertain, produce children in the fullness of time. Then there was work, in another box.'

'And your feelings?' she asked.

'Under lock and key,' he admitted. Callum reached out and pulled her back close to his side. 'That is not fair to you.'

'Or to you,' Sophia said.

'Discussing feelings is not a language I know the grammar of. You must teach me, Sophia.'

It would be easy, and so much safer, to tug his head down for a kiss. He would take her off to bed and all these difficult things could be put aside. After a moment Sophia said, 'Tell me how it was with Daniel. How you communicated. Could you read his mind?'

She felt his body tense against hers and thought he would not answer, then he said, 'Lord, no. That would have been uncomfortable and embarrassing! I felt his emotions as though they were mine and yet I knew they were not, somehow. And I felt those emotions physically as I would my own.'

'That must have been awkward under certain circumstances,' Sophia murmured.

'You learn to disregard that sort of thing,' Callum said, and she heard the trace of a laugh in his voice.

'So…' she struggled to understand '…it was as though his feelings were overlain on to yours, like writing on glass, but slightly awry, so you knew it was not you?'

'Yes.' Callum put her away from him so he could look at her. 'Exactly like that. How do you know?'

Because sometimes I feel your emotions, in just that way, she wanted to say. *Because I love you.* 'I guessed it must be something like that. Do you mind, when I ask about Daniel sometimes? I will not if it is difficult for you.'

There was a long pause. Sophia studied Callum's

face, the lowered lids masking the thoughts she was beginning to be able to read in his eyes. 'Yes, it is difficult and, no, I do not mind. No one else will speak of him, you see. The more I can talk about him, acknowledge that he has gone, the easier it will become, I think.'

Sophia snuggled closer into the curve of Callum's body and let her head rest back against his shoulder. 'We won't forget him,' she murmured. 'Whenever you want to talk about him, I will be here.'

Chapter Eighteen

The long, companionable silence stretched on. The fleeting pressure on the crown of her head must be Callum's lips, Sophia realised, warm with happiness.

'Shall we go to bed?' he suggested, his voice a rumble close to her ear. The familiar heat coiled low in her belly as she heard the hint of a growl in his voice. When he spoke like that, husky with wanting her, his eyes intent, his hands already changing their comforting hold to an incitement to desire as his fingertips stroked across the inside of her wrist, how could she resist him?

'We could certainly do that. There were a few things that I would like explaining, perhaps.' Sophia twisted round so she was looking at him and ran her tongue tip over her lower lip. Callum's eyes narrowed. 'If I did this—' she touched him, cupping her hand over the straining hardness '—and then this, is it better than if I do *this?*' She scratched lightly with her nails and then closed her grip and laughed as he caught her hand.

'Witch! Upstairs with you and I'll discuss every inch

that you want to explore. Or we could simply disrobe here?'

'Callum! We cannot—any of the staff might walk in! Oh, you beast!' Sophia protested as he stopped pretending to untie his neckcloth and stood up to sweep her off the ground and into his arms. 'You cannot carry me upstairs at this time of night with the servants—'

It seemed he could, and would, and when they reached the bedchamber, and Chivers vanished as discreetly as a puff of smoke, Callum was as good as his word, letting her explore just as she would before demanding the same rights for himself.

Sophia woke to find the candles still burning and Callum asleep by her side, sprawled naked on his back, one hand behind his head, one knee drawn up, the sheet rammed to the bottom of the bed by his restless feet. It was the first time he had stayed after they had made love and she lay for a while, listening to the deep, steady rhythm of his breathing, savouring the pleasant tingle in her blood and the way Callum's lovemaking left her limbs feeling as limp as velvet.

A clock struck one. She wasn't sleepy now; in fact, the lassitude had gone. She rolled carefully on to her side and studied the unconscious figure beside her. It was the first time she had been able to study him naked for any length of time and the difference between their bodies intrigued her. Hairy where she was smooth; hard, flat planes where she curved and dipped; hands and feet so much bigger than hers. And his manhood, lax on his thigh—she moved a little closer and studied it, fascinated.

She had to draw him. Sophia slid from the bed, wriggled into her robe and went to find her sketchbook and pencils. She perched on a chair by the side of the bed and began making small studies first: his hand, palm up, the fingers flexed, a scar across the base of the thumb. His profile with the faint morning stubble just appearing, his lashes dark on his cheek, those mobile lips relaxed into a half-smile, his sex with all the detail she would lavish on a still life. Then she turned the page and began to draw the full length of him with every ounce of skill and concentration that she possessed.

When she finished she ran her hand over the drawing as she might over his naked body. It was the best thing she had ever done, she was convinced of it. Sophia wondered if Callum would be pleased with it or embarrassed as she closed the book and set it aside. It was certainly going to take her a little time to pluck up the courage to show him.

'*No!*'

Callum's face was stark with a horror that she could not see, his eyes tight closed, his body twisted. Sophia jumped to her feet, reaching for him. As she reached his side one outflung hand hit her a glancing blow, but she caught at his shoulders. 'Callum! Callum, wake up!'

The wave was enormous, as high as a house, its foaming crest white in the moonlight, foam torn from it by the howling wind. 'No! Dan!' He seized the rail, struggling against the tilt of the deck. Below in the ship's boat faces were upturned, stark with horror. Averil, Dita, Lyndon already reaching for the women. Dan, white, his mouth open, shouting something that was lost in the scream of the wind and the terrible grinding of the ship on the rocks.

'Dan—' *And then the wave hit and he was thrown across the deck to crash into something immovable, the breath crushed out of him as he began to crawl and stagger back to the side. And the boat was gone. Gone without trace. And Dan was gone too, gone from his head, gone from his heart.*

Cal forced his body over the rail and launched himself into the chaos of water. If he could only reach him—

'Callum!' *Hands on his shoulders, a desperate voice. Not Dan, a woman, but he had to help her, had to even if it meant abandoning the search for his twin.*

'Hold on!'

'I *am* holding you. Callum, darling, I have you. You are safe. Wake up, please, wake up!'

Light against his closed lids. Light and silence. Stillness. Seaweed—no, long, unbound hair—brushed his shoulder. Hands held him, fierce, protective. He got his eyes open. 'Sophia?'

Her face crumpled as though she was going to cry and then, with a visible effort, she had herself under control again. 'It was a nightmare. You were having a nightmare about the wreck.'

Somehow he stopped the shivering that was racking his body, got himself under control. 'I'm sorry. I must have frightened you.'

'It doesn't matter. Lie still. Let me get you warm.' She pulled the covers up over their bodies, wriggling close to him. He felt silk slide over his skin, warm hands, cold feet. His wife. Yes, that was it, his wife. Cal shook his head, tried to drive away the remnants of the dream and find reality. He must have fallen asleep in her bed after they made love.

'I should have gone. I didn't mean to expose you to this. I thought I had got it under control.'

She had snuggled down, her head on his shoulder, her body wrapped around his, but at that she came up on to her elbows and stared down into his face.

'You mean you dream like that every night?'

'At first,' he admitted. 'Since we married, less.' He could not tell her that the dreams now were as often of her, of losing her, as they were of the wreck. Her face was appalled. 'It is all right, I am not going mad,' he said to reassure what must be her greatest fear. 'I spoke to doctors, they said the dreams would fade in time. You needn't worry, I won't stay again.' He tried to get up and found himself entangled in soft, determined resistance. Without hurting her he could not move.

'Yes, you *will* stay,' Sophia said fiercely. 'Don't you dare suffer this by yourself, Callum Chatterton. Go to sleep now. In the morning you will tell me all about the wreck, every detail.' Her voice cracked. 'You are very brave, and very pigheaded, but you can't fight everything by yourself. You have me now. Go to sleep.'

He had never tried to sleep after a nightmare. Always he had got up, walked or read or worked until dawn. Cal tried to fight the heaviness in his body, the warmth, the limbs twined around his, and felt himself sliding into darkness.

Cal woke to a clatter of china and hushed voices. He opened his eyes and found himself in his wife's bed and Sophia, in a ridiculous confection of flounces and frills, seated at the little table in the window pouring tea.

'What time is it? And what *are* you wearing?'

'Nine. And it is a morning undress gown according to Dita, who nagged me into buying it.' Sophia smiled, but her eyes were anxious. 'I sent a message to Leadenhall Street to say you were detained. Come and have breakfast.'

'Like this?' He scrubbed one hand over his unshaven chin.

'You had best put your robe on first,' she said with a smile.

'I can't—' He got out of bed. 'I need a bath, a shave—'

'Please, Callum.'

He looked at her sitting there, fresh and lovely and anxious and something in his heart turned over. He could feel her anxiety, her distress for him, so strongly. Where Dan's feelings had once touched him, now he could sense Sophia's emotions. It was different; he and his twin had been born with that link. This was something else, felt different, an empathy that had grown because he knew her now so well. Cared about her. No wonder he was dreaming.

He got up, pulled on his robe, ran his hands through his hair and sat down at the table.

'Drink your coffee,' Sophia said. 'They will bring food up very soon. And then you will tell me about the wreck.' She shook her head in answer to his instinctive movement of rejection. 'You have told no one all the details, have you? Not even Will? Your mind has to let go of the horror somehow, I think.'

'How can I burden you with it?' Cal demanded.

'Because I am your wife,' she said simply. 'And I care for you.'

You do? He didn't ask it out loud. The footmen came in with more coffee, covered plates; the moment was lost. But when they had eaten and he sat nursing his third cup of coffee Sophia murmured, 'Callum?' So he told her everything, every detail, from the lurch when the anchor began to drag and how Averil's laughter at one of Dan's jokes had broken on a gasp of shock to the moment when he had opened his eyes to find himself being nursed by Dita in the Governor's House on St Mary's on the Isles of Scilly and had realised that he was, for the first time in his life, alone.

Sophia was silent for several minutes when he finished and he wondered if he had been too graphic, too frank. How much had he revealed about himself, about his weaknesses? He had to be strong for her, that was what a husband owed his wife. But the relief of speaking, of pouring it all out, was almost shattering.

'When you came to tell me that Daniel was dead you asked me to forgive you for not saving him,' she said at last. 'Do you still blame yourself? Do you truly believe there was anything that you could have done that would have saved him?'

'No,' Cal said and, by some miracle, he believed it. He had told himself over and over again that he had done all he could but, even as he had recovered, some small nagging part of his brain told him that there must have been something. He drew in a deep, ragged breath. 'For the first time I do not feel guilty.'

Sophia smiled and he leaned across the table to run the pad of his thumb gently over the dark circles under her eyes. How much sleep had she had last night? 'You go back to bed and rest. Thank you, Sophia.'

There was more to the way he felt than that burden of guilt lifting, Cal told himself as he rode eastwards. There was a new anticipation, a new feeling that was not quite pleasure and not quite apprehension that unsettled his mind and was giving him butterflies in the stomach, a sensation he did not recall feeling since the day he stood on the deck of an East Indiaman and watched the English shoreline vanish into the haze.

'Damn it, is this how marriage makes every man feel?' he demanded under his breath. Would his nights be utterly consumed with dreams of losing her now? The gelding, confused by his tone, sidled and curvetted across the road into the path of a mail coach and Cal jerked his attention back to where he was and what he was doing.

'What's the matter?' As Cal entered the office George Pettigrew looked round from the huge wall-map of India that he had been studying.

'Sorry I'm late. Minor domestic crisis,' Cal said, as he slung his saddlebags on to a chair and hung up his hat.

Pettigrew's very silence and the way he turned back to his map had Cal glancing at his reflection in the glass over the mantelshelf. The shadows under his eyes did not help, but he looked grim enough for a man going to his own hanging. Sophia was getting under his skin, into his heart where he had vowed never to allow anyone again. What if something happened to her? What if she grew tired of this marriage she had been forced to make? What if he hurt her?

Then the memory of her touch, her compassion, the tough way she would not allow him to shy away from talking about Dan, her sweet delight in their lovemaking, all came flooding back and he smiled.

'Confusing state, married life,' Cal said as he sat

down. 'As complicated as negotiating a contract with a Chinese silk dealer and about as comprehensible.'

'Compromise would be the thing, I suppose,' George offered. 'You've got the good faith—at least you can take that for granted.'

'Yes,' Cal agreed and felt better. Good faith and a wife who came into his arms with a generous passion that took his breath away. Whatever else he felt about this marriage of duty, he knew that their lovemaking at least was right and that act, surely, stripped away all pretence. Was he falling in love with Sophia? Was this what it felt like? It must be love. *My God.*

'Pull yourself together,' George demanded. 'I want to have a sensible discussion about tea warehouses, but if you're going to brood on married life I'll go and see if I can get some sense out of Jorgenson instead.'

'No, I'm not going to brood,' Cal said with sudden certainty. 'I know what I'm going to do about it.' He was going to woo his wife. If it was possible to make Sophia fall in love with him, he was going to do it. And if he failed? His stomach gave a sudden sickening lurch as though he had stepped off a high cliff. If he failed, he did not know how he was going to live with it; it would be the pain of losing Dan all over again with the added torment of having to live the rest of his life with a woman he desired body, heart and soul and knowing all he could ever have were her caresses and her kindness.

Sophia did not go back to bed, but it was a long time before she could stir herself to do anything but sit and think. She had known, theoretically, how terrible a shipwreck must be, but she had not *felt* it, not allowed herself to dwell on the terror and the sheer crushing inevitability of the ocean once it had frail humans in its grasp.

But Callum had not been frail. He had fought and battled and even when he had known it was hopeless, that he would not find his twin, at the moment when he could just have given up, he had battled on to save the others who he did find, had held them on the upturned boat until help came, even though he was hurt and freezing and in utter despair.

He was a hero and even now he could not believe it. But he had forgiven himself, that she did believe. And he had spoken about Daniel and his feelings and perhaps now he would not dream that dream again. If he did, she was determined that she would be there. As she finally roused herself and sat brushing out her hair, it occurred to her that perhaps she had finally been able to repay something in return for Callum's offer of marriage, his payment of their debts, his guarantee of security. And there was the money she had earned from her drawings, the money she had thought to use instead of her dress allowance—she could buy something for Callum.

What would he like? He wore jewellery sparingly and he had any number of good family pieces—links and pins and fobs. A horse? He seemed content with the gelding he hired, but perhaps he was just too busy to think about buying one. Sporting guns? They would all take quite a lot of money, she knew that. But she could save up and that would give her more time to find just the right gift.

More content than she had been since Callum had put his ring on her finger, Sophia went to work on another set of drawings for a memorandum book. She would prefer to draw Callum, or try her hand at imitating one of those wicked caricatures, but she was a professional artist now, and this was what Mr Ackermann wanted. If she sold these drawings, then she would tell Callum. He would see it was all harmless and safely anonymous and he would, she hoped, be proud of the standard of her work.

Chapter Nineteen

There were no fresh flowers on the breakfast table when Sophia came down the next morning after a night alone in her room. Nor was there any sign of her husband. Callum had sent a note from the office apologising for missing dinner and then had come in late and had gone to his own room, hours after she had retired to bed. Sophia told herself firmly that she could not read anything into it, that Callum was not regretting the intimacy of the night before and his frankness. He had simply been overwhelmed by work at the office, that must be it.

'Has Mr Chatterton gone out early?' she asked Andrew who was arranging plates on the buffet.

'He said he would be back very shortly, ma'am. He's gone to the market.' The footman looked as confused by this as she felt.

'The market?'

'Shepherd's Market, ma'am. It's only just round the

corner. It's where I usually get the flowers every morning, ma'am. But the master said not to go today.'

'I will wait breakfast until he returns,' she said. 'Please bring me a cup of coffee in the drawing room.' What on earth had possessed Callum to go to a market of all places? If he wanted early morning exercise after a bad night, surely a walk in the park would be more usual?

The front door opened just before she reached the drawing room and Callum came through it, obscured behind a large bunch of flowers. Country flowers, late wild flowers and foliage, a riot of shapes and colours all mixed together as though a small child had plucked the contents of a hedgerow and thrust them into his arms.

'Callum?' Sophia parted the bunch and he smiled at her, petals on the brim of his tall hat.

'I thought these would be a change from roses and give you something else to draw. I realised when I thought about it that there are hardly any wild flowers in Green Park—the park keepers' scythes and the cows see to that.'

'But they are lovely! Thank you—and you went to fetch them yourself.' Not many gentlemen would battle through a crowded market to buy flowers and then carry them back through the streets just because they thought their wives would enjoy drawing them.

She dodged round the flowers as Callum handed them to Andrew. 'That was so thoughtful, Callum.' He turned his head so their lips met and, with his hands free now, pulled her against him. The kiss was slow, thorough and possessive, his lips open over hers, his tongue taking possession of her mouth until the heat flooded into her and she moaned, wanting him, wanting what he had not given her last night.

Then he set her back on her unsteady feet and smiled, quite as though nothing had happened. She stared at him, breathless. 'I've kept you from your breakfast. I'm sorry. I had no idea the market would be so busy and colourful—I thought I was back in India! You must come with me one morning, I think you would find it amusing—it made me want to paint.'

'I would love to come.' Bemused, Sophia preceded Callum into the dining room. 'I thought perhaps you had not had a good night last night and had gone out to take the air.'

'Because I was so late back? I wanted to clear my desk for a day or two and there were things I needed to plan. There are meetings I must attend today, but I am going down to look at the ship again tomorrow—would you like to come?'

Time with Callum, entering into his world, sharing with him—and he wondered if she would enjoy it? 'There is nothing I would like better,' she admitted. 'But don't be late back tonight; it is your cousin Mrs Hickson's party this evening.'

Callum's parting kiss was lingering too, so much so that Sophia was in a considerable flutter by the time he left for Leadenhall Street. She tried to concentrate on sketching some of the flowers he had brought her, but she found she was drifting into happy daydreams. Was he coming to care for her? Might he, one day, come to love her?

Cal found he was in no danger of becoming so absorbed in his work that he did not leave in time. In fact, he was hard put to concentrate and kept drifting off into thoughts of Sophia.

He had a nagging suspicion that he had always placed rather too high a value on controlling his feelings, controlling everything around him, in the past. He was overdue an emotional storm, he supposed, and falling for Sophia had hit him so hard that he had no idea how to deal with it. How do you tell your wife you love her? Propose to a woman and if she turns you down, you can walk away and lick your wounds, get over it in privacy. Reveal your innermost vulnerability in marriage and then find she does not share your feelings—that would be hell.

He had entered this marriage confident that he could provide for his wife, his future family, and give them position and security. And he had suffered no doubts that he could make Sophia happy in bed. But he had not given a thought to love and now he knew that all his confidence, all his certainties, were nothing in the face of this emotion. He wanted the one thing he knew he could not demand: her love.

The ride home through the crowded streets gave him something else to think about, but when he walked into the house, looked in the drawing room and found his flowers all over the room and her drawings with them, he was shaken and disarmed all over again.

Charmed, he tucked a sprig of something he could not identify into his buttonhole and subsided on to the sofa to study the drawings.

'Mr Chatterton has arrived, ma'am,' Hawksley said. 'Shall I send tea to the drawing room?'

With a murmured word of thanks Sophia ran downstairs. Callum looked up from the sheaf of flower drawings in his hand and smiled and her pulse stuttered. 'These are very good,' he said. 'Very accomplished. You have made art, not simply a good representation of nature.'

'I—thank you.'

'Your work should be displayed,' Callum said, his eyes still on the images. 'Printed.'

'Thank you,' she said again, feeling slightly dizzy. Callum thought her work should be printed? She had been trying to summon up the courage to tell him what she had done and it seemed he would have approved in any case. But what he would not approve, she feared, was that she had done it without discussing it first. Admitting to that was going to take courage and the right moment, and just now, with the intimacy they seemed to be achieving so new and so fragile, she could not risk shattering it. Not yet.

Hawksley brought in the tea tray and she began to pour. 'Tell me who to expect to meet at Mrs Hickson's party,' she said. 'I am so looking forward to it.'

Three hours later Sophia recalled those words and winced. Mrs Hickson, it appeared, did not approve of Callum's marriage to 'some country nobody without even youth to commend her.' Neither did her friends.

Sophia slid deeper into the cover of a display of potted palms and listened as one of Mrs Hickson's cronies passed on this judgment to another matron.

'It was deeply regrettable that young men so close to the earldom should have gone into trade in the first place,' Mrs Dunbar opined.

'Quite, although the East India Company is some-

what different—it has great influence and he will doubtless emerge a very rich man.'

'The earl is betrothed, most suitably, to Lady Julia
Gray, so there is probably no risk that the inheritance
might go in that direction, my dear Lady Piercebridge.
That is one mercy.'

'Oh, quite. Not that I have anything against Callum
Chatterton myself. And he does not mix with cits. The
house is perfectly *au fait*.'

'Such a pity your hopes that he would attach himself
to your Daphne did not succeed. So very suitable for
him; this gangling nobody can only pull him down.'

'And I can see no excuse for it. He cannot even plead
the momentary insanity of a love match, I believe. Georgia Hickson said he seems to have done it out of a sense
of duty because she was betrothed to poor dear Daniel.'

Sophia got out of the other side of the palms, the jabs
from their sharp fronds a perfect counterpoint to the
unpleasant pecks from the sharp beaks of the gossips.

They thought she would pull Callum down, that she
was unsuitable as the match for the heir presumptive
to an earldom. Did he share those thoughts? Had he
put them to one side because of his duty to Daniel's
betrothed?

'There you are. I thought you had run off to flirt with
one of my handsome young cousins.'

Sophia looked up to find Callum smiling down at
her. No, he was not that good an actor, surely? If he
had thought like that about her at first, she was certain
he no longer did. 'Are there any?' she asked. 'If there
are gentlemen as handsome as my husband here I must
have missed them.'

'Now you *are* flirting,' he said and his smile warmed

and held promises of all kinds of things that almost banished the sting of what she had just overheard.

Almost. 'Only with my husband.'

'I would like to lurk here all evening to do just that, but duty calls. Can you bear some more introductions? Great-Uncle Sylvester has just arrived. He's as mad as a trunk full of Barbary apes, but he's an entertaining old devil.'

'Yes, of course. An eccentric great-uncle sounds delightful.'

And so Sylvester proved to be. And she liked the younger set she was introduced to and perhaps, if she had not overheard Mesdames Dunbar and Piercebridge she would not have noticed how haughty Mrs Hickson was to her and the pursed lips of some of the older women.

That sort of snobbery had never occurred to her when she'd agreed to marry Callum, perhaps because there were so many other objections to worry about. Sophia smiled and chatted, sipped Mr Hickson's rather inferior champagne and fumed inwardly. She might be a country nobody, but her family was perfectly respectable. Her father had been a gentleman, she had connections to a number of noble families—distant, it was true. The wretched women had no business to speak as though Callum had married the scullery maid.

She recalled how the inquisitive ladies had reminded her of a flock of starlings at the dinner party when she had first met some of Callum's family. These old witches were just the same, snapping at their prey with no concern whether it might be hurt by their spite. Sophia eyed Mrs Hickson's profile across the room and thought of the prints she had bought. How satisfying to draw the whole flock of them as starlings, pecking some unfortunate creature to death.

'Would you like to come into the City this morning?' Cal stood at the foot of the stairs and watched Sophia coming down. She had the faint air of the cat who had stolen the cream and he rather suspected he was looking a trifle smug himself. He had stayed in her bed last night, dreamlessly, and when he had woken at dawn the candles had guttered out and Sophia was sleeping like the dead beside him.

But under the physical satisfaction that still warmed him from last night, and again early that morning, was the lurking knowledge that a marriage consisted of more than compatibility in bed. Shakespeare had written something about the marriage of true minds, hadn't he? That was what he had to find with Sophia in order to make her happy. *A marriage of true minds.* He had to trust enough to let down his guard with her and pray that she would do the same with him.

'I don't want to come with you if you frown like that,' she said, reaching the lowest step.

'I was thinking about Shakespeare,' Cal admitted and she shook her head in bafflement, dark ringlets quivering. 'I could show you St Paul's and the Mansion House and the Tower and then we can go down to the docks and you can see our ship.'

'Ours?' He liked the way her mouth curled, half-teasing, half, he was certain, genuine pleasure.

'We will pretend it is all ours,' he promised.

'The post, sir.' Hawksley came down the hall with a laden silver salver. 'And breakfast is ready, ma'am.'

'Thank you for enduring last night. At least it means

you have met most of the relatives who come to town regularly,' he said as they sat down.

He thought Sophia's smile looked forced for a moment. Perhaps she was tired; he had certainly kept her awake last night. 'And the day after tomorrow is our own reception,' she said. 'We have had a gratifying number of acceptances.' Her smile became stronger. 'I fear it will be a sad crush.'

'Excellent. And you have a new gown?' He knew she had, he had asked Chivers in secret and looked at the simple column of deep blue silk with its sweeping over-skirt of spangled gauze. The sapphires he had bought her to go with it were hidden in his room. Would she read the message in the heart-shaped gem that made a pendant to the necklace?

'I have one I am very pleased with, if truth be told,' she confided. 'Callum, it will not hamper your career that I have no useful connections, that no one has ever heard of me?'

'Good Lord, no.' Cal grounded his coffee cup with a clatter. 'Whatever put that nonsense into your head?'

Sophia would not meet his eyes. 'I overheard some-one last night saying what a pity it was that you did not marry Lady Piercebridge's daughter.'

'Daphne? She's a pretty peahen and I never had the slightest interest in her.' He reached across the corner of the table, put his fingers under her chin and tipped her face up so she was forced to look at him. 'You, my love, are the only woman I have ever wanted to marry.'

Sophia's face relaxed into a smile and Callum realised what he had said. *My love.* But she did not pick up on it. She would surely think it was just an endearment, not the honest truth. When this reception was over and she saw how well she was fitted to be his wife, how easily she was accepted as his hostess, then perhaps she would be confident enough to believe him when he told her he loved her. And he would have two more days to woo her first, two more nights to make love to her.

'Well, Sophia? What is it to be first? Our ship or the horrors of the Tower of London?'

'Oh, the Tower, definitely. And then we can be cheered by the sight of the ship.'

The warmth that crept through him as she laughed and spoke so happily of 'we' shook him. That moment all those months ago when she had roused herself from her shock over the news of the wreck and Dan's loss and had touched his cheek with her fingertips, forgetting her own distress, murmuring her concern that he be warm again, came back to him. His destiny had been there, then, waiting for him.

'Callum? Are you all right?'

'Yes,' he said, smiling into the questioning blue eyes. 'Never better.'

Chapter Twenty

'Oh where has Callum got to?' Sophia realised she was wringing her hands and made herself stop before she split the seams on her fragile kid gloves. 'In fifteen minutes people will start to arrive!'

'He said he had forgotten something and had gone back to Half Moon Street,' the Earl of Flamborough said. Will leaned on the banister and looked down into the hall of his town house in Cavendish Square from the sweep of landing outside the ballroom. 'He can't be much longer. If the worst comes to the worst I'll head the receiving line with you and tell them all he has been rushed to the dentist.'

As she knew he intended, her brother-in-law's nonsense made her laugh. 'Oh, Will! What would Julia say to you deserting her?'

'My betrothed would immediately find another man to flirt with, never fear—but there, you see? Here he is.'

And there, to her relief, was Callum indeed, entering in a dramatic swirl of black and crimson as his evening cloak caught the draught from the open door. He handed a mysteriously large parcel to a footman, was relieved of hat, cloak, gloves and cane by another and then stood in the middle of the hall, tipped back his head and looked up at her. 'There you are.'

'There *you* are,' Sophia retorted. 'Will was fabricating tales to explain your absence.'

'There is something I wanted to show Will that I forgot when you bundled me out of the house after luncheon. It can wait, we'll discuss it when we are recovering after the guests go home.' Callum ran up the stairs two at a time as though he could not wait to be at her side and she indulged that romantic little fantasy for a moment.

'So it was my fault?' she enquired archly as he arrived at her side. Oh, but he looked handsome and just a trifle tousled with one lock of hair falling over his forehead. She put up her hand to push it back and he caught it and brought her fingertips to his cheek.

'Of course it is your fault,' Callum said, his voice husky. 'You befuddle my brain, my love. Turn around.'

Obedient, Sophia turned. No doubt a hairpin had come loose. She was almost used to Callum calling her his love. It was nonsense to attach any significance to it, it was simply a term of endearment. 'What are you doing?' He was removing her pearl earrings, her necklace. 'Callum!' Then something cold touched her neck and he turned her to face the mirrored wall beside the door and she saw the necklace, the heart reflecting blue fire as it lay cushioned on her breast. 'Oh!'

'Stand still, these are tricky.' With more delicacy than she could have expected he threaded the earrings into her ears. 'There.' He delved into his pocket. 'And the bracelets.' Callum turned her around again.

His hands slipped down from fastening the bracelets and caught her fingers in his, his head still bent. She looked down at the thick dark hair, the vulnerable nape of his neck, the broad shoulders and wanted to cry, and to kiss him and to shout to the whole house that she loved him. Instead she said, her voice shaking a little. 'They are so beautiful. Callum, thank you.'

He looked up and she thought she would drown in his gaze, deep and green and intense. 'No more beautiful than your eyes,' he murmured. 'Sophia, I—'

'Lord, here's the first coach.' Will appeared on the landing beside them. 'Most unfashionably early—they must have heard the lobster patties wouldn't go round.'

'Will!' Lady Julia Gray joined him, shaking her head at his levity. 'We had better… Oh my goodness, Sophia, what wonderful sapphires!'

'Callum has just given them to me,' she explained with pride as Will took his brother's arm and started organising them into a receiving line.

'You here, Sophia here. Me here. Julia next to me. Walker, tell the musicians to start playing. Right, Mrs Chatterton, your first reception is about to begin. Good luck—you look ravishing.'

'Thank you, Will.' She stood on tiptoe and kissed his cheek. 'Thank you for everything.' *For being so kind all these years, for accepting me, for being there for Callum.*

And then the front door opened and people began to come in and Sophia was swept up in the need to smile and shake hands and pretend that she remembered everyone. She even managed to smile when Mrs Hickson stopped dead, stared at the sapphires and exclaimed, 'Well! Those sapphires!'

'Yes,' she said with a sweet smile. 'Are they not the loveliest thing? My husband spoils me.' She looked up and he smiled a smile that curled her toes in her silver-kid slippers. What had he been going to say when Will interrupted them?

'Humph,' said Mrs Hickson and moved on to shake hands with the earl.

By the time the line of guests had become a trickle Sophia knew that she was presiding over a considerable success. It might be out of Season, but there were enough fashionable people in London who were eager for entertainment to create a most respectable crush. The reopening of the Flamborough town house was a draw, of course, and so was the appearance of Lady Julia as Will's betrothed. Will had craftily left the great doors at the far end of the ballroom closed to create a slightly smaller space and the card tables had been set up in the room thus created.

The string-and-woodwind band created a perfect tuneful background to the babble of voices, Callum had not stinted on the wine and it was easy to avoid the ladies that Sophia thought of as the Spiteful Starlings. She was, she realised, floating on a happy cloud and it was not the one glass of champagne that she had drunk that was creating that feeling.

Callum had given her a parure of the most beautiful jewels. They were lovely gems, but, most important to her, he had chosen them carefully for this evening. He had looked at her as though he…as though… She could not bring herself to think the words, but she could hope.

Will's servants were experienced and the footmen

circulated smoothly with the wine and in the card room. When Sophia peeped into the ladies' retiring room the maids were calmly dealing with torn hems and a fainting fit. The butler assured her gravely that all was in hand in the supper room. Feeling alarmingly matronly Sophia circulated, steering shy wallflowers into conversations, listening to the latest *on dit* that she hardly understood from gossiping dowagers and nudging gauche youths towards the young ladies who were inclined to giggle at them.

Sophia stopped to fix a foliage spray in a flower arrangement and catch her breath. Hands caught her around the waist and pulled her back against a warm, hard body.

'Mrs Chatterton,' Callum breathed in her ear. 'Your reception is a great success. Allow me a congratulatory kiss.'

'Mr Chatterton…' His mouth was warm and possessive and quite indecently demanding, considering that they were screened only by a large flower display and a pillar. When he raised his head Sophia saw the same sensual delight in his eyes as she knew was in her own. 'Callum, thank you so much.'

'For the sapphires? It is my pleasure.'

'For them, of course. They are beautiful and it is such a thoughtful gift. But for everything. For marrying me. I was so grudging, so awkward when you asked me. I hope I can make you as happy as you have made me.'

'You have made me very happy.' Callum took her hand and lifted it to his lips. 'I hope we can make each other happier yet.'

What did he mean? Children? Or whatever he had been about to say when Will interrupted? Her conscience gave a little jab. Tomorrow she must confess about Ackermann's. But he admired her drawing, had said himself she should be published. Callum would be proud.

'So do I,' she said. He released her hand and she looked around. 'We must go and mingle, it will be supper soon.'

The supper room was set out with small tables for two and four and six. 'Let's go and sit with Will and Julia,' Callum said. 'I think my capacity for mindless chatter has expired, at least until I have had something to eat.'

They wove through the seats and tables, smiling and nodding. Sophia even managed a gracious smile for Lady Piercebridge sitting with her husband and Mr and Mrs Hickson close to Will's table, which was in the far corner.

'Come and enjoy your triumph,' Will said, pouring champagne. 'I've told the footman to bring a platter of assorted savouries. This is going very well. Do you know, I even saw Lord Eagleton in positively amiable conversation with Great-Uncle Sylvester and I'd have sworn they haven't spoken in ten years. Yes, Paul, what is it?'

Sophia glanced up to find a footman standing holding a parcel.

'I am very sorry, my lord. Sanderson on the door says Mr Chatterton went out in a hurry to get this just before the guests arrived and it quite slipped his mind. He overheard Mr Chatterton saying it was for your lordship. I thought I had best bring it straight up in case it was needed.'

'What the devil is it?' the earl asked.

Callum said, 'No, no, not for now, for later. Take it—'

But the footman, his attention on his master, not on Callum, unfurled the wrapping paper and placed two portfolios on the table.

Sophia gasped. Not only the portfolio she had given to Callum to look at, full of harmless drawings of flowers and scenes from the park, but the old one, with Ackermann's card and receipt for her work and the caricatures and the other sketches she had pushed in there and hidden under her sofa.

'I was going to show you these later, Will. They are Sophia's and I remembered that printer who did such a good job of Grandmama's watercolours for a private family edition.' He glanced at her as she sat frozen, staring at the battered old black folder. 'I found the green one on the side and then I hit this with my foot—it must have slid under the sofa, which does not say much for the frequency with which the carpets are brushed.'

'But I—' Suddenly galvanized, she reached for the incriminating folder, her hand hitting Will's as he, too, leaned across for it. A full glass of wine tilted, Lady Julia made a grab for it and knocked the folder with her elbow. It slid to the floor, the tattered front cover fell off and the papers inside fanned out in a great drift.

In the centre rested the large nude study of Callum, asleep, as exposed as his body had been in reality. Lady Julia gave a small gasp and stared. The ladies at the Hicksons' table were transfixed. A small flurry of caricature prints landed at the feet of Mrs Hickson and she picked them up, her eyes still on Callum's explicitly naked body. A pen-and-ink study fluttered on to the table before her and she glanced at it, then stared and gave a squawk of outrage. 'Maud, look! It is us! As starlings!'

Lady Piercebridge looked from the paper she was holding directly at Sophia. 'This is a receipt! Mrs Chatterton is selling drawings to Ackermann. The wicked creature is selling libellous caricatures of us!'

The disturbance in their corner was attracting notice from all around the room. Callum fell to his knees, swept the tumbled papers together and hissed at Will, 'Get them out of here, for heaven's sake!'

Will was on his feet. 'Cousin Georgia, Lady Piercebridge, do come through to my study, I am sure there is nothing to be concerned about.' He shot a look at Lady Julia who, with admirable composure, moved to the nearest occupied table and sat down.

'Oh dear, what a to-do! A foolish practical joke by one of Flamborough's younger cousins that has completely misfired. Such a naughty drawing! I declare I will be blushing until tomorrow.' There was laughter and Sophia realised that no one else, except the footman who was looking scandalised, had actually seen what had come out of the folder.

Callum stood up. 'Come with me,' he hissed and followed Will, his arms full of portfolios and papers. As soon as they were out into the corridor he demanded, 'What have you done? The truth.'

'I sold some perfectly innocent drawings to Mr Ackermann for a memorandum book, to be used anonymously,' Sophia said. Her voice teetered on the edge of hysteria and she wrapped her arms around her body, hanging on while she fought for composure. 'I bought the prints and I copied the style, because those old cats said such horrible things about me, but I swear I haven't sold anything to anyone, only those little sketches to Ackermann. I was going to tell you tomorrow.'

Callum's eyes were dark with anger, his face as rigidly controlled as she had ever seen it. 'Have you any idea how serious this is? It may be the ruin of you. Why the hell couldn't you tell me what you were going to do? Do you trust me so little?'

Despite his anger and her own distress, Sophia could read the hurt in his eyes, the betrayal. She had not simply failed to trust him with a secret, she had struck at his honour and his career by her actions. 'Callum, I am—'

'They will say that you are a professional,' he swept on, ignoring her words and her outstretched hand. 'They will say that I knew about what you were doing—I can hardly deny it, can I, not with my body on display for the entire world to see? And to add to the general humiliation, the word will go around that I need my wife's earnings as an artist to support us. You had better get out there and circulate as though nothing has happened. Can you do that?'

It could ruin him, too, she knew that even if he did not say it. A wife who was disgraced, exposed as a professional artist with the suspicion that she was selling scandalous prints, would be more than a liability to a man with his feet on the precarious ladder of success. The Company demanded high standards and good judgement. What did it say about Callum's judgement that he had married her, allowed her such scandalous freedom?

'Yes. Of course. I can manage. Callum, I am so sorry.'

'It is a little late for that,' he said grimly and strode off down the corridor.

She could not faint now, or weep. The only way she could help Callum was to put on a mask and follow Lady Julia's lead. Sophia took a deep, shuddering breath, fixed a smile on her lips and opened the door.

Dita, Alistair, Averil and Luc were sitting at Will's table laughing. As soon as they saw her they gestured for her to join them and Alistair fetched a chair.

'Sophia, dear! Such a lovely evening,' Dita said, then dropped her voice. 'What on earth is wrong? We caught some of it—we were sitting just behind Mrs Hickson.'

'And I've got my foot on a sketch of some kind.' Luc bent down and picked up a rectangle of paper covered in pencil studies. A man's hand, a bare foot, his torso and— Luc slapped his large hand over it as Dita said, with some interest, 'Is that Callum? My goodness.'

'Yes, it is. Thank you.' Luc folded the paper and slid it across to Sophia. She stuffed it into her reticule. 'I sold some little sketches to Ackermann's for a memorandum book, just innocent flower and landscape studies. But Callum didn't know what I had done and he brought my portfolio to show Will without telling me and he picked up the one I thought I had hidden and that idiot of a footman brought it to Will and it got dropped and…'

'And now the fat really is in the fire,' Dita said. 'How can we help? Will's Lady Julia is doing an excellent job of spreading a story about a practical joke by the young men and naughty sketches, so we'll support that. Do you want to go home? We'll take you.'

'No.' Sophia shook her head. 'I am the hostess, I have to be seen or it will cause more talk. I do not know how Callum can stop those dreadful women spreading the truth—and what they believe I have done, which is even worse—but for now I must just pretend nothing is amiss.'

'That's true,' said Alistair. 'Right. The three of you spread around and keep the practical-joke story going—with plenty of emphasis on how shocking it was for the Hickson and Piercebridge party to explain their outrage. I'll walk around with Sophia for a bit of moral support.'

'Thank you,' she said through a smile that felt increasingly precarious. 'Thank you so much.'

'Well, of course I knew about it,' Cal said, passing glasses of brandy to Mr Hickson and Lord Piercebridge while Will dispensed Madeira to their fulminating wives. 'Sophia is extremely talented and I was intending to show her work to my brother in the hope he would ask her to do a portrait of Lady Julia. The fool of a footman got in a muddle and thought the portfolios were something we needed urgently.'

'You *knew* your wife was a professional artist?' Cousin Georgia demanded.

'A few drawings anonymously for an Ackermann memorandum book is hardly professional, Cousin.'

'But this is!' Lord Piercebridge brandished a sketch under Callum's nose. Lady Piercebridge, Cousin Georgia and a number of other ladies were perfectly recognisable in a flock of starlings pecking at a huddled female in a fashionable gown. Speech bubbles issued from their beaks. The whole thing was very much in the style of the vicious caricatures on sale in every print shop.

Callum tilted the drawing and began to read the words. 'It is entitled "Some Country Nobody Without Even Youth to Commend Her,"' he said. 'Now, what are these birds saying? *It is deeply regrettable that young*

*men so close to the earldom should have gone into trade
in the first place... The earl is betrothed, most suitably, so there is probably no risk that the inheritance
might go in that direction, my dear Lady Piercebridge.
That is one mercy... This gangling nobody can only pull
him down. Callum cannot even plead the momentary
insanity of a love match.'* He looked up and studied
the appalled faces of the two women. 'I wonder where
Sophia heard those words spoken?

'My wife—whom I love very much, for your information—was so hurt by your vicious attacks that she
retaliated in the only way she could without confronting
the ladies who were so cruel and causing a public rift. I
imagine she felt a lot better having drawn this, which is
for her own relief and to share with me, not for public
consumption.'

'She draws disgusting things!' Lady Piercebridge
interjected. 'There was a naked man—'

'Myself. I am sorry you find it disgusting, I thought
it rather flattering,' Cal said calmly.

'Maud, did you say these things?' Lord Piercebridge
had picked up the drawing and was staring at it.

'Well, I might have intimated that I did not approve
of the match—' she stammered.

'Mrs Chatterton is a charming young lady, very
pleasant to talk to. Most interested in my gout,' the
baron snapped. 'Don't blame her if she *was* upset to be
attacked like this, anyone would be. We'll say no more
about it, do you hear me, my lady? Good evening to
you, Flamborough, Chatterton. Good party. Very good
party, but I think we'll be off now.'

He hustled his wife out, leaving Cousin Georgia pink

in the face and attempting to bluster at Will, 'I have never been so insulted!'

'No, my sister-in-law has never been so insulted, Cousin. If you wish to explain to your acquaintance why you are no longer welcome in my home, or those of my friends, then all you have to do is spread this malicious nonsense.'

'And if anyone were to suggest that my wife is responsible for satirical prints of any kind, then I would have to resort to the law,' Cal said, turning to Mr Hickson, who was tugging urgently at his wife's sleeve and being ignored. 'I suggest that what so shocked you was a naughty drawing by one of our young relatives spread around for a prank, was it not?'

'Of course, of course it was,' he gabbled. 'Georgia, we were quite mistaken, you must see that.'

The internal struggle was plain on Cousin Georgia's face, but after a moment she said with glacial dignity, 'No doubt we were misled. I have been greatly shocked, but I will disregard it out of respect for Flamborough as head of the family. As for you, Callum, I am gravely disappointed, but my lips are sealed. Come, Mr Hickson.'

Chapter Twenty-One

Will waited until the door closed and then flopped into the nearest chair. 'Hell's teeth, Cal!'

Cal went to stand beside the chair and dropped a hand on to his brother's shoulder. Now that was over he found it an effort to uncurl it from a fist. 'Thank you for your support.'

'Did you know?'

'No. I did not know she had been to Ackermann. I had not seen half of those sketches, certainly not the nude.' The sense of betrayal was like acid in his stomach. He turned and spread the drawings out on the desk. How could she draw him, so intimately, so tenderly, and yet hide it from him? Hide what she had done. Surely she knew how shocking it was for a lady to sell her work for public display?

'Did she need the money?' Will said. 'Is there a problem, Cal? If I can help—'

'Damn it, no!' The implication that he could not support his wife and that she must sell her art for pin money was like a slap in the face. 'I paid off the family debts, I give her an allowance that made her jaw drop. She isn't playing cards—I would know if she had got into that sort of company.'

'Her brother? Trouble with a blackmailing female? Racing debts?' Will shrugged. 'No, not that idiot. He's too dull to trip over trouble, let alone go looking for it.'

Cal splashed brandy into a glass and tossed it back. It did nothing for the pain in his gut. Sophia did not trust him and her art and her ambition were more important to her than he was. That was the only conclusion he could draw from this.

'And you love her, or was that a lie for their benefit?'

'Yes. I love her.' As he said it he found it was still true. Betrayal and disillusion did not, apparently, make you fall out of love.

'Have you told her?'

'No. She does not love me—as is obvious from this fiasco. I feel no inclination to lay my heart out for her to trample on.'

'So what will you do?'

'Go back out there, circulate until our guests leave and then take my wife home and attempt to find a way to live with her, I suppose.'

'You defended her, you owned your love for her. That is something to build on, surely?'

'Perhaps.' But the trust was gone and he did not know how to get it back. 'I had better go out, Will.'

'Come on, then.' His brother opened the door and he walked out to do battle.

Callum told her that he had silenced the two women, then they rode home in the carriage in complete silence.

When they arrived Callum opened the door into the drawing room with perfect courtesy and followed her in, then he shut the door and leaned against it and just looked at her as though he had never seen her before. Perhaps he was thinking that he never had—not the real her. *Oh, my love.*

Sophia walked over to the fireplace and waited. She deserved everything he would throw at her, she knew it. He was furious. It burned in his eyes, it showed in the taut line of his jaw, in the very care he took to keep his hands open and relaxed.

'Well? You sell your work to publishers and do not see fit to tell me?'

'Just one. Just Ackermann. He is very respectable. He will use them to illustrate a memorandum book, anonymously of course.'

'So why did you? Do I keep you so short of money, Sophia? You only had to ask and I would give you what you want.'

'No, you are more than generous and I want for nothing.' *Nothing except the love that I certainly do not deserve.* 'I…I know I married you for security, for position, for a family of my own. But my art has always been important to me, I told you that.

'When Daniel was so long coming home I thought I would have to try to sell it so we could make ends meet. The idea stayed with me—I wanted to see if I was good enough.'

Callum looked down at his clasped hands. 'And you did not feel you could tell me about it? Did you not realise how scandalous such a thing is?'

'I know. I know it was wrong as well as deceitful. But my art is so personal to me, so *essential*, that it did not occur to me to discuss it, to share. I should have done. I should have known you would be interested and support me. When I realised I should have spoken to you first, it was too late.'

'Were you ever going to tell me?'

'Yes. I was going to tell you tomorrow, I promise I was. At first I just wanted to see whether I was good enough. And then he gave me the money and it was done. I thought I would sell some more, save up to buy you something, something with my own money. Then I realised that could take ages and I ought to tell you now.'

'And you drew me when I was asleep, unawares. Were you going to tell me about that also?'

'Yes,' Sophia whispered. She searched for the honest thing to say, an apology and a truth that would not reveal that she loved him. Love had never been in the bargain, not a one-sided love that imposed emotional burdens on him. To declare it now would sound like moral blackmail. 'I think you are generous and I am sorry if my actions made it seem that I do not. I trust you to be kind and honourable and to try to do the right thing for me. But I am not sure I trusted anyone to understand me and what is in my heart.'

'Let alone the stranger who has married you.' It was a statement.

'Why should you understand me?' she asked, despairing. He never would now.

'Perhaps understanding comes with love? Or would it cloud it, do you think?' he asked, startling her.

'Lo-love?' Did he suspect her true feelings? 'I am married to you.'

'So you are,' Callum said as he stood up. 'And you do not love me, do you?'

'Do you want me to?' she stammered, thrown off balance by the abrupt question.

'Why should I?' he countered. 'Love is a painful thing to feel, easily broken, easily betrayed.'

'No,' she said. 'I do not think it can ever be broken. Betrayed, yes. What I felt for Daniel was not real love. I know that now. What do we do now, Callum?'

'We go on,' he said. 'What else is there to do? We married for better or for worse, did we not?' He straightened up and held the door for her and Sophia gathered the tatters of her self-possession around her and walked through it and upstairs.

Sophia sent Chivers away and sat for a long time, drawing the brush through the thick mass that waved slightly from its pins and braids. It was soothing and faintly mesmerising. She was very tired, too tired almost to hurt any more, and her focus blurred until she was almost brushing in a doze.

It took a moment to realise that the bedchamber door had opened. 'Callum?'

He closed the door and came in, took the brush from her lax grip. Her hair crackled, sprang up to cling to his hands. 'I think this is brushed enough.'

'Yes,' she agreed and got up. Why was he here? He was wearing the black robe, his feet bare on the carpet. As she looked into his eyes, dark green, shadowed, full of emotions she did not understand, Sophia realised she couldn't bear it any longer. 'I am so sorry.' He would go now, she thought.

'I find I want you,' he said, his voice harsh. 'I am not

sure I understand why. I am angry with you, I am tired, but I want you. Doubtless it is something primitive and I should be ashamed of it. Tell me to go and I will—I'll not take an unwilling woman.'

It never occurred to her until he said it that he might force her, or to fear that he would hurt her physically because of what she had done, but she knew many men would. 'I know,' she said. 'Stay.'

Callum stooped and kissed her, drawing her close against the thick fabric. Beneath it she could smell the familiar scent of him, the tinge of spice, the faint remnants of soap, the smell, so arousing, of male. His mouth was hard, demanding, but not brutal. A tear escaped and trickled down her face.

Callum lifted his head and licked his lips, tasting the salt. He rubbed away the moisture under her lashes with the pad of his thumbs. 'Don't cry.' His harsh voice was at odds with the gesture. 'It won't help.'

'No,' she promised. She would not cry. He still wanted her, his body betrayed that all too graphically. And he was too much a gentleman to punish her for what she had done. All she could give him in return was her passion and her loyalty and her restraint.

Sophia reached up and pulled Callum's dark head down so she could reach his lips and kissed him, trying to give him everything he wanted. 'Make me stop thinking,' she murmured against his mouth, not knowing if he heard her.

He lifted her without breaking the kiss and laid her on the bed, then shrugged off his robe. As she expected, he was naked beneath it. She closed her eyes, shielding the raw wanting, waiting for the bed to dip as he joined her. But instead he sat at the foot and began to run his hands over her feet, chilly from sitting without her slippers for so long.

His strong thumbs massaged under the arches, then moved to her ankles, circling them easily as if shackling her, then he opened his hands and ran his palms up to her knees. Sophia lay still, swallowing tears, trying just to let herself feel.

His hands were calloused from riding. She felt them snag in the hem of her nightgown as he pushed it up a little and she braced herself for his weight to come down over her, but all he did was to explore the hollows at the back of her knees. 'Soft,' he murmured and moved to nuzzle into them, nudging her legs apart to give him access.

Helpless against the need he was stirring in her, Sophia lay there, her legs sprawled wantonly as Callum's kisses trailed up the sensitive inner surface of her thighs. So gentle. She could feel the restraint he was exercising, sense his need to just take her, punish her with his body. This was a worse punishment, this gentleness when she felt she deserved nothing of the kind.

Her nightgown rucked around her hips and Sophia arched upwards so he could push it free. As she lowered herself his hands opened her further and his mouth found her hot, moist core, his fingers parted the intimate folds so his tongue could stroke and torment in long, slow strokes that had her moaning out loud, her hands fisted in the covers.

Callum had done this before, but in the heat of desperate, urgent sex, never like this with deliberate, exquisite patience so she was forced to lie and suffer every lingering touch of his mouth, every gentle scrape of his teeth, every thrust of his tongue, deep inside.

Sophia reached down and threaded her fingers into Callum's hair, cupping the elegant bones of his skull in her palms as wave after wave of pleasure seared through her, tightening her arousal almost to breaking point. 'Please,' she heard herself saying, 'please, please.' He shook his head, just a little. No, he was not going to release her, not until she was screaming. This was a punishment.

He was cruel, so cruel. She arched, straining, seeking her release as she pressed against his clever mouth and he lifted his head, surged up the bed to hold his weight off her so she could not press up against him as he began to torment her breast with the same ruthless expertise.

His tongue fretted her nipples into aching knots and then, finally, as she sobbed in desperation, he lowered himself, thrust and possessed her, sheathing himself deep within her needy, aching centre. Sophia felt herself unravel instantly, as though he had touched spark to powder. She convulsed around him, tight, tight as if to stop him withdrawing, leaving her, ever. But he thrust again, stronger and harder. He shuddered and was still.

The air was cool on her heated breasts. Sophia opened her eyes and found Callum still braced above her, elbows locked, only his hips pressing into her where they were still joined. His hair fell over his sweat-slicked forehead, his eyes were closed. As she looked he opened them, dark and fathomless, on her face. Still watching her, he slid from her body and rolled off the bed.

'Sleep,' he said. He lifted his robe from the floor, shrugged into it and left.

Her body was nothing but boneless velvet. Her heart felt as though it was breaking. The candles flared and guttered round the room. Sophia lay on the bed, dry eyes aching in the light as she stared at nothing and wondered how she could endure this.

'Is Mrs Chatterton at home, Hawksley?' Cal dropped his hat and whip on the hall chest and began to strip off his gloves. He had come home early, although why, what good it would do, he did not know. He had left before breakfast that morning, broken his fast at a coffee house in the City.

It had been hectic enough at the office to keep his mind from last night and to energise him sufficiently to overcome the exhaustion of a virtually sleepless night shredded by dreams of the swirling grey fog. There had not even been the figure of his wife vanishing into it. She had gone.

Last night. He could let himself think about it now. The hurt that Sophia could not trust him, the shock of how close to ruin she had come, the reality of the pain he had dreaded ever since he had found himself in love with her.

And then in her bedroom. He closed his eyes in denial, but his memory and his body would not let him forget. He had set out to punish her, torment her, prove to her that she was in thrall to him here, and in their marriage. The memory of her softness quivering in his arms; the intimate salt-sweet taste of her lingering on his lips; the feeling of her closing tightly around him, a hot, wet velvet fist; her frantic begging for release and her cries as he gave it to her.

It had been a hollow victory, the one who was hurt

most by it, he knew, was himself. But he had not been able to stay or he knew he would have poured out his feelings for her.

'Madam said that I should ask you to be good enough to call at Lady d'Aunay's residence when you returned, sir.'

'She is there?' Cal asked, puzzled.

'Yes, sir. I believe the ladies have been exchanging items from their wardrobes, sir. Chivers took a portmanteau round.'

Something cold and clammy settled in his gut. Callum recognised fear and told himself not to be a fool. She would not—

He stood on Averil and Luc's doorstep, his heart pounding, and made himself breathe. 'Good afternoon, sir.' The d'Aunays' butler opened the door. 'The ladies are in the drawing room. I will announce you—sir!'

On a wave of relief Cal strode into the room and stopped dead. There were only two ladies: Averil and Dita seated side by side on the sofa regarded him with expressions of identical apprehension. It occurred to him, in the part of his brain that was still functioning properly, that he had never seen Dita show fear before, even during the wreck.

'Where is she?' he demanded, ready to shake it out of them if that was what it took.

'We do not know,' Dita said. She stood up and handed him a letter. 'She said she was going somewhere peaceful and warm.'

'Warm?'

'I did not understand it either. She asked that we make sure you understand that she is not leaving you, that she will come back if you want her to. Only not just yet.'

Cal looked at the letter in his hand and then at the two women.

'I swear that is all true,' Averil said.

He turned on his heel and left without a word, pushing past the butler, out and along to his own home. *Home?* Not without Sophia. Without Sophia it was just a house.

He stood in the hall and broke the seal with an impatient thrust of his thumb under the wax. It shattered, blood-red drops across the black-and-white marble of the floor. *My heart's blood.* What was he going to do if she would not come back? Dita's words were like the rudder of the overturned boat he had clung to after the shipwreck and he held to them with as much fervour, *She is not leaving you.*

Callum, the letter read in Sophia's elegant, artist's hand.

> Please forgive me. I am not leaving you, only going away for a little while to regain my courage and my balance. I was wrong to have married you, I know that. I cannot thank you enough for your gallant kindness in offering for me, in insisting against my ungracious refusal. I have betrayed the trust you placed in me by giving me your name, I know that. When I come back I will make you a good wife, if you will let me, I swear it.
>
> But I need warmth. I know you cannot give me that, especially now, and I do not reproach you for it. I am going somewhere where I will find that comfort, I think. Just for a little while. Then

we can begin again and I will try my best to be everything you ask of me, and nothing that you would not want.

Thank you for protecting and defending me last night.

Your Sophia

His Sophia. He had to bring her back, had to tell her he loved her and forgave her. He had to find a way to let her into his thoughts and his feelings and show her the warmth she craved. She said she had betrayed his trust. A splinter of hard wax cut into his finger and he almost welcomed the sharp pain.

He had expected her trust, thought it his right. But he had not earned it, seen it as something that would come with time and nurturing. Sophia had not turned instinctively to him to share her hopes and dreams and fears, and why should she? He had begun to tell her his, because she had teased them from him as a patient woman might untangle a knotted ball of thread. And she had done that because she cared and had wanted to share his pain and to heal it. Was that not a thousand times more meaningful than her error of judgement, her withholding of trust over this one thing?

He had to find her, bring her home safely, tell her this and pray she would understand. But where was she? He doubted she had gone to her family home. She loved her mother, but he had sensed that they were not very close and he thought Sophia was unlikely to want to worry her with fears that the marriage was in trouble. Certainly she would not go to her brother, he would lay money on that.

Flamborough Hall? But Will was here, in London.

Warmth. The word nagged at him, chasing a thread of memory. A good memory and then it had turned sour...

Long Welling. Sophia had stood in the hall of the old house with her hand in his and said *I love it. It feels warm as though it wants to hug us.* Would she have gone back there, even after the way their visit had ended? It was the only place he could think of, the only dice he could roll. If she was not there, then— No, he would not contemplate that.

'Hawksley, did Chivers return?'

'No, sir. I believe her to be with Mrs Chatterton.'

'I see. It appears that my wife has taken it into her head to go down to Long Welling on a whim.' He forced a smile, a man amused and tolerant of his wife's little fancies.

'Indeed, sir?' Behind the bland expression the butler obviously did not believe a word of it.

'Indeed. Have Andrew pack for me—a week in the country. No formal functions. And have Michael go round to the livery stables and secure me a chaise and four immediately.'

'Sir.' Hawksley effaced himself and Cal took the stairs two at a time to his study. There was money enough in the safe. He stuffed notes into the breast of his coat then sat down to write to Leadenhall Street, a note of apology for landing Pettigrew with extra work, enclosing a letter to the Court of Directors excusing himself on the grounds of family ill health.

As he got into the post chaise Cal wondered if their lordships would take exception to his abrupt departure and then found he did not much care. If he did not find Sophia, then what was he working for? Ambition and position and wealth meant nothing if they were not to please her, to support her and their children, to lay whatever she wanted at her feet.

Chapter Twenty-Two

The postillions drew up in the road at the point where the narrow back way to Long Welling turned off. As Cal got out they began to protest that they couldn't risk the equipage down that track, not with four horses, not in the dark.

'I don't expect you to,' he said, paying them. The chaise rumbled off, leaving him standing by the roadside, portmanteau at his feet, the darkness broken only by moonlight breaking through the tree canopy overhead. There was no sign of light from the house somewhere down below him. An owl hooted, an ineffably lonely sound.

He hefted the bag and began to walk, instinctively taking care to move silently until he reminded himself that this was not India with tigers and dacoits lurking in the jungle and he would do better to watch his footing on the potholed track. It was easier to concentrate on that, and the rustling sounds of the woodland night, than to contemplate what he would do if Sophia was not here.

She was safe, he felt certain, not in the way he had with Dan, but with a desperate faith that he would know, somehow, if she were not. Then the bulk of the house loomed out of the darkness and a light flickered and he knew that Sophia had reached shelter.

Cal pushed open the back door on to the cavernous kitchen to find Chivers standing at the table, clearing away the remains of a simple meal. She looked up, startled, as the draught made the candle flames flicker. 'Sir!'

'Is your mistress well, Chivers?' Cal closed the door behind him and came in.

The girl swallowed, searching for words. 'She's safe. We got here without any trouble and we've had some supper and the beds are made up.' She hesitated, then seemed to find courage. 'But she's not happy, sir. She's not crying, but she's grieving. And I don't know what to say to help make it better, sir.'

'You've done all you can, Chivers. Thank you. You take yourself off to bed when you're ready—I'll look after your mistress and lock up.'

The maid met his eyes, seemed to see something there that reassured her and nodded to herself. 'She's in the parlour, sir. Good luck, sir.'

'Thank you, Chivers.'

The house was dark as he moved through it, wary of the uneven floors and odd steps. It creaked around him like a fat old dowager settling into a comfortable chair to the peril of her stay-laces. Cal smiled wryly at his own flight of fancy, then sobered as the spill of light under the parlour door showed him where Sophia was. He took a deep breath and laid his hand on the door latch.

* * *

Sophia put down her pencil on the desk, set both hands in the small of her back and stretched. Now there was nothing to think about but Callum and the fact that she had left him.

The door latch clicked behind her. 'Do you want to go to bed, Chivers?' she asked without turning. 'I don't need any help with this gown and I think I will be too restless to settle for an age yet.'

There was no answer. She swivelled round and almost fell from the stool. There, looking steadily across the long oak table, was her husband, his hazel eyes so dark they seemed almost brown.

'Callum.' How had he found her so quickly?

'What are you drawing?' he asked, as if he had just strolled in from his study at home.

'You,' she said, finding her voice. 'You and Daniel.' She lifted the portraits and put them on the table. They were the best thing she had ever done, she knew it, but while the pictures of Daniel were as good as she could make them, helped by Dita and Averil's descriptions, there was something special about the portraits of Callum. She was aware of it, but would he notice? Would he care?

He picked one of Daniel up, put it back and lifted another. Callum's mouth curved in the faintest smile.

'You lost all your drawings of Daniel in the wreck,' she said. 'Averil and Dita described him for me, I thought you might like to have them one day, when it was not quite so raw. Perhaps you could colour them, or show me how.'

His hand tightened on the paper and he put it down, smoothing out the creased edge with a frown.

'I wanted it to be a surprise.'

He picked up a picture of himself. The best one. The one that had made her weep as she drew it.

He looked up at her then and the breath caught in her throat. She had never seen emotion like that on his face, never seen such uncertainty. 'There is such feeling in this,' he said after a moment. 'Sophia, I know you married me for security and position and to help your family. Was there anything else?'

'Not at first,' Sophia admitted in a rush. Callum said nothing, but he had become very still. 'There was desire, of course. You must have realised that I was hardly indifferent to you! I may have been innocent and inexperienced, and perhaps it took a little getting used to, but I do not think a woman finds such pleasure in a man's bed as I do with you if there is not a fundamental attraction.'

'Or a man in a woman's,' he said.

'Really?' Momentarily distracted, she sent him a quizzical glance. 'I understood that men were quite happy to take sex where they could find it, never mind who the woman was.'

Callum gave a slight huff of amusement. 'The mechanics and the release, perhaps. To find the pleasure I discovered in making love to you, no, that is not experienced without something more. It took me a while to realise that.'

'You feel more for me?' Sophia whispered, hardly daring to ask. Callum seemed in the mood to tell her the truth, but she was not certain she dared to hear it.

'I tried not to,' he admitted.

'Because I had once fancied myself in love with

Daniel?' Was he going to come to her or were they to stay marooned, either side of the wide old table?

'No.' Callum's mouth twisted into a self-mocking smile. 'Nothing as acceptable as that. I did not want to care for anyone else. Not for Will, certainly not for you. It hurt too much and where Dan had been, part of me, all my life, there was nothing. Just a black, aching hole. How could I lay myself open to that sort of loss again?'

'But you looked after me,' Sophia offered. He had done that, and now he had followed her, realised where she had gone. Surely she could take the first step now. She skirted the table until she was standing in front of him, not quite within touching distance. *Your move now, my love,* she thought.

'I'm very good at that,' Callum said. 'I looked after Dan instead of forcing him to stand on his own two feet. I manoeuvred you into marrying me because I thought it was the right thing for you. I immersed myself in Company business so I could become rich, buy you a big house, buy myself a title perhaps. I did not stop to ask myself if that was what I wanted, or ask you what you needed. What I needed to do to earn your trust.'

'I need you to hold me,' she whispered and took that last step forwards. Callum pulled her into his arms, against his chest. She felt the deep, shuddering sigh rack him, then he was still. The weight on her head, she thought, was his cheek. 'This is all I wanted, Callum. Not houses, not money, not a title. Not even the lovemaking, although that is wonderful. I should have trusted you, told you about the drawings. I am very sorry, but I could not reach you, somehow, I could not let go and trust completely. I just need you, Callum, not you behind a pane of glass, keeping me out.'

'I did that?'

'Yes. But then you could be so understanding and gradually I thought you were accepting me. For hours at a time I thought it would be all right and then you cut me off again. But I almost disgraced you in front of your friends and relatives and people on whom your career depends and you defended me.'

'I can speak six languages,' Callum said, the words rumbling against her ear as she stood crushed to his chest. 'I can stand in front of the Court of Directors of the East India Company and convince them to make a change of policy, I can make money and I can administer justice in a foreign country. What I found I could not do was to tell a woman I loved her.'

For a moment Sophia thought she had not heard him correctly. 'Love? You love me?' She wriggled until she could tip back her head and gaze into his face. He looked, for the first time since she had known him, uncertain.

'Yes. I kept trying to tell you, then deciding the time was not right. It seems that neither of us dared take that final step and trust each other. Do you mind that I love you?'

'Mind?' Sophia bit her lip to steady herself because she did not know whether to laugh or cry. 'Mind that my husband who I love with all my heart loves me? No, my darling Callum. All I mind is not knowing sooner.'

He sat down, hard. Fortunately the table was behind him. Sophia found their eyes were on a level as she stood in the circle of his arms. His hazel gaze held all the warmth she could ever want and the dark brown that she had come to associate with pain or worry had gone, replaced with glittering green. 'You love me? We have a love match and neither of us realised?' His grin took years off his age. 'How long? When did you realise you loved me?'

'When I saw Averil in your arms. I was so jealous I could have scratched her eyes out—and then so relieved when I discovered who she was. So I thought about it and realised why I felt like that.'

Callum pulled her tight back against his body, his thighs cradling her, his bristly cheek pressed to hers. She didn't mind; the rasp of his evening beard somehow made this real, believable.

'Thank heavens for jealousy,' he said, rubbing one big palm in comforting circles on her back. 'I found I was beginning to understand your feelings, almost as I would understand Dan's, and I realised I was letting you into my emotions, into my heart. I thought how I would feel if I lost you and realised that I loved you. I had nightmares about losing you. So I set out to court you, so I could work round to saying it—only it was far harder to manage my emotions then. I wanted to be controlled, moderate, do the right thing, but I cared too much, I was too frightened of losing you.' His arms locked tight.

'You *will* lose me if you suffocate me!' Sophia struggled free and found she could laugh. Perhaps she had to, or she would burst with the happiness bubbling up inside her.

'I thought I had.' Callum looked so serious that she sobered, shaken by the intensity in his voice. 'I thought I had driven you away. I was cruel last night, I meant to punish you without words or blows. Dita said you wanted somewhere warm—and I remembered your reaction when we came here that day. I have no idea what I would have done if I had not found you tonight.'

'I am sorry I left, but I wanted to think,' she explained, stumbling over the words. 'I believed I had to resign myself to a marriage without love and I thought I had forfeited all right to hope for it. Somehow I did not have the courage to face you, knowing that, and I had to find it again, find the strength to go on. I have been a sad trial to you.'

'You made a mistake because we had not learned to trust each other or understand what mattered. You are not a trial, wife.' Callum cupped her face in his hands and studied it, the smile coming back to warm his eyes. Her gaze rested on the sensual curve of his mouth and heat pooled in her belly. 'You are, I think, my salvation. I did not understand about your art,' he murmured. 'I am sorry for that. Will you draw family portraits? We will have private editions of your work done, just for the family. You can even sell to Ackermann so long as it is anonymous.'

'Don't you mind?'

'No. I am proud of you and your talent.' Something in the way she was looking at him seemed to register and the smile became provocative. 'Shall we go to the Hall and beg a bed for the night?'

'There is one made up here.' She did not pretend to misunderstand. Callum was not in need of a good night's sleep.

'The same bedchamber as that kiss that made you so angry with me? Don't you mind?'

'Not at all. It was a very good kiss, although I was hoping for a little more this time perhaps…'

'You little witch! If you want more, you shall have it.' Callum straightened, rocked her off balance and swept her up in his arms. He strode to the half-open door, shouldered his way out into the hall and made for the front door.

'Callum! That's the door to the outside—the stairs are over there.'

'Sir? Ma'am?' Chivers came running from the kitchen, a lamp in her hand.

'Open the front door, Chivers.'

'Callum, you cannot be taking me outside—'

He swept past the maid, down the step to the carriage drive, then turned around and walked back in. 'There. I have carried my wife over our threshold, something I failed signally to do in London. Chivers, you may lock up and see to the lights. Do not hurry breakfast in the morning.'

'Sir.' The maid retreated, giggling. 'Goodnight, sir.'

'I sincerely hope so,' Callum muttered and began to climb the stairs.

'Put me down, I am much too heavy,' Sophia protested, hoping very much he would do no such thing—this was the most romantic demonstration she could have imagined. It was also deliciously masterful. She knew Callum was fit, but the feel of his muscles moving as he climbed, the steadiness of his balance, the heat of his body, made her melt with anticipation.

Chivers had turned down the bed and left a lamp burning on the carved chest. Callum kicked the door closed and eyed the huge old four-poster bed. 'The knack with this will be not falling off—you could break a limb from that height.'

'We could stay in the middle,' Sophia ventured.

'I fully intend using every square inch of this piece of furniture,' he said as he deposited her in the centre of the bed which sagged, almost swallowing her into the depths of the feather mattress which billowed around her as she struggled to sit up. 'Ah,' Callum said. 'Once this thing captures us there will be no escape.'

'I don't think I want to escape,' Sophia said, as she wriggled into a sitting position. 'I would rather save all the interesting and adventurous things for another time—I just want you, Callum, holding me, inside me.'

It was the right thing to say, she could see it in his face. He leant over the bed, caught hold of her and hauled her out. 'Come on then, we'll get undressed and then fall into that billowing mass together and hope we don't suffocate.'

They were laughing as they helped and hindered each other to undress, fingers fumbling on buttons and tapes, mouths meeting and lingering, then parting as they twisted and turned. Finally they half-fell, half-rolled into the soft depths of the bed and stilled, tangled in each other's embrace.

'I haven't said it yet,' Callum murmured, rolling over so Sophia was beneath him, her thighs cradling him, her hands caressing his back and shoulders and lean flanks. 'I love you, Sophia.' He eased into her slowly, filling and possessing with a gentle power. 'You have made me complete in a way I never was before. You have made me whole.'

'I love you,' she answered, feeling him within her, answering with the quivering pressure of her intimate muscles, stroking and holding him as he sheathed himself deep in her core, making them one.

They lay there, eyes locked, their bodies hardly

moving as they rocked together, up and up, higher and higher, until there was nothing but the sound of their gasping breaths and their bodies meshing together and the love and passion in Callum's eyes as they read every feeling she could not find the words for, the strength of his body giving her pleasure beyond her dreams.

She broke, like crystal shattering, and knew she called his name because he answered as he surged impossibly deep within her and she felt the heat of his release and clung to his broad shoulders as they sank together into fulfilment and peace.

Cal opened his eyes on to a room filled with swirling dust motes in sunshine that lanced through the uncurtained window. He turned his head on the pillow and saw his wife—his love—standing quite naked in the shaft of light, watching a robin on the sill.

'I used to think you were skinny,' he said. 'I must have been blind.'

Sophia spun round, laughing at him, and the bird flew away, scolding in alarm. 'I used to think you were arrogant.'

'I am. Come back to bed at once, wife.'

She came as far as one of the bulbous Tudor bedposts and stayed just out of arm's reach, tracing a grotesque mask with her fingertip. 'Must we go back today?'

'We need never go back, if you don't want to.' He threw back the sheet, sat up and stretched. Sophia's gaze trailed over his body like a touch, with inevitable results.

'What about the Court of Directors?'

'The Court of Directors will have to make love to their own wives.' He moved to sit on the edge of the bed and Sophia bent and kissed him, open-mouthed, lingering. 'I could just farm the two estates.'

'Give up your position?'

'If you want me to.'

'No,' Sophia said, shaking her head so her hair fell over her shoulder and caressed his chest. 'You are destined for great things and I am destined to be the Countess of Long Welling, wife of the chairman of the Court of Directors of the East India Company.'

'I can't do it alone,' Cal said, knowing it was the truth. Without her, he would never have the heart for the fight; there would be no one to be doing it for except himself.

'We will do it together,' she promised as she pushed him back into the yielding mattress and scrambled up to straddle him. 'The Company, the estates and the three children.'

'Only three?'

'Four, then.' She lowered herself, inch by tantalising inch on to him, purring with pleasure, her eyes half-closed, the sunlight outlining her body.

'Now that,' Cal said, reaching for his wife, 'is something we can put our minds to immediately, my love. Not that we need an excuse.'

'Yes, my love,' she agreed, falling forwards on to his chest. 'Oh, yes.'

* * * * *

HISTORICAL

Where Love is Timeless™

HARLEQUIN® HISTORICAL

COMING NEXT MONTH
AVAILABLE APRIL 24, 2012

A TEXAN'S HONOR
Kate Welsh
(Western)

RAKE WITH A FROZEN HEART
Marguerite Kaye
(Regency)

LADY PRISCILLA'S SHAMEFUL SECRET
Ladies in Disgrace
Christine Merrill
Three delectably disgraceful ladies, who break
the rules of social etiquette, each in need of a
rake to tame them!
(Regency)

THE TAMING OF THE ROGUE
Amanda McCabe
(Elizabethan)

HHCNM0412

REQUEST YOUR FREE BOOKS!

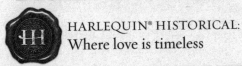

HARLEQUIN® HISTORICAL:
Where love is timeless

2 FREE NOVELS PLUS 2 FREE GIFTS!

YES! Please send me 2 FREE Harlequin® Historical novels and my 2 FREE gifts (gifts are worth about $10). After receiving them, if I don't wish to receive any more books, I can return the shipping statement marked "cancel." If I don't cancel, I will receive 6 brand-new novels every month and be billed just $5.19 per book in the U.S. or $5.74 per book in Canada. That's a savings of at least 17% off the cover price! It's quite a bargain! Shipping and handling is just 50¢ per book in the U.S. and 75¢ per book in Canada.* I understand that accepting the 2 free books and gifts places me under no obligation to buy anything. I can always return a shipment and cancel at any time. Even if I never buy another book, the two free books and gifts are mine to keep forever.

246/349 HDN FEQQ

Name	(PLEASE PRINT)
Address	Apt. #
City	State/Prov.	Zip/Postal Code

Signature (if under 18, a parent or guardian must sign)

Mail to the **Reader Service:**
IN U.S.A.: P.O. Box 1867, Buffalo, NY 14240-1867
IN CANADA: P.O. Box 609, Fort Erie, Ontario L2A 5X3

Not valid for current subscribers to Harlequin Historical books.

Want to try two free books from another line?
Call 1-800-873-8635 or visit www.ReaderService.com.

* Terms and prices subject to change without notice. Prices do not include applicable taxes. Sales tax applicable in N.Y. Canadian residents will be charged applicable taxes. Offer not valid in Quebec. This offer is limited to one order per household. All orders subject to credit approval. Credit or debit balances in a customer's account(s) may be offset by any other outstanding balance owed by or to the customer. Please allow 4 to 6 weeks for delivery. Offer available while quantities last.

Your Privacy—The Reader Service is committed to protecting your privacy. Our Privacy Policy is available online at www.ReaderService.com or upon request from the Reader Service.

We make a portion of our mailing list available to reputable third parties that offer products we believe may interest you. If you prefer that we not exchange your name with third parties, or if you wish to clarify or modify your communication preferences, please visit us at www.ReaderService.com/consumerschoice or write to us at Reader Service Preference Service, P.O. Box 9062, Buffalo, NY 14269. Include your complete name and address.

HH11B

HARLEQUIN® HISTORICAL:
Where love is timeless

SCANDAL NEVER LOOKED SO GOOD
WITH FAN-FAVORITE AUTHOR

MARGUERITE KAYE

Waking up in a stranger's bed, Henrietta Markham
encounters the most darkly sensual man she has ever met.
The last thing she remembers is being attacked—yet being
rescued by Rafe St. Alban, the notorious Earl of Pentland,
feels much more dangerous! And when she's accused of theft,
Rafe finds himself offering to clear her name. Can Henrietta's
innocence bring this hardened rake to his knees…?

Rake with a Frozen Heart

Sparks ignite this May!

*Lady Priscilla and the Duke of Reighland play
a deliciously sexy game of cat and mouse in
LADY PRISCILLA'S SHAMEFUL SECRET,
the third and final installment of the Ladies in Disgrace
trilogy, a playful and provocative Regency series
by award-winning author Christine Merrill.*

He was staring at her again, thoughtfully. "Considering your pedigree, it should be advantageous to the man involved, as well. You are young, beautiful and well born. Why are you not married already, I wonder? For how could any man resist such a sweet and amenable nature?"

"Perhaps I was waiting for you, Your Grace." She dropped her smile, making no effort to hide her contempt.

"Or perhaps the rumors I hear are true and you have dishonored yourself."

"Who…" The word had escaped before she could marshal a denial. But she had experienced a moment's uncontrollable fear that, somewhere Dru had been that she had not, the ugly truth of it all had escaped. And that now, her happily married sister was laughing at her expense.

"Who told me? Why, you did, just now." He was smiling in triumph. "It is commonly known that the younger daughter of the Earl of Benbridge no longer goes about in society because of the presence of the elder. But I assumed there would be more to it than that. And I was correct."

Success at last, though it came with a sick feeling in her stomach, and the wish that it had come any way but this. She had finally managed to ruin everything. Father would be furious if this opportunity slipped through her fingers. It would serve him right, for pushing this upon her. "You have guessed correctly, Your Grace. And now, I assume that this interview is at an end." She gestured toward the door.

"On the contrary," he replied. "You have much more to tell me, before I depart from here...."

If you like your Regencies fun,
sexy and full of scandal then you'll love
LADY PRISCILLA'S SHAMEFUL SECRET
Available May 2012

Don't miss the other two titles in this outrageous trilogy:
LADY FOLBROKE'S DELICIOUS DECEPTION
LADY DRUSILLA'S ROAD TO RUIN

HHEXP0512